Bury the Hatchet
in Dead Mule Swamp

an Anastasia Raven mystery
Joan H. Young

Copyright © 2014 Joan H. Young
Published by Books Leaving Footprints

ISBN: 0990817229

ISBN-13: 978-0-9908172-2-2

DEDICATION

To:

People in any small town who love historic buildings

1

Points of crinkly white tissue paper peeled open under my fingers like the petals of a flower around an irregular umber center. The curved stem ended in a rubber grip. My mind struggled to rearrange the imaginary flower into the actual contents of the carton, and a ragged gasp escaped my lips. I pulled my hands away from the hatchet, its blade stained a dark reddish-brown. It was a good thing I'd placed the box solidly on Cora's desk, or it might have slipped from my hands. Sitting with a thump in the rolling office chair, I skidded into the wall.

"What the...? Holy moley, Cora! Come look at this. Where did you get this box?" It was a Tuesday in late August, too hot and humid a day to be opening boxes containing bloody weapons.

"That one came in the mail," Cora answered. "Why?" She was sorting Depression Glass on one of the work tables of her private Forest County museum, but in response to my alarm she walked briskly to the office space, enclosed by half walls in the corner of her large pole barn.

"Is this some kind of sick joke?" I asked. I'd been working my way through a stack of cartons filled with donated items. I helped Cora once a week, and my task this day was to make lists of the contents of each box. I continued to hold the flaps open so Cora could see, but I didn't want to touch the hatchet, which lay flat and diagonally in the box.

"Is that blood? Who would do this?" Cora asked, peering into the box.

"It looks bloody." I leaned over and sniffed in the vicinity of the hatchet head. "Doesn't smell right, somehow."

"What's the postmark?" Cora asked.

I'd already touched the outside of the carton, as had the mailman, and probably a lot of other people. I folded the right flap in and squinted at the smudged inky circle on the box. "Chicago, I think. It's pretty hard to read."

"Does the Post Office still use that kind of cancellation stamp? Most things that come by mail have a sticker with a bar code."

"I think you can still ask for hand cancellation, but wouldn't that make it likely someone would remember who mailed the box?"

"They probably get so many packages at any Chicago Post Office no one would know."

"What if the person paid with a credit card?"

Cora sighed. "I don't know. I only use mine for online ordering. I suppose we have to call the Sheriff's Department."

She opened the desk drawer and pulled out a battered phone book that was probably out of date.

"I'll call," I said, pulling my new cell phone from my purse. "I've got the number programmed in."

Cora slid the old directory back in the drawer. "I'll bet you do, after that run-in with Larry Louama's gang." She chuckled.

I put my finger to my lips as the number rang through. I was glad to know there was service at Cora's rural location. "Detective Milford, please. This is Anastasia Raven," I said.

"Not going to settle for small potatoes, I see," Cora said with a smile.

I rolled my eyes at her and rotated the bottom of my cell away from my face, leaving the speaker near my ear. "This is a weird thing someone sent you. Milford should know me well enough to realize I'm not joking. I just wish he wasn't so gruff." The phone squawked. "Yes, Detective. I'm fine, thank you. At least I think I am."

"Put it on speaker," Cora requested.

I continued talking to the detective. "I'm at Cora Baker's. I'm going to switch to speakerphone so she can hear too. She's just received something very strange in the mail."

Milford's voice suddenly boomed into the air, sounding oddly tinny on the small speaker, although deep. "... think there's something criminal or illegal?"

"We don't know what to think. I opened this box and there's

a hatchet carefully arranged in tissue paper. The head is covered with something that's dried into reddish-brown flakes that could be blood, although it doesn't smell quite right."

"How is the box addressed?" Milford asked. "Wait. Don't touch it any more than necessary."

"It's all right. I can lift the flap with something, although I've already had my hands all over the outside. And the tissue paper." I slipped a pencil under the cardboard and folded in one edge of the box. "'Mrs. Gerald Caulfield, Forest County Historical Society, Cherry Hill.' There's no street address. That's Cora, you know, right?"

"So I've been told."

"I guess the post office just knew to send it out here since she doesn't live in town any more," I said.

Cora had scurried to her stash of cotton archival gloves. She returned to the office wearing a pair and handed a set to me.

"Is there a note or anything else in the box?" Milford asked.

"We've got gloves on now. Let me look. I'll try not to disturb anything. Oh! Here's a card slipped right down the side of the box where it's easy to find."

"Give it to Cora, since it's addressed to her. What does it say?"

Cora took the card gingerly and balanced her petite frame on an upturned potato crate. "Detective," she began, speaking loudly in the direction of the phone, "I hope you are aware that I haven't been Mrs. Gerald Caulfield...," she enunciated each part of the name precisely, "...for several years now. Obviously this person is unaware of my personal situation."

Cora was being as polite as possible, but I knew she was inwardly seething. Her relationship with the owner and editor of the *Cherry Hill Herald* had not ended amicably, and she bristled whenever Jerry's name was mentioned, even if it wasn't being connected to her. I'd gotten to know Jerry Caulfield earlier in the year and thought he was quite a nice man, but Cora certainly disagreed.

"I understand, but we have to accept that you are the intended recipient," Milford said.

"Well, there is that," Cora said. She sighed and turned the

3

card over. "It doesn't say very much, Detective."

"What, then?"

"'For your museum—found in Dead Mule Swamp.' There's no signature. The printing is plain block letters."

"This hatchet wasn't found in any swamp," I said. "There's no mud on it at all." Cora winced at the sharp edge in my voice.

"Can you tell if there's anything else in the box, without disturbing things?"

I felt carefully under the edges of the white tissue paper. "That seems to be it. What should we do?"

"Better bring the whole thing in here. I'll have the lab look it over. It might just be someone's idea of a joke, but we can tell pretty quickly if there's real blood on it. That would change things a bit."

"We'll come right away. Thanks," I said, and hung up.

Cora picked up the potato crate she'd been sitting on and lifted the carton the hatchet had come in, sliding it into the wooden crate like a drawer into a cabinet. "We can carry it in this without touching the box. I don't feel like wearing gloves all day."

"Cora, let's drop this off and treat ourselves to lunch at the Pine Tree Diner."

Her gaze dropped to the floor. "Maybe not today. I don't want to discuss this in a public place."

"Oh, come on! I bet you haven't eaten out since our treasure hunt earlier this summer." Cora began to restack the remaining unpacked boxes by the desk and didn't look at me. My suspicion was confirmed by her fidgeting. "We can talk about your interesting gift in the car. Have you even been to town since July?"

"Not really; Tom does my shopping, you know." With thin fingers she straightened one of the straps on her faded blue overalls and checked nervously to be sure the ends of her gray braids were tucked tightly around her head. "All right, the food is decent at the Pine Tree. But, Ana, my life was much calmer before you moved to Cherry Hill."

"What? I didn't have anything to do with you receiving this

hatchet."

"Oh, I suppose not, but lots of things have happened since you moved here."

"And you haven't enjoyed that?" I said, winking at her.

"Let's go, then," Cora said. She turned toward the door, still looking away from me. But I saw her grin.

2

There wasn't much to do to prepare for a trip to town. We put the crate with the box inside it in the back seat of my navy blue Jeep Cherokee, and Cora locked the museum and her little house on the south bank of the Pottawatomi River. From her place to Cherry Hill, the county seat, it was sixteen miles. Once we got off the narrow sand roads that led to her house on Brown Trout Lane the drive was easy, straight north on paved Freetown Road.

Cora wasn't usually reticent, but neither was she one to ramble, so I knew the hatchet was weighing on her mind when she began to talk before we'd even reached the pavement.

"Do you think it was meant to scare me?" she began abruptly.

"It was a little shocking—mostly for you when you opened the box—but I've lived a long time, Ana. I've seen much more frightening things."

"If it was meant to be a message of some kind, it's not very clear." I shrugged but kept my hands on the wheel as I navigated around a deep hole in the sand road.

"I certainly don't know what they were trying to say."

The words ran through my mind: *For your museum-found in Dead Mule Swamp.* "The note wasn't very intimidating."

"No, it was pretty bland," she said, shifting her hips and pulling the shoulder belt away from her neck. "Darn cars nowadays aren't made for small people."

"I was thinking about the address."

"There wasn't one, except Cherry Hill," she said.

I thought about that for a minute. "I'm surprised the Post Office delivered it. I heard they were really cracking down on vague addresses, and packages without a return label," But I suspected rural communities were still more forgiving of missing information.

"No, there wasn't a street address, and whoever sent it knew I have a museum, but they still addressed the box to Mrs. Gerald Caulfield. The first part is based on relatively recent events, but I haven't been Mrs. Caulfield for four years."

"That is strange. Maybe it's some kind of warning for Jerry."

"Then they don't know that I'm not speaking to him," Cora said through tight lips.

"Did that box really come in the mail?" I asked. "There were a lot of cartons that came since last Tuesday."

"It was sitting beside the mailbox post when I walked out to get the mail Saturday. The other boxes were brought to me by Kelly Skarvaald last week. She's cleaning her grandfather's attic. But I know that one was by the mailbox because it was taped shut and labeled 'This Side Up.' I just piled it with the others because I was in a hurry to do some baking. I didn't even look at the address label."

We slowed to wind through the small burg of Freetown, at least what was left of it. The road made a small jog and crossed the Thorpe River before turning due north again. All that was left of Freetown was a tiny schoolhouse, now converted to a private residence, an empty commercial building with sagging walls, and the steepled, white frame Freetown Lutheran Church. A clean signboard displayed the service times and a pastor's name, so I was pretty sure they were still viable, but the building was so small it could probably seat fifty people, at the most.

I'd lived in Forest County long enough by that time to have a pretty good map of the main routes in my head. My house is northeast of Freetown by several miles, near the confluence of the Thorpe and the Petite Sauble rivers, and east of Cherry Hill. Dead Mule Swamp, where the hatchet was said to have been found, is associated with the floodplain of the Petite Sauble River, not the Pottawatomi River, by which Cora lived, nor the Thorpe. One thing the area has is plenty of rivers.

"Do you think the officers will tell Jerry about this?" I mused.

"Oh, probably. It's really a bother. I suppose they'll question us about all sorts of old nonsense, and we'll be forced to talk to each other."

"Cora, why do you dislike Jerry so much? I know I'm rather new here, but I know you both, and..."

She cut me off. "It's really nobody else's business."

I stiffened, realizing I'd probably crossed an emotional line. But Cora had become one of my favorite people, and this hatchet seemed destined to open some old wounds, not just with its sharp blade.

She pulled against the uncomfortable seat belt again, sighed and said, "It's really not all that private, and there's no reason I shouldn't tell you. You've been a good friend since you moved here."

"Thank you," I said.

"I've always been set in my ways—remember I told you about my single-minded interest in local history since I was a child?"

I did remember. When I'd first gotten to know Cora in the spring she had told me how she'd been collecting things for a museum since grade school. It had been her life-long obsession.

"So, I suppose my stubbornness is part of the problem. You know it was a second marriage for both Jerry and me?"

"I know your son Tom's father was John Baker, and you told me he died in an explosion at the canning factory. But I didn't know Jerry had been married previously."

"Oh, yes. His first wife was Bernice Foltz. Old money, just like Jerry. They had a boy and a girl. Neither one of them gives a fig about Cherry Hill. It's such a shame; the paper will probably pass out of the family."

"That has to hurt," I said. It was hard to imagine who might keep the paper going if Jerry were gone. He produced the weekly almost singlehandedly, except for some employees who came in to do the actual printing. Jerry had proudly told me how his great-grandfather founded the *Cherry Hill Herald*, but he had not shared anything of the questionable continuation of the legacy.

"Anyway, Bernice died in 1995—pancreatic cancer. It wasn't pretty. Jerry rattled around in that big old house like an empty rowboat on the open ocean. He and I started talking about organizing an historical society. He was really excited about it at the time. One thing led to another, and by 1998 we decided to get married. We liked each other a lot..."

"You weren't in love?"

"We were, I guess. It wasn't the kind of love one feels at eighteen. Neither Jerry nor John was the same as Jimmie."

I grinned. "Three J's. You seem to have a lifetime theme." I knew she was comparing them with Jimmie Mosher, her first love. Jimmie's family had once owned the house I had recently purchased on East South River Road. Long ago, Cora had fought with Jimmie over her fanatic love of history and they broke up.

"Not really. Jerry is Gerald, with a G, you know." She turned her face away.

"OK, I'm just being a smart aleck. I didn't mean to interrupt," I said, somewhat abashed, because I didn't want her to stop talking. I stole a glance in her direction. She was gazing out the window, and her eyes seemed focused far away.

"We got married and started to make plans to convert that huge Victorian house of his into a museum."

"Cora! That would be great. The tall square tower with the picture windows on the front would make a beautiful showcase."

"Yes it would. But it's all behind us now. I wanted to make some changes to the building, things that made sense for a public place. Jerry wouldn't have it. He said I was meddling with his ancestors' ghosts. One thing led to another, and I got stubborn."

She stopped talking and sighed. I wasn't sure if I should pursue the topic. "You didn't care about each other enough to work it out, or find a different building?"

"Well, you've heard how I pushed Jimmie away when he didn't accept my love for our local heritage. I guess I did the same thing all over again. I'm just an old fool. More to be expected than when I was a young fool, I suppose."

"Cora, you are passionate. Someone who really cares about you will accept that and help you realize your dreams." I heard myself giving advice on relationships and nearly gagged. My own marriage had ended in divorce less than a year ago. "Listen to me," I said with a nervous laugh.

I tapped the brakes as we passed a speed limit sign and

approached the southern edge of Cherry Hill, where Freetown Road became Mill Street. We cruised past Jouppi Hardware and Aho's Service Station. I was learning that in a small town every business owner soon became an acquaintance, perhaps even a friend. I'd spent many hours in the hardware store, picking up supplies for the extensive remodeling project my house had become. John Aho and I served together on a church committee, and his willingness to share the unpleasant details of an assault he'd experienced years earlier had contributed, in July, to the apprehension of a local bad boy grown into an adult menace.

I was somewhat startled to realize how connected I felt to this small community, after only four months.

Just south of the center of town, the printing offices of the *Cherry Hill Herald* occupied most of the block between Polczyk and Meadow. With the Caulfield house on our minds, we both looked through the vacant lot beside the *Herald* building to peer at the back of Jerry's imposing family home, which faced the next street over. The only other building facing Mill Street on this entire block was a small, plain structure on the corner of Meadow and Mill, which had recently opened as a real estate office. At the center of town we made a left on US 10/Main Street and drove the two miles to the Sheriff's Office in comfortable silence.

"Here we are," I announced unnecessarily, as I pulled into the parking lot.

"Let's hope your detective can provide us with some answers about this bloody hatchet," Cora said. "I'll carry the box and keep it level if you open the doors."

3

Detective Milford wasn't nearly as awed with our boxed weapon as we had been. In fact, he was brusque.

The deputy at the desk led us back through the small maze of concrete block hallways to the Detective's office. He rapped on the narrow glass window in the plain steel door and opened it without waiting for a response. Dennis Milford rose from his desk and motioned us toward two straight chairs. He was a large man, solidly-built, with short salt-and-pepper hair and a neat mustache. He had on the same gray suit I'd always seen him wear. Perhaps he owned several identical ones.

Cora placed the box with its potato crate sleeve on his desk. Milford didn't show any interest in looking at the contents. I was reminded of his apparent initial disinterest when I'd first had to talk with him about the critical situation that had developed near my home only a month prior. After Cora and I again answered all the same questions we'd covered on the phone, Milford called in a young female technician who carried the box away with latex-gloved hands.

"I think that's all, ladies," he said, rising to his feet and clearing his throat.

"But, you didn't even look at the hatchet! We thought you might have some ideas about what it means," Cora protested. "Do you think it's a warning, or someone's idea of a joke, or did someone simply find it, as they claim?" Her voice rose, as close to a whine as I'd ever heard from her.

"We have no indication of what direction our thinking should take just yet, Ms. Baker."

I was glad he realized the importance of using the name she preferred.

"Can't you analyze the handwriting?" Cora pressed.

"It's printed in plain block letters, which aren't as anonymous as you might think, but we have to have something to compare them to. We can't ask everyone in Forest County and Chicago for alphabet samples."

"Oh. I suppose not."

He continued, "It's not a crime to mail a hatchet, and as you have both pointed out, we don't even know if the substance on the blade is blood or only something similar. Now, if you'll let me get back to work, someone will call you when the lab has given us some facts to work with."

"All right. Thank you for your time, Detective," Cora said, but she shut her lips in that thin line which served as an indicator of her annoyance level.

I touched her arm. She turned to me and her eyes opened wide. "Let's go get lunch," I said, picking up the potato crate.

We drove the two miles back to town in silence, but it wasn't as comfortable as the outward trip. Had I offended her with my touch? Cora was twenty years my senior, and perhaps local people of that age group expected even their friends to keep a certain distance.

However, as we pulled up in front of the Pine Tree Diner, she grinned at me and said, "That man infuriates me, but let's try to enjoy our meal. I'd rather not talk about the hatchet in the restaurant if it's all right with you."

"Sure," I said, opening the door. "I'll fill you in on my renovation project."

"That will be perfect," Cora said, as she jumped lightly from the Jeep.

We mounted the two steps to the glass door of the diner. If there was handicap access it must be through the back. Funny how I'd never thought about that before. I looked around at the small crowded storefronts and realized how difficult and expensive it must be to re-fit an aging downtown to meet modern standards.

A few other people were seated in the restaurant, but most of the breakfast regulars had left, and it was still a bit early for the lunch crowd. The odor of grilled hamburgers and onions hung about the room, with overtones of black coffee. Two older men in jeans and work shirts looked up and nodded at us as we entered.

For the most part, the Pine Tree hadn't tried very hard to keep up with the times. From past experience, Cora and I headed directly to a booth to the left of the door but not the one by the front window. I knew the vinyl benches we chose had fewer duct tape patches than the others, even though it only mattered when you slid in and out, and the rolling corners of the tape caught against your pants. Actually, I supposed it only mattered to those who didn't wear blue jeans. Most people in Cherry Hill wore jeans nearly all the time, at least the ones who ate at the Pine Tree.

I sat facing the front door and Cora slid in the other side. We pulled the dingy plastic-coated menus from behind the table's condiment rack and opened them to the sandwich section. Not that I really needed to. I'd eaten there enough to know exactly what the choices were. The food was always good, and the servings generous, but the selection ran to open-faced hot roast beef, with gravy and mashed potatoes, served with a side of canned corn, or hamburgers in various weights with assorted toppings.

In short, this was where many local people ate meals on a regular basis. The Pine Tree was not out to attract upscale tourists if Cherry Hill had any.

Suzi Preston, my favorite waitress, came to the table with glasses of water. "I'll have a tuna melt, and iced tea," I said. I'd learned that the tuna sandwich was one of the healthiest and least greasy choices.

"Grilled ham for me," Cora said.

Suzi looked at me. "Chips and cole slaw, like always?"

"Yes, please."

"How about you?" she turned to Cora.

"I'll have the applesauce. No potatoes."

"Something to drink?" Suzi smiled at Cora. Her style had been improving over the course of the summer. She was much more friendly and engaging than she had been in June when she nervously began at the diner, right after graduating from Forest

County Central High.

"Iced tea, also, if you don't mind," Cora smiled in return. "Are you Janice's girl? You look very much like her."

I knew that Janice Preston baked pies before dawn almost every morning to supply both the Pine Tree, and Volger's Grocery store. I couldn't imagine facing that task every day.

"That would be me," Suzi said with a flip of her blonde ponytail.

"Do you help with the baking?" Cora asked.

Suzi glanced at the dessert board. I followed her eyes and saw: *PIE- apple crumb, lemon meringue, local blueberry.* "No, I don't make pies as good as Mom's."

"It takes a lot of practice to get the crust right, my dear," Cora said.

"Suzi! Order up," came a man's voice from the kitchen.

"Gotta go," Suzi said, turning on her heel and heading for the back of the room.

When my attention returned to Cora, she said, "Tell me what you've finished in your porch."

She was referring to the enclosed, upstairs screen porch I'd added to the old farmhouse I was remodeling. The house was originally built in a basic T-shape with the east section having two stories and the west only one. I'd added a complete second story and a screen porch above the concrete terrace. It was a project that should have consumed all my time over the summer. However, I'd managed to become entangled in more than my share of local adventures involving police and dangerous situations.

My new lifestyle was being funded by a very large settlement from my former husband, Roger. He had announced over dinner one night, about a year previous, that he preferred a friend named Brian over me. It still made me grind my teeth, and yet I stifled a smile every time I was reminded that he had to pay handsomely to make that permanent. My investments guaranteed a good monthly allowance for life.

However, the income wasn't large enough that I could pay for all the renovations at once. Since I enjoyed doing a lot of the work myself, spreading it out was more fun, anyway. Finishing the screen porch was my current project.

I answered Cora, "I've painted the walls a bright teal."

"Sounds like a lot of color," Cora said. I knew she liked pastels most. She had a large collection of softly checked, plaid, or flowered blouses she wore with her faded denim overalls.

"There isn't much wall space between the screens on the two open sides, and since I always sit to look outside, the solid teal wall behind will set off some white wicker furniture very nicely."

"What about the floor?"

"Bamboo. I haven't picked it out yet, though."

Suzi brought our iced tea, and Cora took a sip before saying, "I think you'll have to shutter those screens every winter to keep the snow out. I'm not sure how practical your porch is here in the north."

"I suppose so. Robert Gorlowski—he did the work, you know—said the same thing. I'll have to get him scheduled to make them. Or maybe he can just give me a design drawing."

"Ana, you are so handy! I envy your abilities."

The front door opened, and Adele Volger, a widow and owner of the local grocery, entered carrying a large cardboard carton. Adele has ample bulk, but she moves it with surprising speed. She didn't look around but headed straight for the kitchen. I had thought to help her, but she was well past us before I could swallow my tea and set down the glass, ice clinking against the sides.

Cora's eyes narrowed as she followed Adele's back. I tried to keep the conversation going.

"I do like to putter around with projects that aren't too big for me. I was always handy with tools, but Roger preferred I keep my fingernails long and my hands soft. It's a mystery to me why I let him tell me how to be for so long." I realized Cora wasn't paying attention. She was looking toward the kitchen door. In another minute I knew why, as Adele walked over to our booth.

"Ana, Cora," she began.

"Adele," I said brightly. "Why don't you join us for a minute?"

"No thanks," she said, turning her back to Cora. "I just

delivered some emergency supplies. Jack called and said they were out of eggs and running low on cabbage. He has to pay retail price on these extra orders, so it's worth my time to run over here."

Why would Adele tell me that?

I saw Cora's lips tighten in that telltale straight line. "Adele, one would think you'd not need to make an extra nickel off your local friends," she said with her precise diction.

Adele whirled to face her. "Cora Baker, you don't have one business cell in your brain. If you want a grocery to stay open in Cherry Hill, I have to turn a profit. Some of us can't afford to play with doo-dads all day and not work."

I swallowed hard. These two women had become my best friends since I'd moved here, but they barely tolerated each other. It was as if Adele had picked a fight on purpose, but I couldn't imagine why.

"Jack isn't rolling in cash either," Cora said with flashing eyes. She picked up her fork and almost managed to look menacing. The women were referring to Jack Panther, owner of the Pine Tree.

"Not a one of us is," Adele countered. "You know that perfectly well. Jack gets wholesale on any regular orders; it's just special deliveries where I charge full price. He knows that. We've operated that way for years without your help."

Suzi intervened. "Excuse me," she said as if there were no tension in the air. "I have your sandwiches. This should settle the hungries." I predicted a good future for Suzi as a mediation specialist.

"Nice to see you," Adele said, looking pointedly at only me. She turned and walked out the front door without a backward glance.

4

Adele's behavior didn't leave either Cora or me feeling warm and fuzzy. I was embarrassed and slightly angry. Adele hadn't needed to create a scene. Maybe she was jealous that I'd been spending more time with Cora than with her. Could she really be so childish?

Cora seemed to fade into the vinyl seat, and she ate in silence. I listened to the clinking of dishes being washed in the kitchen and a hot fly buzzing in the sun on the front windowsill. Cora swallowed the last bite of ham sandwich, and wiped her mouth with a carefully folded paper napkin. She tucked it neatly beside her empty plate. Then she picked up the check, which Suzi had already left on the table, reached into her pocket, and pulled out a few bills. Her eyes rose to meet mine, a silent message.

"Sure," I said. "Any time." I quickly added my share to the money on the table and slid out of the booth, taking one more gulp of tea before following Cora toward the door. She already had it open and was headed for the steps. I caught Suzi's eye and looked toward the table. She nodded and grinned.

"She does it on purpose, you know," Cora finally said, when we were well on the way back to her house.

"Why?" I asked.

"Just to annoy me. She and her husband were great friends with Jerry and Bernice. Prominent citizens and all that. I think she was sweet on Jerry after Bernice, and then her husband Henry, died."

"Well, if she likes Jerry that much you'd think she'd be happy he's free to date again."

"I suppose. But instead of trying to be nice to Jerry, she just goes out of her way to be unfriendly to me."

The last thing I wanted was to get entangled in a local lovers' spat. Or lost lovers' spat. Or whatever this was. I sighed and kept my eyes on the road until Cora was safely back in her own yard.

"See you next Tuesday?" Cora asked.

"Maybe sooner, if anything interesting comes up with your hatchet."

"You know where to find me," she added, before she shut the Jeep door, just a little harder than was necessary. I doubted Cora the Hermit would venture away from her house and museum for quite a while.

The day had taken on a dark tone, and I didn't want to go home to an empty house. I thought about running back into town to ask Adele why she had been so pointedly rude but didn't feel up to more tension. Then I thought about dropping in on one of the other people I'd met since moving to Cherry Hill. Young Jimmie Mosher, grandson of Cora's former sweetheart, and his mom lived in town now. But that would remind me too much of Cora, who thought of the boy as a grandson. The girls, Sunny and Star Leonard, might be happy to see me, but I didn't feel like driving all the way out to Hammer Bridge Town either.

"Why do my two best friends have to hate each other?" I asked out loud.

What I wanted was dessert. I wanted some of Janice Preston's pie, but I wasn't going to settle for one piece. Her house was actually on my way home if I didn't take the shortest route. I drove straight up Centerline until I reached Otto Road and turned east. Prestons lived at the corner of Otto and Fishkill Roads, and from there I could follow dirt roads home.

Janice had a cheerful painted sign in her yard with red and white checks around the edge and a rooster crowing from the left side. "Fresh Pies" was lettered above his beak. Smaller tabs hung from hooks with the flavors of the day. I was happy to see blueberry as well as lemon meringue.

Two cats watched me from the porch railing as I got out of the Jeep, and an aging beagle heaved himself from the grass and waddled toward me. "Ar-oooo," he said without much enthusiasm, but he had his duty to do. I reached down and scratched behind his ears.

"Hello, Bub," I said. Janice appeared on the porch. Her face was red, and she was wiping purple hands on a towel.

"Hi, Ana," she called. "I was just washing elderberries, darn tiny things. Come on in."

"Ar-oooo," Bub added, and returned to his spot in the shade of a large maple, where he plopped down heavily. According to Suzi, his full name was Bubbles, having been fat since puppyhood. No one called him that to his face, though. One should never insult a beagle.

I entered Janice's large airy farm kitchen and sat at the breakfast counter. Without even asking, she filled two glasses with ice and water from the refrigerator door and placed one in front of me then sat down with the other glass already on its way to her lips.

"Sure is a hot one," she said.

"It is," I agreed. "How do you keep on cooking and baking in this heat?"

"The breeze'll pick up in just a little while," Janice said, pushing a strand of damp hair out of her eyes. I'd gotten to know Janice when Adele asked me to return some of the plastic racks on which pies had been delivered to a church event.

"Even so, I think I'd go crazy cooking all the time," I said.

Janice laughed, a genuine, cheery laugh that was a real bright spot after the way the rest of the day had been going. "Some days it does seem a bit much. But, it brings in extra cash. It's hard to live on just a farm income, and it paid for this kitchen."

I looked around. The room was huge, and featured commercial appliances, expensive countertops and two double sinks. At the same time, it was homey, with crisp white eyelet curtains, and red and white checks, as on the signboard, for accent.

"Are you just visiting, or did you want something in particular?" Janice asked, glancing at the huge pile of elderberry heads with their minute purple fruits.

"You've lightened my day already," I said, "but I really came for a pie."

"I have one of each flavor left. Most went out on orders. Which one would you like?"

"Blueberry. Definitely," I said. "You aren't making elderberry pie to sell, are you?" I wondered how many hours it took to prepare those fruits.

"Gosh, no. I haven't completely lost my mind. I'm making jelly for my family and maybe Christmas presents."

Janice opened the commercial refrigerator and pulled out a pie, already boxed. "That's twelve dollars, for you, neighbor."

"Janice, that's not enough," I protested. I opened my purse and laid a ten and a five on the counter.

"I'll get your change," she said.

"You'll do no such thing." I grabbed the box and scooted for the door. When I reached the Jeep, I looked back at the house. Janice was standing in the open kitchen door, smiling. She waved at me. Bub raised his head, but didn't waste his breath to bugle at someone who was leaving.

I soon arrived at my own old farmhouse, but it wasn't nearly as big or as nicely kept as Janice's. Seeing hers inspired me to keep working on my renovations. I looked up at the freshly painted white siding, and the new screen porch, mentally counting the number of sheets of plywood I'd need to make storm shutters, then pushed open the kitchen door with a sigh. I set the pie box on the counter, tossed the keys in a basket, and pulled a plate from the cupboard and a fork and knife from a drawer. I cut myself a slice of blueberry heaven and sat at the kitchen table silently blessing people like Janice.

Of course, pie alone wasn't quite enough to overcome the disturbing events of the morning. I dialed Chad's cell number. Chad is my son, soon to begin his junior year at Michigan Tech. However, he was spending the summer studying wolves on Isle Royale in Lake Superior. I knew I couldn't reach him if he was actually on the island, but he was supposed to show up here for a visit some time this month. His phone rang four times, then went to voicemail. I left a message but had no idea when he'd actually receive it.

I looked around my kitchen. It was the one room I'd hardly worked on at all. Secondhand appliances and cracked vinyl went well with the old-fashioned wallpaper featuring faded green twining ivy. I wasn't exactly jealous of Janice's kitchen. I'd made my choices about which rooms to fix first, but sometimes it was hard to be patient.

I wandered into the living room and ran a finger along the spines of my CD cases. Jazz? Ragtime? Easy listening? Classical? Nothing fell into the nagging hole inside me. I'd cut all my ties with friends from the Chicago area when Roger and I broke up. Chad was essentially grown. We'd always been close, and I knew he was excited to see the house I'd bought, but his visit was possibly a couple of weeks away, and I hadn't heard his voice since mid-July when he'd placed a hurried call one night on a mainland trip to do some shopping.

Although I'd known for months that Cora and Adele did not like each other, I'd never been in the middle of an actual confrontation. Mostly they just avoided one other. Today's spat made me feel distant from both of them. I hadn't felt this alone since I'd moved to Forest County.

I went back to the kitchen, cut another slice of pie, and poured a glass of iced tea. I wouldn't be rushed through this glass. If I couldn't have nice friends, at least I could have comfort food.

After I'd licked the plate, and the second piece of pie and the tea had pleasantly expanded in my stomach, I headed for bed.

My bladder woke me the next morning; the sun was already up. Inevitably, the phone rang just as I was finishing up in the bathroom. It was the home phone, not my new cell. Thinking it might be Chad, I didn't want to miss it and rushed downstairs.

On the fourth ring, I grabbed the handset. "Hello?" I gasped, trying to catch my breath.

"Ana? Is that you? You sound funny." It was Adele.

"It's me. It's really early. I had to rush to catch the phone. What's up?" I wondered if she wanted to talk about the events at the Pine Tree the day before.

Adele was never one for preliminaries. She launched right into the meat of her news. "I was just opening up the office at the store and I heard something coming over the police scanner. I called my neighbor to verify the news, because I wasn't sure I caught it all."

"All what, Adele?"

"I'm trying to tell you. Jerry Caulfield's body was found in the river, downstream at Jalmari. They said he'd been cut up! What am I going to do? Oh, Ana, what am I going to do?"

5

At six-forty-five, Wednesday evening, I sat uncomfortably at a roll-out table in the multi-purpose room at Forest County Central School several miles north of Cherry Hill. It looked like nearly a hundred other residents had already turned out for the meeting. If only we knew what the meeting was for. I'd gotten a call around two in the afternoon via the Crossroads Fellowship telephone tree. Geraldine Longcore had told me that Sheriff Newt Sullivant and Cherry Hill Police Chief Tracy Jarvi were requesting all county residents to attend a brief informational meeting at seven at the school. Geraldine said she had no idea what it was about. She made sure I remembered the next person on the phone tree list, and hung up.

Newton Sullivant was practically a stranger to me, but Tracy was our young female Chief, a friend, whom I liked a lot. The law enforcement agencies almost always worked together in this rural area.

I did my duty and passed the message on to Marie and John Aho, the service station owners. "Maybe it's about Jerry," Marie said with a catch in her voice, and then she hung up just as abruptly as Geraldine had.

The *Cherry Hill Herald* comes out every Wednesday; however, my copy comes in the mail on Thursday. I really wanted to see if someone had managed to get anything about Jerry's death in before it went to press. But driving to town, potentially having to talk to grieving locals, was beyond my courage level. I hunkered down in my bedroom for the rest of the afternoon to read a few chapters from *East of Eden*, with Beethoven's *Eroica* symphony mournfully echoing my mood. Cherry Hill wasn't looking so innocent and friendly to me any more.

Judging from the folks who had turned out for the meeting,

more than one telephone tree had been summoned to action. In addition to those from the Crossroads church, there were plenty of Catholics and Lutherans in attendance, and dozens of people I didn't know at all. John and Marie Aho approached the table section where I sat alone.

"Ana, it's so good of you to show up for this... this, whatever it is." Marie struggled to speak.

"She means— because you're pretty new to Cherry Hill," John added.

"Does anyone know why we're here?" I asked.

A tall, thin woman wearing a tropical print dress, one of the strangers to me, slipped into the bench on the other side of the table. She held out a narrow hand covered with rings. "Virginia Holiday," she said in a husky smoker's voice as we shook. "Holiday Real Estate. I bought that little building on the Caulfield block. Great location." She twisted on the seat and also shook hands with John and then Marie.

"I'm Ana Raven," I said. "It rhymes with ca-bana." Apparently, the palm trees and flowers on her dress made me think of beaches and small pointed tents.

"Nice to meet you," Virginia said. "What's this all about?"

"We assume it's something about Jerry Caulfield's death," John said. "You haven't heard?"

"Caulfield's..." she began tentatively, but was cut off by Adele who swept toward us.

"This is one sad day for our community," Adele announced loudly, shaking her head.

From a couple of tables away, a man yelled, "Where's the Sheriff? It's six-fifty-eight."

"Danged mysterious, if you ask me," said a woman I identified as a Lutheran, because she had served me a hot dog at the St Johh's lunch tent on the Fourth of July.

People had continued to drift in, and now the room was packed. I saw Cora and her son Tom, but they took seats on the far side of the room and didn't respond when I waved.

"But, I just spoke to Jerry Caulfield about the..." I heard the woman across from me begin. My attention was distracted as two men entered the room from the school hallway, rather than through the outside doors. Harvard Brown, a Sheriff's Deputy, and Kyle Appledorn for the city, were in full uniform, including hats and holstered guns. Harvey walked through the room and took a formal stance beside the double doors that led to the parking lot, while Kyle remained near the hallway opening. Neither man said a word, but everyone quieted down. Adele motioned for me to slide in along the bench, and she sat down at the end.

Harvey and Kyle had their eyes focused on a shorter table that was marked "reserved" on which rested a portable podium and microphone. It was positioned near a windowless door that probably led to the kitchen, since there was a closed, long metal rolldown window in the same wall.

The kitchen door opened, and Tracy Jarvi, also in full uniform, came out. Behind her was Sheriff Sullivant. A third person was behind the Sheriff, and by virtue of his height we could all see at a glance who it was: Jerry Caulfield. I swear I felt a breeze from the collective gasp.

Beside me, Adele moaned and laid her head on her arms on the cold Formica. Her body was shaking so hard it tickled my arm. After the sudden quiet, the room erupted in a wave of babble as people reacted to the presence of the not-so-dead newspaper owner. Sheriff Sullivant produced a gavel from somewhere and rapped on the short table. A chair screeched as Tracy pulled it out and sat down. Her eyes roved over the people in the room, searching for information in their reactions. Jerry remained standing in full view of everyone. I thought he was working very hard not to smile.

"Ladies and gentlemen," said the Sheriff. The microphone squealed, and everyone flinched. Sullivant began again from a better distance, "Ladies and gentlemen, as you can clearly see, Jerry Caulfield's alive and well. First off, I'll give him a chance to speak to you and verify that assumption."

Jerry stepped to the podium. He was wearing a light blue dress shirt, open at the neck, and crisply pressed navy slacks. A summer tan contrasted with his wavy white hair, which glowed, even under the unflattering fluorescent school lights. He cleared his throat, adjusted the microphone to his height and spoke in a perfect tone, slightly cynical, but jocular. "Hello, friends. It would be overly trite to quote Mark Twain and say something like 'the reports of my death have been greatly exaggerated.' So I won't say that. Actually, it hasn't even been reported, and I was quite surprised to hear the news myself when I awoke late this morning after a busy night at the print shop. I'll let the Sheriff explain. Please note," he added, "that the *Cherry Hill Herald* did not carry any false headlines."

Jerry pulled out the remaining chair—no grating sound when he did it—and sat down on the other side of the podium. He relaxed, and a grin broadened across his face.

Sullivant stepped forward again, but he was not smiling. "Now that we're relieved to learn our newspaper's still in business, let's discuss how this rumor got started. I believe that any number of private citizens own police scanners." He paused and glared at several people in the room, including Adele, who had recovered enough to sit up.

"Lordy, Lordy," Adele whispered to me as she lowered her eyes.

"That's perfectly legal," Sullivant continued. "However, I have to say that it'd be a good thing for people to be certain of what they think they hear before calling all their friends and neighbors with the latest news."

"I know what I heard just fine," piped a woman in a bright lavender sweat suit.

"You know what you think you heard, Helen," the Sheriff said, his voice threatening to make the microphone squeal again. "Just hold your horses for a minute."

Everyone squirmed; there were a few coughs, and Sullivant went on. "The partially decomposed body of a man was discovered on Tuesday, down the river at Jalmari. Without doin' a lot of fancy testing, it's pretty clear that he's been whacked on with a hatchet, although we don't have an official cause of death just yet."

I searched for Cora's eyes across the room and found that she was also looking for mine. She raised her eyebrows.

"We found a wallet in his pants pocket, making tentative identification gol-darned easy. The man's name is Jared Canfield." Sullivant let this information sink in for a few seconds and then asked, "Anyone here think they know this fella?"

6

I awoke Thursday morning with a pounding headache and scenes from the meeting playing through my head. No one had a clue who Jared Canfield was, but there had been plenty of speculation, none of it meaningful. The Sheriff gave us some facts, but they were meager. Canfield's laminated driver's license showed him to be from Royal Oak, a suburb of Detroit, five-foot-eight, with brown hair and eyes, and fifty-two years old. In the wallet had also been two credit cards, some damaged pictures, and a few pieces of paper which were soggy and unreadable. These had been taken to the State Police lab. If the Sheriff knew more, he wasn't sharing.

We citizens had been sent home with admonitions to keep our ears open, and our tongues more tightly under control.

Strong coffee and some pain killers were first on my agenda for the day. Before long, I was sitting in my living room reading and thinking about what I might try to accomplish. My brain was seriously foggy, and I must have dozed off because I jumped at the sound of a knock at the front door. I hadn't heard anyone drive in.

The knocking was repeated, more insistently, and I hurried to the door. Whoever was out there was standing to the side, out of sight. I couldn't see anyone through the old wavy glass panels, and no vehicle was within view.

"Who's there?" I called.

There was no answer, but a squarish shoulder eased into sight and the person knocked again. I pulled open the door and blinked in the morning sun at the sight of a thin but muscular young man, about six feet tall, with light brown wavy hair, a little wild. He wore jeans and a brown t-shirt with a white silhouette of a moose on the front. His blue eyes were twinkling.

"Hey, Ma! I thought I'd surprise you."

"Chad Allen Raven, you are impossible! Get in here." I swiped at his arm as he entered, but he sidestepped and instead encircled me in a bear hug and swung me around the room. When he put me down, we were both laughing and a little dizzy.

"So this is your 'new' place," he said, looking around.

"What are you doing here now?" I asked at the exact same time.

We laughed again.

"My project finished a few days early."

"I've still got a lot of work to do." Once more our sentences collided.

"Me first, I'm the mom," I said, retrieving my shoulder length hair and tucking it behind my ears. "I thought you'd call first. How'd you know how to get here?"

Chad rolled his eyes. "Ever hear of GPS? I just keyed in the address and followed the directions."

"Where's your car?"

"Out there around the curve. I didn't want you to see me drive in."

"You scallywag. Have you had breakfast? Did you drive all night? How long can you stay?" My mind flooded with mother questions.

"Slow down, Ma!" Chad said. "I camped with some friends last night in the National Forest, and we split up early. It was only about two more hours to get here." He rubbed his stomach.

"OK, I get the hint," I said, leading him toward the kitchen. "I think I've got eggs, and maybe some ham."

While I fixed omelets and divided up the rest of the blueberry pie—the smaller piece for me—Chad pulled his battered Toyota up to the house and brought in his backpack and guitar case.

As I beat the eggs and poured them into a hot pan, I realized my headache had disappeared. I was delighted to see Chad. He and I had always been close, but one never knows what might happen when a son begins to discover his adult self, especially when his parents have recently split up. Chad looked a lot like a young Roger, with his blue eyes and wavy hair. My mind drifted as I waited for the eggs to cook; I buried my nose against a small warm head of blond curls while the other young man squeezed my shoulders and smiled down at us. Wasn't that just a few months ago?

"Ma! This old place only has one bathroom? Upstairs? Where should I sleep?"

Reality always cuts to the immediate, rather than the important questions. "How about one of the little rooms off the living room? I don't have an extra bed yet, but it would be more private for you."

"That's perfect. I'll use my camping pad and sleeping bag. No big deal."

For the rest of the morning, Chad and I brought each other up to date on the events of the summer. We'd talked by phone a few times, but the connection was never good enough to really visit. Of course, I wanted to hear what he'd been doing on Isle Royale, but I was surprised and pleased that he was interested in my summer, too. I gave him a tour of the house, and he liked what I'd accomplished, but he mentioned the lack of a television and an internet connection.

When I got to telling him about the recent confusion over a body washing up at Jalmari, he held up a hand. I stopped talking.

"I think you've found a new hobby, solving mysteries," he said.

"Oh, no, I don't have anything to do with this one," I said, bugging out my eyes and shaking my head. I changed the subject. "How long can you stay?"

"'Til Saturday, I think. I need to go see Dad, too, before I have to be back on campus."

I knew this was the outline for my future, having to share Chad with a man who made my stomach contract into a hard knot. I wanted to protest that two days was too little time, but I knew my desires couldn't make Chad stop caring about his dad. I didn't want him to hate Roger. Well, maybe just a little bit.

"How about if I help you get those shutters for the screen porch started tomorrow?" Chad said, pulling me back to the conversation.

"That would be great," I said, "But why not start today?"

"I have something I'd like to do, if you don't think it's too stupid." The impish grin I love broke across his tanned face.

"What's that?" I asked, wondering what on earth he might have cooked up in just a few hours.

"I drove in to Cherry Hill pretty much along the river. This part of the state is beautiful. Can we go look at cabins on the water? I'll be in work-study this fall, and maybe I could make payments on something small."

"But you don't have any idea where you'll be working after college, or anything yet," I protested.

"Yeah, but you plan to stay here, right?"

"I think that's settled," I said. "But what difference does that make?"

"If I had a cottage, I could have my own place and still see you without being a bother. Even if I end up with a family some day, it would be a great vacation place."

"Chad, I don't know. Anything on the water will be expensive. Who will take care of it?" I didn't want to get saddled with the upkeep on another old building.

"Oh, c'mon. Looking is free. It's probably just for fun. Are you worried about high-pressure realtors bugging you after I leave?"

"Maybe a little bit," I admitted, picturing the lady in the tropical print with the husky voice. She had seemed very forward, but I supposed realtors had to be. "All right. It's a good trade for help with all that plywood tomorrow. Where shall we start?"

In about an hour, we were driving into Cherry Hill, past the park beside the river where I'd faced off with a really bad man in May, and over the Mill Street bridge. Chad had talked me into letting him drive my Jeep, so I was in the passenger seat. We turned west on Liberty Street. I'd never seen this part of town, since it wasn't really on the way to anywhere.

"Hey! There's the old school," I said. I pointed at a large red brick structure on my side of the street. "Stop a minute."

"That's a really cool building, but not quite what I had in mind," Chad said dryly as he pulled to the curb.

I recognized this place from pictures Cora had shown me. The two-story school had a central bell tower, and a third-story dormer with small diamond-shaped panes. Close behind the building was a chain-link fence, with the Petite Sauble River just beyond. I hadn't realized the building was so near the river. I wondered where the schoolkids had played. The structure obviously hadn't been in use for a long time. Some windows were broken out and covered with plywood. Nevertheless, it was a handsome building.

"Ma? Hey, are you in there?" Once again, I'd been lost in thought until Chad's voice brought me back. Maybe I had been spending too much time alone lately.

7

"Sorry. I'm still discovering things around here, too. A friend told me about this building, but it's even more beautiful in real life."

"Beautiful?" Chad asked with some disdain. "Looks pretty spooky to me. A great place to scare some friends on Halloween. Maybe I'll come back in October and bring my buddies."

He put the car in gear again, and we continued straight for a couple of blocks till Liberty ended where West South River Road veered off to the right, close to the water. I pointed. "Take this. It's even closer to the river than US 10."

"Now we're getting somewhere."

We drove for a few minutes past several large year-round homes, stately Victorian mansions, until the road narrowed, and the space between the pavement and the river became filled with black willow trees, brushy sumac, and overgrown grape vines. Occasional clumps of deep purple asters brightened the scene. The water wasn't visible, and there appeared to be no cottages along this stretch. "I don't know which sections have been built up by summer people," I apologized. At least I'd been in Cherry Hill long enough to know what cottage owners were called.

"We'll find them," Chad said with the confidence of the young. But, the landscape still didn't reveal any driveways on the water side. "I've been thinking about your dead body."

"What? It's not my body!"

"You know what I mean. It's just too weird, a name so much like the newspaper guy. Doesn't seem like a coincidence," Chad said.

"I agree, but he's much younger than Jerry Caulfield. Shorter, too. Even if someone was trying to hurt Jerry, they couldn't have mistaken the two men."

"No, the similarity isn't their looks, but their names. It's more like some kind of threat."

"Seems awfully far-fetched."

"Maybe. But it's pretty unlikely that a man who lives hours away, that no one seems to know, would come up here and get himself murdered by accident in a town with someone whose name is so similar."

I grinned. "Murdered by accident?"

"My point exactly."

"But what could it mean? It doesn't make much sense any way you look at it. And I don't think they know where he was killed." I was sure the Sheriff hadn't mentioned it, but maybe he knew and wasn't telling.

"I think it's a warning. I think someone wants to tell Jerry Cauliflower that he should be careful."

I clucked my tongue, and tried not to smile. "Caulfield, Jerry Caulfield. But who would have that big of a grudge against Jerry?"

"Don't ask me. It's your town. Think about it. People with that much power always have enemies. And he's old. He's had time to collect lots of them."

"Maybe, but I haven't been here long enough to hear much against him." Jerry didn't seem that old to me, but he did have control of considerable property in town. And I knew that four generations of Caulfields had lived on the upper edge of Cherry Hill society. Poorer folks always resented those with money. However, if this was a warning, a lot of planning had gone into it. Luring Jared Canfield to Cherry Hill had taken some cunning. Unless only his dead body had been brought here.

"Look, Ma, there's a road with a whole bunch of house numbers on that board, and a couple of 'For Sale' signs." He turned the wheel and we bounced into a pot-hole-riddled sand track. The road broke into three forks almost immediately, and names handpainted on slats nailed to trees suggested how one might find certain owners. However, the placement and angles of the boards didn't convince me that one could be sure of locating any particular cottage on one try. At the corner, some small realtors' signs on wire posts had been pushed into the ground. One of them had a blue arrow and read "Holiday Realty." I thought that must be the new lady I'd met Wednesday night. Both signs directed potential buyers to the left fork. Chad slowed down and took that road.

We bumped along for another half mile until the road widened into a sandy clearing containing three homes which seemed to have open space beyond. Chad parked the Jeep away from any of the buildings and practically leaped out his door. I followed a little more slowly.

No one seemed to be at any of the cottages, if they could be called that. All of them were full-size homes; one was modern, and the other two were older. We were drawn immediately to one of the older ones that was for sale.

"This is great, Ma! Vintage, and in really good condition."

A long set of dark green steps climbed to the main level of the house. A carved sign above the screen porch read "Chippewa Lodge." The building was square with an open porch, connected to the screen porch, and wrapped around the river side of the building. White clapboards and more green trim completed the classic look. A stone chimney rose from the roof. We quickly discovered why there had been a void beyond the houses. A high bank fell off steeply to a bend of the river. The water seemed deeper and swifter here than it did at my property.

I told Chad, "It's absolutely wonderful. But, this is probably worth two-hundred thousand dollars. A little out of your range, don't you think?"

"Yeah, but who knew there were awesome places like this in such a sleepy town? Most of it looks like a dump compared to home."

A stab of pain shot through my chest. Of course, he would still think of home as the place he grew up. But it no longer held fond memories for me. "This is my home now, Chad," I said in a quiet voice.

"Oh. Yeah. I didn't think about that. I'm sorry, OK? Let's try to find something smaller." He headed for the Jeep.

We continued downstream on West South River Road, driving

slowly. We stopped a couple more places, but everything we saw was either too large for Chad's potential budget or dilapidated almost beyond repair. I wasn't surprised. People didn't seem to want rustic cottages for vacations these days; they preferred secondary mansions.

About three o'clock, a small road sign notified us that we were entering Jalmari.

"Jalmari!" I said. "I didn't know it was so close. This is where the body was found."

"I think I see exactly where. Isn't that crime tape up there on the right?" He sounded excited.

We drove through remnants of the small town. It appeared to be somewhat viable, with a large gas station/convenience store, a pizza place and a canoe livery.

The yellow plastic tape was completely blocking the public access to the river. I was pretty sure that wasn't making the livery owners happy in August. We pulled slowly past the access, and as we crept by, I had a glimpse of two divers wading from the water. I also caught sight of a solid man with short grizzled hair and a scowl on his face, Detective Milford. He wore a tie, but no suit coat, and his sleeves were rolled part way up his arms. He looked hot and frustrated.

"Pull over, I want to talk with the Detective," I said.

"Sure, but I thought it wasn't your murder," Chad said with a grin.

Milford spotted me and began walking toward us. "Well, well, well. Look who turns up at the scene of the crime," he said.

"Detective Milford, this is my son Chad Raven. Actually, we were out looking at riverfront properties, and sort of wandered into Jalmari." I paused, but Milford just looked from Chad to me. "Is this where Mr. Canfield was killed?" I asked.

"Probably not, but we're checking the river for evidence since he was found here," he said, jerking a thumb toward the divers who were peeling off equipment behind him. "Hello, Chad. Are you planning to live here with your mother?"

"Oh, no. I'm just visiting. I'm still in college. We were sort of checking out cottages for fun."

"Did you find something in the water?" I asked. I was searching the concrete launch ramp for anything the divers might have brought in that looked out of place.

Milford responded. "Not here. But it is very interesting that the murder weapon has been identified as a hatchet, and so far the only extra hatchet to be found is one you brought to me."

I suddenly felt slightly dizzy. "So, that was blood on it?"

The detective shuffled his feet and sighed. "Yes it was."

My stomach turned over. The thought that I'd almost handled something which had been used to kill someone, even someone I didn't know, was not pleasant.

Chad was watching Milford closely, and his eyes narrowed to slits. "There's something he's not telling you, Ma."

"Your son is very observant," Milford said. "There was dried blood on the hatchet, but it was chicken blood."

"Chicken blood!" I said, taking a step back. "What on earth?"

Milford ran a hand over his short hair, and shook off drops of sweat. "That hatchet wasn't used on Jared Canfield unless that was earlier, and then it was cleaned exceptionally well before it was used on a chicken. Nevertheless, I don't think you should take any overnight trips until we get this cleared up."

"Me? You think I had something to do with this?"

"At this point, I'm not thinking. I'm just collecting data."

"What about Cora?" I said in my defense. "It was sent to her."

"She's already had a call from my office. You'll find a message in your own voicemail." He turned to Chad. "Nice to meet you, son. Will you be here long?"

"Just a couple of days."

Detective Milford rolled his eyes toward me and spoke to Chad in a man-to-man sort of tone that infuriated me, "See if you can keep your mother out of trouble."

Chad stuck out his hand to shake with the detective and said, "I doubt I'll be very good at that."

8

We headed back toward town with Chad still at the wheel. I was lost in a brown study featuring hatchets, local animosities, and derelict dwellings. Chad, however, was hungry. After just a few miles he said, "Your refrigerator was pretty empty. Is there somewhere we can get some food?"

I pulled myself back to the present, embarrassed that the recent events of my newly adopted county could so completely block out the limited time I had available to spend with my only child. "Sure. Let's go to Volger's Grocery. If Adele's there, you can meet her. She's one of my best friends."

It didn't take long to drive back to Cherry Hill, since we were no longer looking down every driveway or two-track. However, when we passed the old school, Chad pulled to the curb and studied the building carefully. I found this quite curious since he hadn't shared my enthusiasm for the architectural beauty of the brick building.

"Would you try to find out who owns it?" he asked.

"Why?"

"It really would be a great place to bring some friends for Halloween weekend. We could have a party and creep each other out."

"I don't know if the neighbors would appreciate that."

"What neighbors? There aren't any houses nearby in any direction. That makes it spookier. And the whole block across the street is empty. That must be where they played ball and stuff."

I was dubious. "I'll ask around, but don't expect miracles."

"You can come, too. Invite your friends. Make it a town party."

"That's not the point. I don't know what to tell you, but I'll try."

"Good." Chad nodded his head and pulled back into the traffic lane. "Now let's get some groceries."

I directed him to Main Street and to the parking beside Adele's store. Volger's Grocery looks like a holdover from another era. There is no wide, sliding-glass double door for a front entry. Instead, one passes under the shady branches of a large maple tree which has broken the sidewalk with its roots, steps up onto a large stone slab recessed between thrust display windows and then opens a squeaking wooden door secured with a thumb latch. Once inside, the sense of entering a time capsule is somewhat overcome. One can see the thriving business has expanded to fill two adjacent buildings, and sturdy metal beams support openings to those spaces. A side door with a ramp allows better access to the parking lot for rolling filled carts to vehicles.

Adele stocks more than convenience foods. She offers a full line of groceries, produce and meats. There's even a limited deli case. Without the success of Volger's Grocery, Cherry Hill would likely shrivel and die. Speculating with Chad about people in town who wield power made me realize that Adele was certainly in the upper ranks of influence, even if she didn't power dress.

She was working this day, and I introduced Chad to her.

He was cheerful and polite. "Hello, Mrs. Volger. I'm glad to see my mom makes friends with people who can supply food."

"Call me Adele, Chad. It's nice to meet you. Let me guess, her refrigerator is empty again."

I squirmed and tried not to look sheepish.

"It is," Chad said. "But I'm picturing something lean and red that could be cooked on a grill."

"Yes, indeed. A young fellow like you needs more than a salad to keep you going. I have some nice T-bones on sale."

"Now we're talking."

Before long we had a cart filled with steaks and hamburger, fresh corn on the cob, potato salad from the deli, more staples for the next day, assorted snack items and a bag of charcoal. Adele followed us around, chatting with Chad about Isle Royale, while keeping an eye on the cash register.

Chad seemed quite willing to talk to Adele. This was a side of him I hadn't seen before. He clearly thought of himself as an adult and soon barged right into the topic on his mind.

"My mom's been telling me about the unsolved murder. In fact, we just came from that place with the funny name..."

"Jalmari," I put in.

"Yeah, that's it. They had divers in the river and everything. But the detective said the guy hadn't been killed there. So that means he came from somewhere upstream. Like maybe from a cottage, or here in town."

"I heard on the scanner about the divers being called out," Adele offered tentatively. Maybe she was feeling less inclined to gossip after the debacle with the Jerry/Jared name mix-up.

Chad continued, "What I'm wondering, I mean, it would take someone who's lived here a long time to know..."

"Hold on," Adele said, scooting for the checkout line. She quickly rang out another customer, Harold Fanning, the city manager. He was picking up milk and bread. I also spotted a package of heat wraps for muscle pain in his pile. Maybe his wife was dragging him to exercise classes again.

I turned to Chad and whispered, "What are you trying to do? I thought you were teasing me for getting involved in all these local crimes."

He just grinned at me and shrugged. Adele motioned us to the checkout lane and began scanning items from our cart.

"Well, what is it you're wondering, son? I've lived here all my life. If you want answers, estimates, or even wild guesses, I'm the best source of information," she boasted.

Chad glanced my way and smirked. "I'm an outsider, for sure, but it looks to me like someone is trying to send a big fat warning to your Jerry Caulfield. So, who would want to see him out of the way?"

"Now that's an awfully serious question." Adele sat a full bag of our groceries back in the cart with a solid thump. "I've been thinking about that myself."

"Well?"

"Could be a lot of people. There's Jack Panther, of course."

"Jack Panther!" I exclaimed. I had no idea the owner of the Pine Tree had bad blood with Jerry.

"What's his beef?" Chad asked.

"Oh yes, Jack and Jerry go back a long way. When the Cherry Blossom Restaurant closed Jack tried to buy it. Jerry didn't think Jack had enough class to run a nice restaurant like that. He used his leverage with the officers at the bank, and Jack couldn't get a loan."

"What's this Jack do now?" Chad asked.

"He owns the little diner down the street," I said.

"But that's nothing compared to what the Cherry Blossom could have brought in, right?"

"Definitely," Adele said. "Jerry Caulfield is a good man, but he has a lot of influence over what happens in this town."

"I wonder if Jerry is making a mental list of people who might have something against him," I mused aloud.

Chad guffawed. "Ma, by now the police have sat him down and told him to make that list on paper. For them."

9

Chad complained about my tiny tabletop grill, but he managed to get a nice bed of coals going, and while I worked on shucking and boiling the corn, he watched the steaks.

Although it wasn't yet fall, sunset was coming noticeably earlier. We sat on the concrete terrace and angled our chairs toward the swamp, to keep the low orange sun out of our eyes. We watched the slanting light set the tops of the trees aglow. I still didn't have a picnic table, but the card table served well enough for the two of us. Chad was devouring his steak like a lumberjack. I was enjoying mine, but this was way too much food for me; I was already planning two more meals from this slab of meat. I'd add some vegetables and rice...

"Ma, I want you to think about something," Chad intruded on my thoughts, as he set down his fork. His tone was serious.

"What?"

"I don't think you are taking very good care of yourself. You don't have a television or an internet connection..."

My initial reaction to this statement wasn't positive, and I interrupted. "I don't miss having electronic toys at all. When I do, I'll get them."

"It's not just that. I don't like the way you live out here all alone at the end of a dirt road. You don't have furniture in all your rooms or any curtains at all. You hardly keep enough food in the refrigerator for your next meal."

"Hold on, there! I'm not very alone. I talk on the phone with Cora or Adele almost every day." Chad didn't need to know that was a bit of a fib. And, since when did college students worry about furniture and curtains? "I've been able to fix up this house just the way I want to, and I'm enjoying working on it a little bit at a time without your father telling me what to do. And, do I look like I'm starving?" I patted my hips which were neither skinny nor excessively padded for a woman of forty-two.

"Do you even know your closest neighbor?"

That made me stop and think. I had to admit I didn't know him very well. When I lived in the suburbs, there had been hundreds of people living within a half mile. Here, the closest house was two-plus miles away at Cherry Pit Junction. An old widower, Eino Tangen, lived there alone. He had been polite but hadn't encouraged me to contact him again when I'd knocked on his door in May to introduce myself.

Chad continued. "I'll bet you don't take your cell phone out with you half the time."

I wasn't willing to confess to the truth of that crime. "I'm on a first name basis with the Chief of Police, Tracy Jarvi," I protested. "Look, living in a small town is different. I don't understand it completely yet, but it's not about how physically close you are to other people. It's more about the connections. People who care and watch out for you."

I thought about Janice Preston, Cora's son Tom, Jerry Caulfield, the Leonards in Hammer Bridge Town, Jimmie Mosher and his mother Dee, and so many other new friends I'd made in the past six months.

"Yeah, but you've already gotten mixed up with three bad characters. Now there could be another murderer around, and I'm worried about you."

"Listen to me. I married your dad when we were just out of college, and then it was all about going where we needed to for his job, and what he wanted. I worked very hard to be the perfect corporate wife. But, he's decided to go in a different direction, and I'm getting a chance to start over. I'm not about to let someone else tell me how I'm supposed to live or what my house should look like. I don't need you to be Roger Junior."

"Aw, Ma. Don't get mad."

I stood up and collected the dishes from the table. I might have done so with just a teensy-weensy bit of excess vigor. Chad also rose and put his arms around me, tipping the plates. I watched a glob of steak sauce slide over the edge and land on the leg of his jeans before I could set the dishes back on the table. It was very strange to be held by my son who was now more than a head taller than I.

He squeezed me and then released his hold.

"You have steak sauce on your pants," I said with a sniff.

He reached down and wiped up the red spot, then licked his finger. "You're the mom," he said with a shrug.

We carried the dishes inside and washed them, avoiding any heavy topics of conversation. With no way to watch TV or a movie, Chad shut himself in his small room at ten. I climbed the stairs, undressed, and fell into my own bed. The harmonies of guitar chords and Chad's soft baritone voice floated up the stairway. As I drifted into unconsciousness, I wondered who was working harder on growing up, Chad or me?

10

Friday was clear and warm with a light breeze. It was as if the unpleasantness of the night before had blown away. Over breakfast, we sketched out plans for some narrow, hinged shutters that would be easy to store and maneuver into place in the fall. Toggles would hold the sections over the screens. The lumber company said they could deliver the plywood right away, and I also ordered paint, hardware, and a new circular saw blade.

While we waited for the truck, we set up sawhorses in the front yard, got out the tools, and hooked up a heavy-duty extension cord. Then we ate an early lunch, making sandwiches from the rest of the ham, so we'd be ready to work as soon as the delivery was made.

By noon we were cutting out simple shutters and lining them up in pairs to be sure the sizes were right. The whine of the saw made conversation impractical, but I kept rehashing all the events of the Caulfield/Canfield puzzle in my mind. After a while the cutting was done, and screwing on hinges and painting were quieter tasks.

"I've been thinking," I began.

"Yeah?"

"I'm not sure it makes a lot of sense to threaten a man by killing another person with a similar name, and by sending a hatchet to his ex-wife. Maybe this whole thing is just some weird coincidence."

Chad wiped the sweat from his cheekbones with the back of a hand, and managed to smear paint on his face. "Maybe, or maybe Jerry has gotten some direct threats. That would pull it all together. Have you asked him?"

"I thought you wanted me to stay away from this mystery."

He grinned. "I do. But it's hard to resist trying to figure it out, isn't it?"

I wasn't sure Jerry would share any personal information with me, but it was certainly possible there was more going on than what I was aware of.

By late afternoon, we had almost all the pieces of plywood painted with primer and one finish coat of Liberty Dusk, a deep charcoal blue, and all the hardware was ready to put in place.

"How about if we carry a picnic back by the river?" I asked. "You haven't seen that part of my property yet."

"Sounds good. If you pack up the food, I'll finish painting this shutter and put stuff away."

"Very traditional roles," I teased, giving Chad a light punch on the shoulder. But it was a good deal, and I headed for the kitchen to pack up some food.

Before long, Chad was carrying a small cooler loaded with hot dogs and soft drinks, and his guitar, and following me down the narrow trail that led directly to the river. I carried a bag of potato chips and a blanket. This was not the wider and higher mowed path that I walk almost every day for some exercise; this was barely more than a deer trail. Soon we entered the clearing Sunny Leonard had found earlier in the summer.

"Hey, this is wicked cool," Chad said.

"I like it." I'd done a bit of cleaning up since July, and had rolled a couple of logs around the brick-lined fire pit. I laid the folded blanket over a rough log.

"Is that an old foundation?" Chad asked, pointing at a rectangle of chipped and angled concrete blocks.

"It seems to be, but the cabin was demolished before I was ever here."

"How 'bout that rowboat?"

I laughed. "It's too rotten to be any use in the water. But I like the atmosphere." The overturned boat's faded and peeling red paint contrasted nicely with the green leaves, and blue-brown water.

Chad started a fire, and after a few minutes we had threaded hot dogs on peeled sticks and were holding them over the crackling flames. The river gurgled quietly against its banks as it flowed from our right to left. Sparrows twittered amongst the maple leaves which were shivering in the slight breeze. The earth smelled warm and damp, and the hardwood smoke tickled our nostrils. Opening the potato chip bag was an intrusive, rustling sound and crunching the chips was even worse. I tried to soften them first by holding them in my mouth so eating wasn't so noisy, but finally gave up and munched along with Chad, who felt no similar urge to be quiet.

We squirted ketchup and mustard into buns and snuggled a blackened hot dog into each one. Sitting here with my son, enjoying this simple meal, called up memories of family picnics from years past. Chad wiped greasy hands on his jeans, pulled the guitar from its case, and began to fool with the tuning pegs.

"I see why you like it here," he said, strumming a few chords.

"I really do, you know."

"I'm sorry I bugged you last night, Ma. You're doing fine without my advice."

"Thanks," I said. "It's nice that you care."

He played quietly for a few more minutes. "Instead of buying someone else's cabin, would it be all right if I rebuilt one here? It would give me a place to stay when I visit, and you'd have it to use, too."

"That sounds like a great idea."

"I'll work on some plans over the winter, and start building during spring break."

The sun was slipping lower and the flames had died down. I pulled my sweatshirt over my head. "Don't you want to go to Daytona or Las Vegas with your friends for vacation?" I asked.

"This place is lots nicer."

"I think so, too." I said.

We sat quietly, and I poked the fire up a bit while Chad strummed tunes. After a while, he sang "Blue Moon." It had been a family favorite.

"Ma?"

"Yeah?"

"I have to leave early in the morning so I can visit Dad and then get back to campus on time, you know."

"I know." I'd miss having him around, but I really was enjoying my new life, so my feelings were mixed.

"Don't forget to find out if I can use that old school for Halloween."

"OK," I said, but it still didn't seem like a great idea.

"Just do one thing for me."

"What's that?"

"Make a habit of carrying your cell phone, will you?"

I thought about when I'd tried to call 911 from my mobile phone in July, and there wasn't enough service to connect. But Chad didn't need to know that. I looked at him and smiled. "I'll try."

11

Chad drove away before seven o'clock. I was left with some nearly finished shutters and a big empty space around my heart. But I wasn't about to get down in the dumps over a son who was turning out to be a really nice person and who enjoyed my company. By the end of the day, I'd finished painting all the shutters and cheered up. There were some leftovers from our picnic to eat, but the refrigerator was nearly empty again by the end of the day. Maybe I really should try to do better with meal planning.

Over the next two weeks, life at the edge of Dead Mule Swamp settled into a calm and easy routine. Everyone pretty much forgot about the body of the stranger washed up at Jalmari.

I did call Harold Fanning to ask who owned the old school building, but didn't get any useful information. He told me the plat book still showed the city as the owner, but he knew the property had recently changed hands, and couldn't or wouldn't say anything more. I asked him if the building might be available to rent for an event, but his voice became tense, and he said I'd need to contact the owner. But I didn't know who that was. End of story.

Detective Milford didn't call Cora or me with more information about the hatchet, and we didn't call him. Perhaps we were uneasy with what we might learn. Maybe there just wasn't anything more to know, except that a chicken somewhere was also dead and probably even less-mourned than Jared Canfield. The citizens of Cherry Hill knew nothing about Canfield's family or friends, but he was human rather than a farm animal which should have brought him a bit of respect. I thought of Milford's order not to leave and wondered if we were supposed to stay in the county indefinitely. I wasn't sure if I'd get in trouble if I wanted to go to Emily City. But I had no plans to travel far, anyway.

Leaves began to turn to gold and red, and farmers and gardeners were speculating on the date of the first killing frost.

Janice Preston's mother-in-law died, and the locals were much more interested in this death. The funeral was at Crossroads Fellowship, where I'd been attending church. There was more rejoicing than sadness at the service; Eula Preston had been ninety-three and suffered from Alzheimer's. Everyone celebrated her long life and homegoing.

At the luncheon after the service, Adele hustled me into the kitchen to help with dishes. She wanted to be sure I knew that the Family Friends committee had a meeting coming up the next day. While I washed plates and forks, Adele's voice flitted through my consciousness like a bird. "Justin headed back to college, so now I don't have any good help at the grocery store," and "I hear Virginia Holiday is going to the Lutheran Church. That makes sense; it's where the money is," or "Jack Panther told me, just today, that he might have to close down for part of the winter, expenses are so high."

Before the dishes were done, I wiped my hands on a towel, draped it over Adele's arm, and excused myself. I could feel Adele's gaze boring into my back as I left, but I didn't care. I was in a funk and just wanted everyone to leave me alone.

If I'd been in a better mood and been willing to chat, Adele would have sent me home with enough leftovers from the luncheon to keep me in food for at least a day and a half. As it was, I knew I'd have to either eat peanut butter sandwiches or scrambled eggs made with water unless I made a trip to the grocery store. I didn't want to go to Volger's. Although Adele was at the church, she could return to the store any time, and I didn't want to talk.

So, not taking Detective Milford's warning literally, I drove to Emily City, a fairly large community in Sturgeon County, one county to the east, and pulled into the ample parking lot at the IGA. The anonymity of shopping in a larger store held a lot of appeal just then. If there had been a Wal-Mart in town, I probably would have gone there just to be surrounded by lots of shoppers I didn't know.

Inside the store, I was cheered by twelve numbered aisles of canned and boxed goods and three long outside walls lined with coolers containing produce, meats, and dairy products. I hadn't realized how much I'd missed having lots of choices. I pulled a cart from the rack and began wandering through the produce section, selecting tropical fruits, novelty squash, and an assortment of salad greens that weren't iceberg lettuce.

I was filling a paper bag with bulk coffee beans when behind me a deep, familiar voice said, "How are you, Ana?"

I nearly jumped out of my skin. Beans scattered on the floor. Fortunately, not too many. Turning, I tried to kick the errant brown ovals under the display rack. I found myself face to face with Jerry Caulfield, who was looking highly amused.

"Jerry!" I said. "You scared me."

"I see that," he said. "Are you feeling guilty for shopping outside Cherry Hill?"

"No. Not really." I looked around for a way to escape. "Maybe a little."

Jerry also had a shopping cart. I noticed he had picked out several bottles of regional wine and some expensive cheeses.

"Let me guess. You just didn't feel like talking to Adele any more today."

"Sometimes I do feel a little overwhelmed," I admitted. "What are you doing here?"

"I have an idea," Jerry said, ignoring my question. "I've been meaning to talk to you. Why don't you let me take you out to dinner tonight?"

"Dinner? Out?" I looked toward the store entrance again.

"Yes, the evening meal." Jerry drew his hand across his upper lip, smoothing his mustache. "People dress up, go to a restaurant, eat, talk, drink a little wine..."

"Um... I have these groceries. I'm wearing clothes for a funeral."

"Oh, the service for Eula Preston. Well, it's early anyway. Why don't I pick you up at your place about seven?" he asked.

"That would work," I said. I shook my head. "Are you serious?"

"I am. I would very much like to have dinner with you. As for 'serious?' I'm not immediately proposing a long-term relationship, but dinner seems fairly safe."

I heard myself say, "I'd like that a lot."

"Good. We'll come back to Emily City. I had something a little nicer than the Pine Tree in mind."

Jerry reached out and lightly touched my upper arm. I was too stunned to comment as he turned and pushed his cart toward the meat section.

12

After putting away over a hundred dollars worth of groceries and household supplies I turned on the water in the bathtub and began to shuffle clothes in my closet in anticipation of the evening. I hadn't paid this much attention to what I would wear since attending *Mosè in Egitto* over a year ago at the Chicago Opera Theater. My plum-colored skirt, coupled with a deep gold silk blouse, accented with a scarf in swirled fall tones, which included the plum and gold, seemed subtly elegant, but not too dressy. Jerry was tall, so I also laid out a pair of heels.

As I slid into the warm bathwater, I realized I was both excited and apprehensive. Jerry was a sophisticated and respected man, not to mention good-looking. I'd been treated to a light breakfast at his home, back in May, when I'd first met him. Since then, we'd never exchanged more than a few words at a time, always at public gatherings. His position as owner and editor of the newspaper kept him from slipping into the quagmire of gossip that Adele so loved, and yet his ability to gain information and insight into local happenings was excellent, as borne out by the fact that the *Cherry Hill Herald* enjoyed a large subscription base. I was looking forward to conversation with him, although I had no idea what we might find to talk about. Had he said he wanted to talk to me about something specific?

There was always the mysterious Jared Canfield of Royal Oak. Maybe Jerry would share with me any connections he might have found with the dead man. Maybe he knew something about the reason the body had been dumped in the Petite Sauble River. The topic didn't seem like it would fit into a romantic dinner, but I certainly could feel my curiosity rising.

And the whole idea of "romantic" was somewhat terrifying. Of course, I was flattered to be asked to dinner by a handsome, available man, but the truth was that I didn't yet have a desire to get into an intimate relationship of any kind. Above all, I didn't want to place myself into some sort of odd, awkward triangle. Adele made it abundantly clear that she liked Jerry very much, and considered him extremely eligible. Cora, at the opposite extreme, was his ex-wife, and had no use for him at all. Although she'd shared some of the basic reasons things had gone wrong, I couldn't help but suspect there was more to it. If either of my friends thought I was dating Jerry Caulfield, I was pretty sure they wouldn't be my friends for long. And, Cora and Adele already despised each other.

The water was almost cold, and my skin was pickling. I let my anxieties over the coming evening drain away with the water; I dried off and dressed. My hair, a light-brown pageboy, was too short to do much with, but I brushed it and straightened the part. Makeup or not? I added a bit of lipstick and mauve eyeshadow. That would have to do. Maybe a spot of cologne. I was just rummaging in an unpacked box of cool weather clothes for my light wool cape when I heard a car pull into the yard. It was Jerry.

When I opened the door I was pleased to see that he hadn't dressed too formally either. He wore pleated gray slacks, a pale gray shirt, and a blue blazer. His conservative tie was striped in tones of blue.

"Come in," I offered, "or do we have a reservation deadline to make?"

"We have a few minutes," Jerry said, stepping into the living room. "You look wonderful! And you've done a huge amount of work on this old place. May I have a tour? My parents were friends with Jed and Hazel Mosher, but I haven't been inside for decades."

I was gratified to have a reason to show off my progress to someone who was familiar with the old house. As we walked from room to room, Jerry explained that he'd spent some time here as a child. Despite the progress I had made, it was a little embarrassing to realize how much there was yet to do, especially when Jerry mentioned that the faded and stained kitchen wallpaper was just as he remembered it. However, he praised me for the upstairs addition and liked the blue and white I'd chosen for the living room.

Jerry was driving a silver Chrysler Sebring.

"I just had the car fitted with an aftermarket sound system. Do you like classical music?" he asked as he opened the passenger door for me.

"Very much," I replied. So, on the way to Emily City our conversation was confined to a few comments about the weather and local landmarks. We drove past forests hinting of the red and orange splendor which would soon be at its peak, while the strains of Vivaldi's *Four Seasons* filled the car in quad stereo.

Shortly before eight we reached Chez Léon, on a side street in the downtown section of Emily City. It was not yet fully dark, but a soft golden glow was spreading from the lighted windows. Jerry opened the door and motioned for me to precede him. I protested that this was the twenty-first century, but he smiled and said that he was a twentieth century kind of fellow, which reminded me that he was probably twenty years my senior. We were soon seated at a quiet corner table covered with burgundy linen. A candle with a faceted amber globe thrust warm rays of dancing light across the cloth. The hostess left us with menus and a wine list.

"I recommend the baked salmon with herbs," Jerry said. "If you'd like that, I'll order a bottle of Sauvignon Blanc."

"That all sounds good," I answered, thinking it had been a long, long time since I'd let someone else choose what I was going to eat.

The waitress took the order from Jerry and returned quickly with the wine and a basket containing a small loaf of warm brown bread. Jerry poured and I sliced. While we sipped at the wine and nibbled the crusty, nutty bread, Jerry began to tell me stories of Cherry Hill from his boyhood. Seeing the inside of my house had opened a flood of memories. He seemed to be lost in another world.

Abruptly, he stopped and looked directly at me. "How rude of me," he said. "My small-town roots have overcome my manners.

Please tell me more about yourself. I know you're recently single again, but I know very little about you. If it's not too painful, I'd like to hear where you're from and how you came to move here."

I began to tell Jerry bits of information about Roger, my ex. I didn't want to dump a lot of emotional rhetoric on him, but it was nice to have someone new to share with. As I talked, I realized that I'd gained some perspective on the situation over the past year and didn't have as much need for a shoulder to cry on as I had several months ago. Jerry asked probing but gentle questions at several awkward moments, and we were nearly through the main course—the salmon turned out to be delicious— before the topic was pretty well played out. I'd been doing most of the talking, and less eating, so Jerry's plate was emptier than mine. It was time to turn that situation around.

"Enough about me," I said. "I can't help but be curious about your feelings concerning the murder of Jared Canfield last month. Do you think it was just a coincidence, or have you felt threatened?"

Without any indication that he was startled at my bold question, Jerry switched topics with me. "Detective Milford and Tracy have certainly been asking me that, also," he began. "The truth is, and I think I can trust you not to spread this around, some strange things have been happening lately. I've found several notes under the door at the newspaper office."

"What kind of notes?"

"Just heckling sorts of messages, like 'You know you've abused your privileges. Time wounds all heels,' or 'It won't be long until Forest County knows the kind of person you really are.'"

"Those sound ominous," I said, alarmed.

He shrugged and stabbed a broccoli floret. "Well, maybe. They don't say anything specific. There's no actual threat included in any of them. They're just harassment, nothing you can guard against. And they could be from anyone. There's no mention of Jared Canfield. Someone might have simply taken advantage of that situation to air some unspecified grievances."

"Is that all?"

"Some minor vandalism, if it's even that. Flower pots knocked off my porch rail, for instance. Did some person do that, or was it a neighborhood cat prowling at night?"

"What do the police think?"

"They've taken the notes, but there are no fingerprints, and the paper is from a cheap tablet one can buy anywhere."

I recalled something Chad had predicted, and asked, "Have the police asked you to make a list of people who might have something against you?"

"Oh, yes. It's a difficult task. I've lived here all my life, and in any small town the paper and its owner hold a lot of power. I might have angered any number of people. The *Herald* has supported certain political candidates, for example. Losers, or even losers' families, might hold me responsible. Someone might feel socially snubbed and be holding a grudge. Bernice, my wife..."

"Yes, Cora told me she died. I'm sorry."

"Thank you, but it was quite a while ago. Anyway, Bernice had an impeccable social conscience. She would invite all the right people to parties and keep things on an even keel when those with differing opinions got too vocal. I'm afraid I haven't even tried to keep up any sort of calendar of entertainment for publishing colleagues, or even friends."

"Would someone find that worthy of a serious threat?" I thought that was a silly motive for any kind of physical retribution.

"It seems unlikely, but then, my thinking just doesn't travel in those directions. For some, being socially snubbed can be quite important."

If you're in junior high, I thought. Feeling bold, I ventured, "I heard that Jack Panther might be angry with you over a lost chance to buy the Cherry Blossom."

"It's certainly possible," Jerry said thoughtfully. "I had forgotten about that, and I guess the Pine Tree isn't doing so well. The town could definitely support one or even two restaurants, but Jack is letting the diner become a wreck. That doesn't encourage anyone but a few regulars to patronize it."

I smiled as I recalled the peeling duct tape and fly-spotted window sills.

Jerry continued. "Jack's lack of pride in the physical facility, even though the food is good, bears out my conviction that he couldn't have adequately managed a nice restaurant like the Cherry Blossom."

We finished our fish, and Jerry poured some more wine. The waitress cleared the dishes and placed a small plate of layered chocolate-mint candies between us. She added a carafe of coffee and two cups.

"Would you care for dessert?" Jerry asked.

"No thanks, these mints are perfect," I answered, unwrapping one and popping it in my mouth to demonstrate my satisfaction.

"Now it's my turn to change the topic," Jerry said, also taking a mint. He unwrapped it carefully with his long fingers and smoothed the foil wrapper into a neat square. I noticed his nails looked professionally manicured.

"OK," I said. "Fair enough."

"I've really enjoyed getting to know you tonight. I didn't realize you had taught Literature at the college level. I'd never say that Cherry Hill lacks culture, but once in a while it's nice to have a friend who might be able to discuss a serious book with some animation."

"Thank you. I've had a good time too. You've given me a chance to reflect on my situation in a new way."

"You are a beautiful woman, Ana. I'd love to have dinner with you occasionally, if you are amenable."

"Jerry, I, I..." I stammered. The truth was, that as much as I had enjoyed the evening and Jerry's company, I was sure now that our age difference, and some other fundamental differences, kept me from being attracted to the man in a romantic way.

"Ana, don't jump to any conclusions. Actually, I want to be quite clear on what I'm proposing."

I watched the light from the candle flicker across the tablecloth and sparkle on the wine glasses. "Go on," I finally said. I held my breath apprehensively.

"I need to be quite clear on one thing. I'm not looking for a relationship beyond one of friendship."

I let myself breathe. "Friendship would be perfect," I said with a sigh.

"However," he continued, "what I have in mind is actually more risky. I'd like to involve you in a conspiracy, if you are willing."

13

"Conspiracy?" The word itself was shocking. "I thought you were an upstanding citizen, Jerry. What on earth do you have in mind?"

"Oh, probably nothing illegal, but it's definitely on the sneaky side. You seem like the right person to help me."

I wasn't sure if that was a compliment or not. "You think I'm sneaky?"

"No, no, that's not what I meant. But you are certainly in an excellent position to accomplish certain things," he added cryptically.

I poured a cup of coffee and took a hasty swallow. I wanted a clear head for the rest of this conversation, wherever it was going. The coffee burned my tongue and I spilled some of the hot liquid on the tablecloth. Apparently, Jerry assumed I was shocked or anxious about his intentions. He rose and reached across the table, intending to take the cup from my hand, murmuring, "Oh, bother. I've upset you."

Waving him away, I set the cup down without help. "The coffee's too hot," I explained with a tentative smile, wiping my lips on my napkin. "It's nothing. Tell me what grand perfidy you have in mind."

Jerry took his seat again and hitched the chair nearer to the table. He leaned in close and spoke softly. "You know Cora's still in love with me, right? We just have to help her realize it."

I was very glad I didn't have a mouthful of anything just then, or I probably would have gagged. Or spit it all over my potential co-conspirator. My surprise clearly showed.

"Oh, yes," Jerry continued, nodding. "That's why she's so adamant in saying negative things. She has to keep convincing herself she's angry."

"She certainly doesn't sound like a person in love with you," I said dryly.

Jerry's lip twitched. "You know Cora pretty well, but perhaps not quite well enough. She's so committed to her history project that she's afraid if she actually loves a person there won't be room in her heart for both. I didn't have that figured out when we were together before."

"And now you think you understand her better?" I was skeptical.

"Definitely. What she wants, what she needs, is an interesting historical building in town for her museum. For that, she needs money. I have plenty, and I don't need nearly as much as I have. What I do need is Cora, a happy Cora."

I thought I'd probe the topic with what little I did know. "I know she was interested in turning your house into a museum."

"Yes, but that wasn't very practical."

"Listen, Jerry. If you are thinking of buying some building to make Cora happy with the expectation that she'll re-marry you, I'm not sure that's very realistic. And it doesn't sound very romantic, either."

"It's romantic enough. The way to Cora's heart is through a building. Trust me. No one's ever appreciated what she does to any great extent. She doesn't give people much of a chance because she's overly defensive about how poor her set-up is."

"Poor set-up! You must be kidding. Her displays are wonderful," I said.

"Of course they are," Jerry said without missing a beat. "But not compared to what she sees in her head. She has visions of different rooms for different eras, whole clusters of rooms with themes, a searchable database for researchers..."

"I know about that," I interrupted. "I've been working on it with her."

"And you know how much time that will take to bring it up to Cora's standards."

"I do." I took another sip of coffee. It was cooler now, but I could feel Jerry warming to the topic.

"Anyway, my strategic plan has two prongs. First, a building.

The other is to make her jealous. That's where you come in." He leaned back and smiled broadly, showing his teeth.

I leaned back myself, in reaction. I felt my eyebrows rise and tried to buy some time by looking around. I realized the restaurant had emptied and quieted. Only a few other diners remained. The candle on the table was burning low and guttering, throwing shifting shadows on the wall. I pinched the flame out and tried to focus, surprised at how much darker the room was without that tiny light. The implication of Jerry's plan clearly was that Cora would see me dating Jerry and suddenly want him for herself. But, did Jerry know about Adele's designs on his future? I thought she wouldn't be at all pleased if Jerry decided to take up with the newcomer— me. Would Cora actually be jealous, or would she just write me off as someone who chose to consort with the enemy? I could end up with no friends at all as a result of this scheme.

"Tell me what you're thinking." Jerry broke my concentration.

"I think it's pretty far-fetched," I blurted out.

Jerry smiled broadly again. "But worth a try?"

"I'm not sure. You are asking me to risk losing my best friends."

"Friends, plural?" he asked.

"Yes, you must be aware of how Adele Volger feels about you. She wouldn't be happy at all to see you dating me."

"Ana, Adele is an old friend. She likes me a great deal. I like her. We tried seeing each other for a while after our spouses died, but we aren't suited for each other as a couple. If I let Adele in on the plan, and have her blessing, would you agree?"

"You know Adele can't keep a secret for ten minutes," I challenged.

"There is that. Hmm. All right. I'll have to think about how to handle Adele.

I switched to discussing the other prong of attack. It seemed safer. "You have a building in mind for the seduction of Cora?" I twisted my lips into a grin that I hoped looked ironic rather than sarcastic.

"Of course. I've bought the old school building."

I laughed loudly, and one of the remaining couples in the restaurant stared at us for a moment. I shook my head and added, more quietly, "I should have known."

"I had a moment of concern. It has sat empty for over thirty-five years, and then when I went to make the city an offer, they said someone else had put in a bid. That lady who bought the small building on my block..."

"Virginia Holiday?"

"Yes. She managed to get herself listed as the realtor, and she wouldn't even talk to me. Then, one day, Harold Fanning called me up and said Ms. Holiday had dumped the property back on the city, that her potential buyer fell through. He wanted to know if I was still interested."

"So you worked through Holiday Realty?"

"No, I bought it directly from the city. They weren't happy with the cost of all the paperwork they'd done, just to have it revert to them in a month."

"How do you propose to tell Cora?" The word "propose" seemed eerily appropriate.

"I'm not sure yet. I'm still working on that part of the plan."

"This is sort of crazy," I began, unwrapping another candy and popping it in my mouth for the fortifying effects of the chocolate. "My son, Chad, was here last month."

"I heard about it, but I didn't have the pleasure of meeting him."

"He thinks that old building is creepy, and he wanted me to find out about renting it for a weekend so he and some friends could come here at the end of October and scare each other silly. But I couldn't find out who owned it. I also talked to Harold, but it must have been when that new woman had it tied up. He wouldn't tell me a thing."

"A Halloween Party, eh?" Jerry mused. "Not bad, but too narrow an appeal."

"What are you talking about?"

"I need an adult audience. A spooky event wouldn't draw enough townspeople."

"To what?"

Jerry leaned in and took my hand. "How about a Harvest Ball? Would you do me the honor of attending with me?"

I let Jerry continue to hold my hand but shook my head and said, "I'm not following you."

He released my hand and held up four fingers. "I need four things. One, I need the building. That's accomplished." With the other hand, he folded his index finger into his palm. "Two, I need a reason to start cleaning it up, check the plumbing and all that, without having to make up some outrageous business adventure that no one would believe. I was so concerned someone else was trying to buy it that I haven't even checked out the interior condition, I just bought it.

"Then, I have to get Cora and a large group of citizens all in the same place at the same time, so I can present it to her. Last, she has to be shocked enough and off-balance enough to realize that she cares about me." His fingers were now all curled and enclosed in his left hand. He opened both hands and held them out, palms up, as if presenting the world with a gift, Cora with a future.

"And, you think she'll actually be jealous of me and want you back?"

"I do. And of course, our game will be over that night. We'll tell her it was part of the secret to get the building ready."

"You'll be lucky to get her to come. She hates big social gatherings like that."

Jerry sighed. "I know. Maybe we can figure out a way to make the ball have some historical context, where her expertise is needed."

"What if we reenacted the shooting of that Judge? What was his name? She'd have to be involved to be sure we get it all right." I heard myself slide right into the conspiracy but didn't have enough sense to put on the brakes.

"Ah. Reuben Pierce Oldfield. A local legend of infamy."

"She'd want to bring in the exact furniture. She has it all, you know."

"I don't feel very good about turning a bunch of young people loose to have paintball fights in the building or whatever kids do nowadays, but I wonder if Chad and his friends would want to be actors in a murder drama."

I felt a bit slighted at Jerry's opinion of my particular college student's respect for private property, but then again, I knew that boys' pranks could get out of hand. "I can certainly ask him," I said. However, I had some misgivings at Chad's possible reaction since he wouldn't be in charge of the plot.

Jerry now took both of my hands in his. He smiled warmly but seemed intensely preoccupied at the same time. "Ana, this is going to be the biggest social event Cherry Hill has had for a decade. We'll draw in people from four counties. I'll have food catered..."

"Maybe give Jack Panther some business?"

A frown creased Jerry's face. "Jack doesn't do fancy foods, but, yes, surely there would be some work for him."

"Maybe Cherry Hill folks prefer plain, solid fare, nicely served," I suggested.

The frown lines disappeared and Jerry was off and running with ideas again. "Of course. Janice and Suzi Preston could be in charge of the presentation. It all looks better without the backdrop of the Pine Tree Diner. Small pulled pork sandwiches, fruit and vegetable trays, tarts."

"Slow down," I said. "Create an atmosphere; you said a Harvest Ball, and turn it over to Janice and Jack. I'm sure they'll do a great job."

"You're right, of course."

"Assuming you have plenty of money to fix up that wreck of a building, and have correctly deduced Cora's reactions, that leaves us with just one major problem."

"What's that?" Jerry asked.

"Adele."

Jerry released me again. He sighed and rose from his chair, placing his napkin on the table. I stood up too, stretching my back, which was stiff from the extended time we'd spent in concentrated discussion.

As he helped me drape my cape over my shoulders, he reiterated the problem. "Adele," he echoed pensively.

14

Jerry and I arrived back at my house well after ten o'clock, and he escorted me to the front door where the small porch light bleached a pale oval on the white clapboards.

"Do you have time to begin the plan tomorrow?" he asked.

"Doing what?"

"If we meet at the school and start going through the rooms we can compile a list of immediate repairs that need to be made. Someone is sure to see our cars and start the rumor mill working." He winked.

"That's practical, at least," I admitted. "Wait. I have a meeting of Family Friends at ten. But I could meet you at the school building around eleven or a bit later."

"Perfect," Jerry said. He leaned forward and gave me a brotherly kiss on the cheek. As he unbent I saw he was grinning. "The gentleman should always thank the lady for a lovely evening," he said.

"It was very nice. Thank you," I said. "I'm not sure your plan is going to have the full outcome you're hoping for, but we should have fun finding out."

Family Friends is a committee of the Crossroads Fellowship church. We organize help for families who are experiencing medical problems or who might be having a tough time financially. Sometimes there is a lot of need in the community, and the meetings last quite a while until everyone agrees on what is the best way to use our resources. Thursday's meeting, thankfully, wasn't one of those. Adele was the committee chairperson, and after we'd all filled our coffee cups and helped ourselves to generous squares of coffee cake, she called the meeting to order. The pleasant aroma of cinnamon filled the room.

Shelby Nickerson had just had her baby, and committee member Geraldine Longcore had already arranged the schedule of people who would take in hot meals for the next week. We heard a short report on Corliss Leonard's progress in the adult literacy program. As usual, John Aho made a brief appearance. He had to take time out from his work at the service station and generally arrived late in his greasy uniform. He always smelled strongly of industrial hand cleanser which didn't combine well with the cinnamon. A couple of other people were being given rides to medical appointments or having casseroles delivered several days a week. But no new crises were brought to our attention.

The most challenging part of the meeting for me was to interact with Adele. I'd left the funeral the day before in a way that Adele might have taken as an affront. And now, I also had the guilty knowledge of Jerry's plan. Adele kept looking at me during the various reports, and I struggled to meet her gaze.

Afterwards, she gathered up her committee notebook and large purse and approached me. "What's bothering you, Ana?" she asked.

"Nothing much," I lied. "I was overly tired yesterday, and I miss Chad. I'm sorry I wasn't paying attention to you. Was there something important you wanted to tell me?"

"Not really. I think we are all waiting for the other shoe to drop on that hatchet murder. It's pretty strange that the police can't seem to get any leads. I'm sure you are jumpy about that—knowing you are involved."

"Involved? Adele! That's pushing it. Really. The one thing the police do seem sure of is that the hatchet Cora and I found wasn't the murder weapon."

"Nevertheless... And something's made you nervous today, too," she added. "I can tell your thoughts are miles away. You can't fool me."

"No, I suppose not," I said absently. But I had no idea what to say since Jerry and I hadn't decided on what to tell her.

"Ana! You're drifting again. Well, I'm not going to pry into your business. You know I don't meddle where I'm not wanted. But you let me know if you need to talk, all right?"

Adele's assertion brought a genuine smile to my face even if it was for the wrong reasons. "Thanks," I said. "You're a good friend. I'll let you know if I need anything."

I glanced at the clock and it was ten fifty-six, just enough time to drive the few blocks to the old school to meet Jerry. Adele and I walked out of the building together. But when I turned north out of the parking lot instead of south which would have taken me home, I could almost feel Adele's gaze boring into the back of my head.

Jerry's Chrysler was already parked in front of the red brick school, and he was standing at the top of the entrance steps holding a large wad of keys in his hand and fiddling at the lock. I parked my Jeep behind his car. Let the gossip begin! He pulled the heavy door open just as I reached the bottom step and stuffed the ring of keys into the pocket of a down vest he had layered over a blue denim shirt. He was wearing jeans, and I was glad I had done the same.

"Ah, my partner in crime," he called cheerfully.

"Hey! Watch what you call me," I shot back. "I'm in enough trouble over that silly hatchet."

We entered the cold, damp entrance hall together. We were in an open squarish space that teed into a hallway at the far side. The space was dingy with smudged, yellowing painted walls. The lower half of each wall had dark varnished wainscoting. Small off-white floor tiles had been set in a mosaic pattern encircling a large maroon cherry, on which we now stood. The cherry's stem was made to look as if it was on fire.

"The Cherry Hill Bombers," Jerry explained, pointing to the pattern in the tiles.

I rolled my eyes.

Jerry took my elbow and turned me slightly to the right. He pointed to a door with an extra-large pane of glass. "The main office," He explained. "Mrs. Sergeant kept everyone under control. And she was only the secretary. The last principal was Harold Fanning."

"Harold Fanning!" I exclaimed. "You're kidding. The city manager? I didn't know he was in education."

"He's retired now, of course. He was a young principal then. After this building closed, he became a vocational counselor at the new Forest County Central consolidated school."

Jerry steered me left again to face the east-west hallway. There were solid wood double doors straight ahead. We crossed to them, and he pulled one open. It gave a wretched creak, something of a cross between a screech and a moan. We stepped through, and it crashed shut behind us.

"I guess that door closer is broken," Jerry said, with a small laugh.

The place was beginning to give me the creeps, and we'd only been here five minutes. I decided Chad had been right.

"This room sure brings back memories," Jerry said. We were now in a large room that had served as both a small gymnasium and an auditorium. Narrow blond floor boards had mellowed golden, and a dark red velvet curtain hung crookedly at the edge of the low stage. "School dances, roller skating parties, dodgeball, plays, assemblies..."

"This was your school, wasn't it?" I asked rhetorically. I could see the memories playing behind his eyes.

"Mine and my father's. And my children's, too. I completely understand why the consolidation had to happen, but buying this building is as much for me and the entire town as for Cora. There are some things you just can't let disappear, or you lose your bearings."

Although I saw decades worth of dirt and could smell the mold in the dank curtains, I knew that to Jerry this building was beautiful.

He continued. "This auditorium is where the Harvest Ball will need to be. It's not in bad shape, just needs cleaning. Maybe fresh paint. We'll have to check out the kitchen, and of course the plumbing and furnace. There are a few broken windows, and I'll have someone replace them to make the building weathertight before winter. Any other remodeling and repairs can be done later."

"Still, that's a lot to accomplish in a few weeks. When are you thinking of having this Ball?"

"I like something mid to late October. It can't compete with Halloween, or the small kids will feel cheated. We'll get it done." He spoke with the confidence of a man with money.

"What do you think will be the biggest problem in getting even this part of the building ready for public use?" I asked.

"The boiler, certainly. Well, unless kids have thrown cherry bombs in the toilets."

"That would be ironic," I said with a smirk.

"Let's go to the basement right now," he said. Once again, he grabbed my arm and led me back through the double doors. We turned left and followed that hallway to the end. A wide flight of stairs led upward to a landing where it turned back on itself and continued to the upper floor. The hall where we stood made a turn to the left, toward the back of the building. We followed it. About halfway down that hallway was an unmarked door with no window. Jerry tried it, but it was locked. "That's a good sign," he said, pulling out the wad of keys. "Not so easy for vandals to get in and make mischief."

In a minute he opened the door. With no landing at the top, a flight of metal industrial steps led immediately downward into total darkness.

"Did you have the electricity turned on yet?" I asked.

He flipped the switch up and down a few times with no response. "I called and requested it, but I guess they have to inspect things first. Don't worry, I brought a light."

From the left pocket of his vest, Jerry drew a flashlight. It was small, but had a strong, although narrow, beam. He started down ahead of me. He'd worn leather-soled shoes, and his footsteps clanked with a hollow sound on the stairs. My sneakers were quieter, but the whole adventure was beginning to feel like some sort of juvenile mystery tale.

"Bah," Jerry said, swatting at some cobwebs that had caught him across the face.

"Thanks for clearing those out for me," I said.

"My pleasure, I think. The boiler probably hasn't been fired up since 1972. I'll have to get Todd Ringman over here. He still knows how to deal with these old systems. Ah, I thought I remembered they were over here."

We had reached the bottom of the steps and Jerry shone the light to the right. The cone of illumination was small, but at the far end of the room I could see two large boilers raised on legs, with dozens of pipes disjointedly angling out from them like the legs of a dying spider. Various gauges and other unknown projections were covered with a thick layer of dust.

He moved the beam of light back until we could see down the passageway which extended straight from the bottom of the steps.

"What's down there?" I asked.

"Should be the electric circuit room, and the custodians' break room. Storage. Things like that. I think the electric service was upgraded just before the building was abandoned. It would be great if there are breakers instead of fuses."

The light stabbed down the hall. "Look at the floor," I said. "I think someone's been down here recently."

Jerry lowered the flashlight, and we could see that the dust was definitely scuffed up. No clear footprints, but something had disturbed the thick coating that covered every other surface.

"Well, remember, the building was almost sold to someone else. Unlike me, they probably looked around before buying. Or, not buying, as it turned out."

"True enough."

We proceeded down the hall on a concrete floor. Here the dust muffled our steps, but as we loosened the old dirt, a fusty smell rose with it, and swirls of tiny particles and threads danced in the flashlight's beam. A cold breeze was coming from somewhere. The first room on the left had no door and one side wall was lined with lockers. Two tables with benches filled the center of the space. A coffee pot and hot plate stood neglected on a table pushed against the opposite wall next to a chipped and stained porcelain sink. A small window, high on the far side, had one broken pane of glass.

The next room did have a door, but it wasn't locked. "Here's the breaker panel," Jerry said as we entered.

I hadn't needed the explanation, but it was reassuring to hear his voice. I don't consider myself skittish, but this place was getting on my nerves. He played the light across the tall gray electric boxes, whose doors were hanging open.

"Everything here looks pretty good," he continued. "Each switch is labeled. Here are classroom numbers, and 'front office,' 'west boys lav,' 'west girls lav,' etc. This shouldn't be difficult to put in working order." He flipped a few switches back and forth. "They feel solid," he added.

"What else do you want to check?" I asked. "I'm getting chilly."

"Let's look in the rest of the rooms as long as we're down here. Do you want my vest?"

"I'm okay, but let's speed things up a bit."

Jerry closed the panel boxes and returned to the hallway. I had stepped out of the room ahead of him and turned to the next room, hoping to hurry us along. The door was ajar, and I pushed it open. Jerry came up behind me and shined the light over my shoulder. He angled the beam downward slightly as he lifted the flashlight high.

In the middle of the floor, a metallic wedge shape reflected the beam. Surrounding the hatchet was a large pool of a dark substance, curled and flaked at the edges, but which was smooth and shiny near the middle, and cracked into irregular polygons. It looked like a pool of dried liquid. I was stunned.

"I think we've found where Jared Canfield was killed," I finally said. My voice caught in my throat. I'd never seen so much blood. I turned and buried my face against Jerry Caulfield's comforting chest.

15

Jerry kept one arm around me, and I didn't try to escape. With the other hand he produced a cell phone and deftly thumbed in some numbers. "I'm calling Tracy Jarvi," he explained. "It looks as if the city police will have the lead on this now. Let's go wait in the break room."

We retraced our steps down the hallway, and sat at one of the tables in the dank, chilly room with the lockers. Jerry flicked off the flashlight.

"Bob? Let me talk to Chief Jarvi will you? It's important." In the glow of the phone's screen I could see Jerry's eyes, which seemed filled with concern. The phone squawked. "Tracy? Jerry Caulfield here. I'm in the basement at the old Cherry Hill school building. Ana Raven is here with me. We've found a hatchet and what appears to be a pool of blood."

"Tell her it's all dried up," I said.

Jerry nodded at me while speaking into the phone. "No, it must have been here a while. We didn't touch anything in that room, except we've walked down the hallway, and someone else had also done that recently. We've touched light switches and walls. Oh, and door handles." He paused. "All right. We'll do that."

He pushed a button to end the call, leaving us in darkness except for the dim light filtering from the high window. Its glass was nearly black with dirt, but a single ray from the high sun shone through the broken panel and illuminated a spot on the floor. It was too small to reveal any information about the room.

Or the truth, I thought. "What happens now?" I said aloud.

"She wants us to meet her at the front door. And we're supposed to try to stay out of the tracks in the dust, even though we've been through them once."

I stood up. "We'll need light to do that," I said.

Jerry produced the flashlight again, led the way back upstairs, and around to the main entrance. We arrived there just as a Cherry Hill police cruiser pulled into the block and parked behind my Jeep. Both Tracy— the Chief, and Officer Kyle Appledorn, stepped from the car; they'd only had to drive a few blocks. Tracy's Finnish bone structure gave her a look of solid competency, and her tightly plaited blond hair indicated a no-nonsense attitude. Kyle was dark and spare, always appearing a bit anxious, but ready for action.

"Show us where you were," Tracy began.

"Do you have extra flashlights?" Jerry asked. "The electricity isn't on."

"OK. Then we'll wait right here," Tracy said, opening the rear door of the police car and motioning us inside, all business. She nodded at Kyle. He knew what she wanted, produced his phone, and in a few seconds we heard him demanding that the electric service be restored immediately.

We began to explain where we'd been in the building and tried to remember anything we might have touched. When Jerry described unlocking the basement door, she wanted to know who else had keys. That led to an explanation of all the various people who'd suddenly been interested in the school after decades of being ignored. Any number of people could have gotten keys or been given tours.

In less than half an hour, a Mid-State Electric truck pulled in behind the police car and Kyle went off to talk to the driver.

"Let's go in," Tracy said.

By late afternoon, crime scene tape had been strung around the school. A Sheriff's car had taken the place of the electric company truck, and a State Police Crime Lab van had also arrived. Detective Milford came in an unmarked car. A knot of children on bicycles gathered in the empty lot across the street, and the casual traffic on the usually empty Liberty Street was much heavier than normal. The drivers craned their necks as they passed, trying to discover the secrets constrained within the yellow tape. A few of the older boys kicked a soccer ball around the field, but most of the younger children just stared at the school, not trying to hide their curiosity.

Jerry and I had a lot of time to observe all this, since we hadn't been allowed to leave, even after showing the police where we'd been. We'd led Tracy and Kyle back to the basement. With lights blazing everywhere, the building seemed only sad rather than spooky, but the dark stain on the basement floor remained genuinely sinister.

It didn't take a specially trained crime technician to see that one edge of the blood pool was feathered and smeared as if something had been dragged out of it and then onto something else, perhaps a tarp or a big piece of cardboard. From that point, leading out the door and on down the hallway, beyond where Jerry and I had walked, a wide pathway striped through the dust. It led to a stairway which opened directly to the outside of the building.

We'd seen that much, but then Kyle had escorted us back outdoors. He'd driven us to the police station where we'd been fingerprinted. "For elimination purposes only," he'd assured us. Jerry took it in stride, but pointed out with some pique that they should also compare Jared Canfield's and probably the realtor, and city council members.

We'd been allowed a bathroom break but then were taken back to the school where some hot dogs, bags of potato chips and bottled water had been delivered, probably from the Pine Tree Diner.

Time dragged on. Jerry and I still sat in the back of the police car. Kyle had asked us to stay there rather than to sit in our own cars. We kept the window rolled down since the afternoon had warmed, and also so we might hear of any new developments. I closed my eyes and attempted to nap, but sleep didn't come. I finally quit trying, but we continued to wait silently. Apparently neither of us could think of anything to say. Jerry fiddled with his cell phone, but I couldn't tell if he was playing a game, texting someone, or making notes for a news story.

A city truck pulled up at the end of the block and removed a small cover plate from a pipe at the curb. The workman inserted a long bar with a handle into the opening and began twisting it.

"Nothing like an emergency to get the utilities turned on in a hurry," Jerry said dryly. "If I work this right, maybe I can get the city to pay for the boiler inspection too."

"You're joking, aren't you?" I asked, suddenly aghast at the possibility that Jerry had just played a huge trick on us all. In response, he smiled, raised an eyebrow and settled deeper into the seat.

One or two at a time, the children began to leave, and even the rubbernecker traffic thinned out.

Tracy came by and told us, almost apologetically, that so far, no fingerprints except ours had been found, which looked suspicious, and could have been taken as an indication that one or both of us was there to confuse the evidence. Obviously, the murder had taken place days earlier, but if one of us had killed Jared Canfield, putting new fingerprints over old ones was quite clever.

I gave her a look that I hoped made her think she had two heads. She shrugged and said, "I'm just offering commentary. We certainly don't have enough cause to arrest either of you."

Just after five, a light green sedan pulled up across the street and Adele emerged, carrying a white box and a thermos.

"It took me forever to get someone to come watch the store," she began, as if she assumed we'd been waiting for her. "I brought you carrot cake and coffee. Why are you still here? Surely they don't think you're suspects? What were you doing at the school?"

Adele's rapid fire questions were always startling, and I hardly knew which one to answer first. Jerry took over.

"Ana was helping me inspect the building," he said. "I've bought it. It's about time this town did something to preserve its heritage."

"Oh, my!" Adele said. "You were together?" She glanced from Jerry to me and back again, rather pointedly, I thought, but perhaps I was feeling guilty.

"Yes, we were together," Jerry admitted. It seemed as if he

was going to stop there, but then he added, "We're planning something. Something big." He smiled at Adele and somehow winked at me, simultaneously. I winced.

Adele lowered her voice. "There's really a big pool of blood and a hatchet in the basement?"

"And a wide drag mark leading to the parking lot," Jerry expanded on the basic facts, smiling broadly now. He crossed his arms and stared directly at Adele. He seemed pleased to be able to produce a fact she hadn't already heard and was almost challenging her to some sort of duel of information.

I wasn't feeling confrontational at all and tried to take the conversation in a different direction. "Thanks for the dessert. All we've had is some hot dogs from the Pine Tree," I said.

"You're welcome," Adele said with a smug look on her face. She was about to win the information war. "Those weren't from the diner. I heated them up in the back room at the store. Jack Panther put a sign on the Pine Tree's front door this morning instead of opening for breakfast. 'Closed until further notice.' Didn't give anyone a heads-up. Just locked up and walked away. No one's seen him since."

16

By Friday noon, the town was buzzing with the news of the discovered crime scene at the old school and Jack Panther's disappearance.

I knew this because I was in Cherry Hill, at Jerry's house, drinking a perfectly brewed cup of coffee and munching on a turkey pastrami and provolone sandwich. His well-appointed kitchen was nicely insulated from the gossip, but before arriving there I'd been to the Post Office, the drug store, and Volger's Grocery. Almost everyone had stopped me and asked if I'd really seen the bloody floor. I assured each person it was no joke. This exchange was usually followed by a comment like, "Why do you suppose Jack left town?" delivered with waggling eyebrows.

I even drove past the old school again. The yellow crime tape bellied outward in a light breeze from the north. There were still people across the street staring as if they thought the tape restrained secrets that were about to burst forth into public view. One couple had even brought a thermos of coffee and lawn chairs in which to wait for the revelation. The day was cloudy and the building dark. It had seemed radiant in yesterday morning's sunshine; now it only looked dirty.

Adele had called me at eight in the morning and asked me to stop by the store. I certainly didn't need groceries, since I'd just stocked up in Emily City on Wednesday, but a good dose of guilt over my cart-full of IGA betrayal sent me to Adele's dairy case for something small. I chose a carton of cottage cheese. I approached the checkout where she waited.

"Ana, I wanted to ask you what's going on," she began as she ran the bar code of the tub over a glass panel and the cash register beeped.

"You know as much about it as I do. You've got the police scanner," I replied.

"No, not the murder. I mean with you and Jerry."

I shifted uneasily from one foot to the other. Jerry and I never had agreed on what to tell Adele.

"Why are you so jittery, Ana?" Adele continued. "I'll tell you what I think. You're dating him!"

"Not really."

"'Not really!' What does that mean? I saw the way he was looking at you in the car. There's certainly something going on between you."

I couldn't tell Adele the whole truth. She'd blab it all over. "We did go out for dinner. He wants me to help him plan a community event."

"Hell's bells. You don't expect me to believe that do you?"

"It's true. You can believe it or not." I was feeling defensive and unsure of myself, and I knew my voice betrayed my emotions, but I smiled at the old-fashioned expletive. Apparently that softened my tone a bit, and I was able to continue calmly. "He wants to host a Harvest Ball in the old schoolhouse. But now I don't know if the police will clear it in enough time to fix it up. Jerry is really impatient. He wants the gala to be in mid-October."

"October? That's only a few weeks away. Even Mr. Old-Money might have trouble pulling that off."

"It was pretty amazing to watch him get things accomplished yesterday. He certainly has a lot of authority," I said. It had seemed like Jerry had been in control, even though it was the police who had gotten all the utilities turned on.

Apparently I'd diverted Adele's attention. She mused, "A Harvest Ball. That sounds interesting. People will like the theme. Corn shocks. Apples, and cherries and pumpkins. Pies! We need to call Janice and warn her."

"Adele!" I cut in. "Wait. You can't just jump in and take over the planning for Jerry."

"Oh, he'll want my help. Don't worry." She bustled to the bakery case and extracted two large muffins. "With Jack Panther gone, there's no one in town other than Janice and me who can do mega-food. You take these right over to Jerry's house and tell him not to worry about the catering. But, have him let me know if he wants a meal or only desserts. That's important."

My head was spinning as the store's front door creaked shut behind me. Adele always seemed about three steps ahead of anything I could handle. But I did as she said. It was only three blocks to Jerry's house. I was tempted to walk, but I didn't want to take up space in Adele's parking lot on a Friday by leaving my car, so I drove west on Main and turned south on Cherry. This was one of the oldest streets in town. It was lined with stately, mature maple trees. The homes were large, of the Victorian era. Obviously, when they were built there was one mansion per block. Since that time, the majority of the estates had sold off side lots, and smaller, newer houses now huddled in the shadows of the huge homes. Towers, porches, dormers, cupolas and gingerbread trim were the hallmarks of the Victorians. Most had been well cared for, and were painted to enhance the fancy detailing. It was clear that this street was where a lot of the Cherry Hill money resided.

The one block that had not filled in was 200 South, the one owned by Jerry Caulfield. His family hadn't needed to sell lots to survive financially. Except for Holiday Real Estate, there was nothing in the entire block except the newspaper office, the Caulfield home, and one large, but less imposing, home to the north, built in a style similar to Jerry's. I wondered how the Mill-at-Meadow-Street corner had come to be sold. I thought it must be galling to Jerry, and I couldn't understand why he didn't buy it back.

I parked beneath one of the maples, grabbed the bakery bag, and headed for Jerry's front door. The cottage cheese would have to take its chances on the floor of the warm car.

Of course, I knew what the front of Jerry's house looked like, but I'd usually seen it from the back, from Mill Street, through the vacant lot. After talking with Cora about the museum idea, I now looked at the front side with new eyes. The house was painted white with maroon, muted teal, and mustard trim. The center section was a large square of three stories, with a widow's walk on top. This seemed unusual in the Midwest, but since no two of the Victorian mansions were alike, I decided the goal of the builders had been to create something more outlandish than any previous structure. This design would have won the contest.

On each side of the second floor front was a steep-roofed dormer, with a tall narrow window that also seemed to function as a door, since each opened to an upstairs porch. The entire central square was thrust out in front into a tower with picture windows on the three sides. The top was adorned with a railing that matched the widow's walk. This tower was the portion Cora had thought would make such a wonderful display case. She had been right. Jerry seemed to be using it this way already, museum or not. In the main window an ornate carousel horse reared with bared teeth and pawing hooves.

And on the first floor, each side of the square tower was filled in with a porch which wrapped around to the sides of the building. The roof shingles couldn't be original, but must have been replaced with ones of expensive restoration quality. They were hexagonal, in a soft gray. Ornate railings and complex detailed trim completed the busy architectural wonder.

From my previous visit, I knew that the main living room was on the left side, so I climbed the steps to that porch and rang the bell. Even though it was covered by a lace curtain, I could see Jerry approach through the large oval pane of wavy glass in the door. When he opened the door, I thrust the small white bag of muffins into his hand.

"From Adele," I said. "Watch out. She's totally on board with the Ball."

In a few minutes, as we ate the sandwiches, I asked him to tell me more about Jack Panther.

"Jack's parents moved to Cherry Hill around 1960," Jerry began. "They were young, dirt-poor and worked at the canning factory. Jack was born in 1970, and then the big explosion was in 1971. Do you know about that?"

"I didn't know what year it happened. I know Cora's first

husband died then."

"Yes he did, and Jack's father too. His name was Edgar something."

"Not Panther?" I asked.

"That's a long story. Jack was just an infant when his father died. His mother never remarried, and she was Mexican. She kept her maiden name; Gonzales, I think, and I don't remember Edgar's last name. I'm sure Cora could tell you. Jack grew up in the Hispanic community. But when he was a young buck he started going to Native American Pow-Wows. Found out he was an eighth Pottawatomi, and took the name Panther."

"How did he get the diner?"

"His mother had kept the settlement money from the explosion in the bank all those years. It was enough to buy the whole building the Pine Tree is in. Jack moved into the upstairs apartment. He's been there ever since."

"Until yesterday," I noted.

"Yes. Apparently, he's closed the entire building. Added new hasps and padlocks to the doors. It looks quite permanent. His car is gone too. I'm sure Tracy has an APB out to track him down for questioning, if only because of the timing."

Jerry reached for the bag of muffins. The smell of cinnamon and sugar burst into the room as he pulled open the paper wrapper. I could see whole pecans emerging from the muffin tops when he set them on the counter.

"Let's split one," I suggested. "They're huge."

"Sure." Jerry pulled the biggest chef's knife from a wooden holder. It seemed much larger than necessary for the job. He turned to me with an evil grin, lifted the knife over his head and glared at me. "Murder and mayhem!" he shouted.

"Jerry!" I cringed as he lunged at me. But then he laughed, turned and brought the knife down carefully on the muffin, which waited without expression for its execution on the butcher block.

17

I was so full of lunch and questions that as soon as I returned home, I took a walk on the trail that led from my yard through Dead Mule Swamp for about two miles until it ended at the seasonal extension of East South River Road. My thoughts were in a muddle, and the hike settled my stomach but not my mind. I still couldn't figure out what the connection might be between the body of Jared Canfield and the very lively Jerry Caulfield. It was confusing, even if coincidental, that the Judge whose murder we had talked of reenacting was named Oldfield. Too many fields! And, maybe it would be bad juju to add that to the mix, even for the sake of enticing Cora to the Harvest Ball. If there would be a ball... with the building controlled by the police... possibly without enough people in town to fix food... without being sure we could even get Cora to come... without a cast to dramatize an old murder if Chad didn't like the idea. And who needed to bring up an old murder? We had a new one right in the building. Unsolved.

I pushed open the kitchen door and heard the house phone ringing. Fortunately it was in the cradle, so I didn't have any trouble finding it. I flipped my hair away from my ear and pushed the talk button.

"Hello?"

"Ana Raven?" It was a woman's voice.

"Yes, who is this?" I asked.

"A fray-und."

I was already frustrated by all the questions I'd just been mulling over. My patience was thin. "Friends generally give their names," I snapped.

"You aren't very observant. Ah'm surprised. You've already gotten quite a reputation for solving mysteries around here, and yet you overlooked my message," she continued.

"What are you talking about? What kind of message?"

The voice took on a harsh tone. "In your car, bee-itch. Pay more attention."

The connection broke. I looked at the display on the phone. Just like when I had received a threatening call in May, the caller's number was displayed. The closest thing to write on was a paper napkin, and there was a pen on the counter, so I quickly jotted down the digits. *Maybe this time the number will lead us to the caller*, I thought. The connection had ended without the tell-tale click of an older mechanical phone, so I suspected the call came from someone's cell. Funny, how much more attention I was paying to details than I used to although not according to my mystery caller. I'd get Tracy to check out the number, but first I wanted to see what was in my car.

I slapped my forehead; I knew one thing that was in the car: a warm carton of cottage cheese. So much for paying attention to details.

Looking around as I opened the kitchen door again and stepped into the yard, nothing made me suspicious that the caller was hanging around the house. Some lazy afternoon bird songs could be heard from the direction of the river, and two squirrels were chasing each other around a tree at the edge of the woods.

The Jeep was exactly where I had parked it. No surprises there. I walked to the passenger side and peered in the window which was open about an inch at the top. When had I rolled it down? On the way to Cherry Hill that morning was my best guess. There was nothing on the seat. I opened the door and looked for the cottage cheese. Lying at an odd angle on top of the carton was a plain piece of computer paper with printing on it. I grabbed a tissue from the packet I kept clipped to the visor and picked it up.

The note wasn't hand written, but was computer printed in a plain font in large capital letters.

"YOU AND YOUR RICH BOYFRIEND BETTER STAY AWAY FROM THAT OLD SCHOOL IF YOU KNOW WHAT'S GOOD

FOR YOU. LOOK WHAT HAPPENED TO THE OTHER GUY. A FRIEND."

I put the paper down on the car seat and went back to the house for my purse and keys, and the napkin with the caller's number on it. Threatening calls and notes were getting tiresome. I was taking this to the police right away.

Chief Tracy Jarvi was stacking a pile of file folders on her desk as I walked into the city police station. There was just one large room, and no one had a separate office. Tracy and Bob Clay, the all-purpose assistant, had desks on different sides of a low railing, but there was no privacy. The one officer, Kyle Appledorn, was probably out in the police cruiser. Bob nodded at me, and I pushed open the gate in the railing to enter Tracy's area.

Tracy looked up. "Ana," she said. "What's wrong?"

I guess my face gave away my growing anger. "I seem to attract threatening people," I said. "Look at these." I laid the note and napkin on her desk, and started to tell her about my afternoon.

As I began talking, she held up a finger, then handed the napkin to Bob, and asked him to run the phone number. She slipped the note into a plastic sleeve and placed it carefully on the corner of her desk.

When I finished my story, she asked, "You didn't recognize the caller's voice?"

"Not at all. Of course, it wasn't a very long call, but I'm sure it's no one I know well," I responded.

"Did it sound disguised?"

"Not really, but how could I tell? I mean, it wasn't distorted, or weird or anything."

"You're sure it was a woman?"

"Yes, as sure as one can be these days. But it wasn't husky like that new real estate agent's, or androgynous, or falsetto. A bit of a Southern accent."

"What does this mean in the note, 'your boyfriend?'" Tracy asked with a smile. "Are you keeping secrets?"

I sighed. It sure didn't take long for tongues to start wagging in a small town. "I think she means Jerry Caulfield. We went out to dinner once, and now everyone is leaping to conclusions."

Tracy grinned and her blue Nordic eyes twinkled. "Are they leaping in the right direction?"

"No. I don't know. He wants me to help plan a big Harvest Ball for the whole community." By now, so many people had probably heard of Jerry's potential plan that not having a ball wasn't even an option. "He's been nice to me," I added, remembering that part of the scheme was to let people think we were dating.

"Is that all?" Tracy asked.

"What do you mean? I had lunch at his house today," I added, feeling guilty. "Do you want to know if we're, um..."

"No, no," Tracy's eyes got wide. "That's none of my business. At least at this point. But you were together at the school."

"We told you. He bought the building on a whim and wanted to look it over. It's where he wants to have the Ball. Do you think you'll be done with the crime scene soon? There's a lot of work to do to get the place ready." I couldn't believe I was even asking. Apparently, I was already invested in the plan.

Tracy shifted in her chair. "I think we'll be done soon, although it's the state lab doing the work, so I can't really speak for them. A Harvest Ball would be fun. It would do a lot to boost local morale."

I had a little trouble shifting from the official policewoman to a community-minded Tracy.

She continued, "Kyle and I would be happy to provide some security. You know, control parking and watch for anything unusual. Now that the building is a crime scene, the killer might be watching for something we don't understand yet. Hopefully, we'll catch the guilty party soon."

"Do you think it's this woman who called me?"

"A hatchet is an odd choice of weapon for a female, but this whole case is pretty strange. I'll call Detective Milford about your note. Maybe it's from the same person who sent the package to Cora."

"Maybe." I had no opinion.

Bob spoke up from across the room. "Just got word back on that phone number, Chief."

"Good. It's all right to share that information with Ana."

"OK, then," Bob said. "It's a disposable cell phone. There was one recent call made on it, this afternoon."

"That had to be the call to me," I put in.

"Yup. It pinged off a tower in Emily City, so that's not going to narrow the choices down a lot."

Tracy looked sad. "Thanks, Bob. Follow up on tracking the purchase."

"Already started, but it's after five. OK if I go home for the day?" Bob asked.

"Sure," Tracy said. "Let's all go home. This case is like an octopus— too many wiggly arms."

18

Before I left the police station, I asked Tracy for a photocopy of the threatening note, which she made without taking it out of its plastic sleeve. I thanked her and headed for Jerry's place.

"Are you out of food at your house?" he teased as he opened the door. He held a pasta fork in his hand. "I just fed you lunch."

"What? No. I'm not even hungry. Look at this." I thrust the copied threat into his hand as I entered the living room. Admittedly, this house was beginning to feel comfortable to me. But Jerry's reaction was anything but comfortable. He seemed to expand to fill the room with indignation.

"Who would do this? When did you get it?"

"It was put in my car through the window. I left it down about an inch. Probably when I was parked right where I am now, but this morning." I pointed across the street.

Jerry walked to a desk, put down the fork and plucked his cell phone off the charger. He began stabbing at it. In a moment he asked, "Is Louisa there?"

Louisa who? I thought, but I just listened.

In a moment, he continued, "Lou, this is Jerry. Were you home this morning? Did you happen to see a car parked in front of your house?... Yes, the Jeep that's there again now. It's Ana's. Ana Raven."

"Jerry, what are you doing?" I protested.

He turned to me and put a finger to his lips. I felt chastened and a bit put out. "All right. I thought you might have been home. Someone tampered with her vehicle, and we would like to find out who that was."

As he hung up, my exasperation got the better of me. "You can't just start calling people," I said. "I've been to the police already. They won't like having someone investigating on their own."

"I'll pretend I didn't hear that," Jerry said, staring at me intently as he poked at the phone again. His voice softened. "Karen? Hello, it's nice to hear your voice too."

Interesting tone.

"Say, I was wondering if you were home this morning... You were?... Well, yes, she is here again, in fact." His smile twisted into a conspiratorial grin and he winked at me.

This is too much! Oh, wait; it's part of the plan.

"What? We're planning a community shindig, some sort of Harvest Ball, to be held later this fall. We'll have the details worked out soon. I'd never leave you out, Karen. By the way, did you happen to notice anyone stopping near Ana's car this morning?... Really? That's interesting, but her office is in the block, so it's probably not significant."

Jerry looked at me and raised his eyebrows. I glared at him, although I wasn't sure if I was annoyed at his aggressive pursuit of the culprit, or feeling slightly jealous.

"Thank you. Love you too, Karen. I'll be sure to let you know when we get a date finalized."

"Who was that?" I asked fixing Jerry with what I hoped was a withering glare.

"My neighbor, Karen Ames. I thought that would be obvious from the conversation."

"No, not who you were talking to. I heard you call her Karen. Who did she see?"

"Whom, Ana, whom did she see."

"Whatever. You're the newspaper man."

Jerry's eyes twinkled. "Are you feeling testy because I told her I love her? I thought our relationship was just a ploy, and you weren't looking for anything more."

My emotions collapsed in a puddle of nerves and remorse. "Oh, Jerry, I'm not. I guess it's just that all of this drama is getting to me. I've had about enough of getting mixed up in local crimes. Why is someone targeting me? I just seem to be in all the wrong places at the right times." I sniffed.

Jerry pulled a tissue from a holder on the desk and handed it to me. "Karen is a cousin of mine, second cousin, if it matters."

I dabbed at my eyes, which had gotten misty for some reason and suddenly laughed. I tossed my head and tried to smile. "Whom. Whom did your second cousin see?"

"My very second cousin saw Virginia Holiday cut through between our houses on the way to her office, my dear. Does that sound suspicious?"

I laughed harder. "No, it does not! But it reminds me that I've wanted to ask why you don't own that corner. The rest of the block is yours, right?"

"That's true. I own it all except that little square. Karen's is the only other house on the block, and it's in the family estate. Used to be the carriage house. She rents from me."

"How did that squat little block building get separated from your kingdom?"

"That's a story in itself, but perhaps not interesting to anyone except me. My great-grandfather sold the corner lot to his best friend, whose son opened a shoe repair shop. That was in 1914. The friend was grateful but a bit of a tightwad who didn't trust old Charles. He had legal wording put in the deed that the property couldn't be sold back to a Caulfield or any close relative for 99 years."

"What about Karen? Is she too close?"

"She is for the purpose of buying the lot. Believe it or not, there have to be five degrees of removal for a sale."

"Unbelievable." I shook my head. "But, that provision runs out soon."

"It does. It's no secret that I'll be reacquiring the corner and pulling that eyesore down. Even with the new wood shake awning Ms. Holiday put on the front, it's just an ugly building. I'm hoping no one else cares and tries to drive up the price."

"Does she know she bought a building with a limited future?"

"I'm not sure. As I said, it's in the deed, but does she realize I really do want to buy it back? I haven't talked with her about it. I've barely seen her, actually, since she first moved in."

"I suppose it's not relevant to this note, anyway. The letter was put in my car, and is focused on the school building," I said.

"That would be my conclusion, also."

"Jerry, you really shouldn't be calling people about the note. Tracy's going to get uptight."

"I suppose you're right," Jerry said, draping an arm around my shoulder and steering me toward the back of the house. He picked up the pasta fork. I was glad he seemed willing to give up control of the situation, but I should have known better.

"Come on in the kitchen and I'll feed you again. I was draining spaghetti when you knocked."

19

I spent the weekend trying to focus on tasks that would need to be accomplished if there was to be any chance of having a Harvest Ball, with a dramatic reenactment, in just a few weeks. Getting the old school building in good enough physical condition was Jerry's problem, but I promised to take care of a number of the other arrangements.

Chad hadn't been very excited at first about changing his plans, which had been for a spooky game of what was essentially hide-and-seek for college kids, but promised to talk to his friends and call me back. As it turned out, some of the girls were a lot more interested in an activity where they could dress up and pretend to be part of something scary, without actually being chased down dark hallways, even by boys they knew. He said they were now eager to receive the details of the story and hoped that Cora would let them write a script. One of the girls, Brittney, was in the thespian club, and she wanted to give it a try. She was even hoping to get credit for the project in her Directing class.

I felt a lot more hesitant about calling Cora. I debated between chatting by phone and waiting until Tuesday for our regular work day. In the end, I decided that fretting over it was too stressful, and I punched in Cora's number on my cell. Despite her hermit-like ways, she had heard of the plans for the Harvest Ball, thanks to news delivered with her groceries by her son, Tom. She wasn't impressed.

"That two-faced Jerry Caulfield has some ulterior motive. You mark my words," she sputtered. But when I shared the idea for the drama featuring Chad and his friends playing the roles of Judge Reuben Oldfield, the murderer Zeke Bradley, and other contemporaries, she thawed like an ice cube on a hot sidewalk.

It was so cliché, but it was all I could picture. She reacted as predictably as Jerry had claimed.

She offered to look up the old records and open the boxes with any artifacts she had, even more things than the furniture from the room where the murder took place. "I'll show you everything on Tuesday. Wait until you see what I have!" she said.

Jerry and I had talked over bowls of spaghetti with clam sauce the night before— it turned out I was hungrier than I thought— about the music. He wanted live music. I wasn't sure what resources the small town of Cherry Hill and rural Forest County had to offer.

"You'll be surprised," he said, and began jotting down names of groups with their genres: The Blue Grass— bluegrass, Hot Sauce— jazz, Jim Frank and Friends— swing. He couldn't recall the names of the groups for light classical and soft rock but had run ads for all of them in the paper at one time or another, so he knew he could locate them.

"What mood are you looking for?" I asked.

"Let's ask around. Just poll the people you talk to and see what kind of reactions we get. I think bluegrass would appeal to most people."

I'd asked Chad. He'd responded with a snort, "Those are my choices? How about none of the above?"

Cora had immediately said, "Light classical." My own opinion ran to jazz to keep the party up-tempo. As much as I liked classical, I didn't want the guests going to sleep.

At least getting the food organized was straightforward. Adele was right that Jerry would rely on her. He'd simply said, "Call Adele. She'll handle it, and it will be perfect. Let's start the Ball at seven in the evening, and just offer small desserts and free drinks like coffee and cider, but there should also be a cash bar."

I decided to talk to Adele after church on Sunday and maybe spend some time with her if she was free. In preparation for this plan, I gathered some pears from a tree at the edge of the woods and made loaves of fruit bread. Then I put together a tossed salad.

My idea worked out perfectly. The Sunday service had been

upbeat, and the drafty church building was pleasantly cooler now that we'd reached September. I approached Adele as she was walking through the foyer toward the exit door and asked if she had plans for the afternoon.

"What do you have in mind?" she asked.

"I have some almond-pear bread I just made. I thought it might be nice for you to have something that probably didn't come from your own store. And I've got salad. Maybe we could pool our resources?"

She laughed. "I suspect you have something in mind besides food, but you know I can't resist news, so come on over. I put a roast in the crock pot this morning. I think we've got ourselves a lunch."

Adele lives on the northeast side of town, on Birch Street, north of the river and northeast of the old school. Her home is a squarish two-story, with an enclosed front porch. It's newer than Jerry's Victorian mansion, probably built during the second spurt of town growth, when farmers and entrepreneurs moved into the area after the timber was cut. Her grandfather-in-law had founded the grocery store that bears the family name.

She let us in through the side door, and we stepped up to her cheerful kitchen which had deep, solid cupboards, painted white. The trim was a soft green. I noticed there were new drawings from the grandchildren magnet-pasted to the refrigerator. All the appliances and decorations were slightly out of date, but neat.

She opened a tall closet door, extracted a bibbed apron and covered her dress. "I'll put on some water for tea right away. You can set the table."

An hour later we were full, the dishes were done, and we had placed fresh cups of tea on the low table in front of us as we settled into the plush cushions of her old-fashioned living room couch.

"I've been very patient," Adele began, as she spooned some sugar into her tea, "but now you have to tell me what you and Jerry are up to."

"Up to?"

"Yes, as in what's going on behind this idea for the Harvest

Ball."

I could feel my palms begin to sweat and my neck redden. What had I been thinking to come to Adele's house today? Jerry and I had never decided what to tell her, and the truth certainly wasn't going to do.

"Jerry wants to create a community center where events can be held, closer than the consolidated school building. He thinks this Ball will be a great kick-off for the project. You know, revive the basketball courts for kids, rent the auditorium and kitchen for dinners, maybe even conferences. Fix up some of the classrooms as suites for business conventions." I paused for air. "There's a lot of potential for that sort of thing, don't you think?"

Adele squinted at me and pursed her lips. "I certainly do not. And neither do you."

I stared back at her with as open an expression as I could muster.

She continued, "Ana, you've come to be one of my best friends since you moved here. Your contributions to the Family Friends Committee have been fresh and welcome, and you are financially generous. You usually have positive things to say about people. You are willing to sit and drink tea with an old busybody like me and laugh at our small town ways without making me feel like an idiot for liking it here. But you're a terrible liar."

"But it's true," I protested. "Jerry bought the building for a community purpose. I don't understand his reasoning either. But he's determined to fix it up. Some parts have to be done in a hurry so we can stage the Harvest Ball." At least this was all true.

"You're still fibbing, but I don't understand why. I'll figure it out before long."

"He thinks you'll be the best organizer for the food table."

"Didn't I tell you that?" Adele said, leaning forward and lifting her teacup to her mouth. She took a long sip, and licked sugar from her lips.

I took advantage of the pause to drink some tea, too. My mouth was dry. "Small finger desserts that people can sample will be perfect."

She glanced sideways at me and set the cup down on the table. Her blunt, work-worn fingers tapped impatiently on the edge of the saucer. "I know that Jerry was not the only potential buyer for the old school. This sudden interest in that dump, and then learning it was the location of the Jared Canfield murder is quite peculiar, don't you think?"

I jumped on the opportunity to change the subject. "Do you know who else wanted to buy it? I do think that's strange."

"Oh, that part's easy. Mavis Fanning. It's why that has me stumped."

I shook my head, agreeing to our mutual confusion. We ignored Mavis' motives and stuck to discussing food for the Ball the rest of the afternoon. Adele called Janice Preston, and even suggested we recruit young Jimmy Mosher, since he was still talking enthusiastically about a career in the restaurant business. She said we'd have to think about who could run the cash bar. I recalled my experiences in the Dead Dog bar and fervently hoped that wasn't the best of the choices, but I planned to leave those arrangements to Jerry, anyway.

As I left, I mentioned the possible music styles to Adele and asked her opinion.

"Swing, of course. It will make people want to get out on the floor and dance."

20

Monday morning, first thing, I drove in to Cherry Hill. I wanted to talk with Tracy. If Harold Fanning's wife was interested in the school building, maybe she was the one who was trying to threaten me away from it. I wasn't sure what she thought she could accomplish, since Jerry officially owned the building now, and I couldn't imagine him being swayed by anonymous notes.

After I told Tracy that Adele claimed Mavis Fanning was the other person who had been trying to buy the old school building, she promised she'd get someone right on it. She also had some news of her own to share.

"Ana, I haven't been told to keep this information to myself, so I think you should know something."

"I don't want you to get in trouble with your colleagues," I countered.

"There's a lot of confusion surrounding that old school building. Too many people are interested in it."

"I agree with you on that."

"You've got every right to be there, now that Jerry owns it, and you're working with him, but please be extra careful." I could see the concern in Tracy's eyes.

"Why? Is there something more? Of course there is, you just said you had news for me."

"We don't know for sure why Jared Canfield was in the school, but we think he wanted to buy it too."

"Whatever for?"

Tracy shuffled her feet and glanced over at Bob, who was studiously looking at papers on his desk. "We have no idea, but he had something in his wallet. The crime lab managed to salvage quite a bit— even the paper things."

"Had he made an offer? Did he have a receipt for a down payment or something?" Tracy looked even more nervous. It was very uncharacteristic. "Look, don't tell me anything you aren't comfortable with," I said.

She tossed her head and the single braid that trailed down her back landed askew on her shoulder. "It's not that. I don't want to cast suspicion on someone we know nothing about."

"Canfield? What does the community care about a stranger from the city? Well, that sounds callous, but, really, he's dead, you know."

"Not him." She sighed. "I'm making it worse by not telling you. There were business cards in his wallet. All of them from Royal Oak, except one. That one was from the new real estate agent here, Virginia Holiday."

"That string bean? She's new in town, and so everyone is being wary, like they were of me at first, but she's not much of a mover and shaker. I haven't even heard of any properties she's actually sold."

"Give her a chance. It takes a while to get established and win trust. Anyway, on the back of the card he had written the address of the school building, and the number 1-8-4-5."

"1845. Is that the year it was built?" I couldn't see how this meant very much.

"The brick school was built in 1896. We checked," Tracy said.

Bob's deeper voice intruded on our conversation. He'd been talking quietly on the telephone, but it had only provided background noise until now. "Chief, I just got word on the sale of that disposable cell phone. We got lucky. It was paid for with a credit card."

"Whose?" Tracy barked.

"Charged to Mavis Fanning. Two years ago."

I sucked in my breath. Why on earth would the wife of the city manager be endangering her position in the community by making stupid phone calls from a number that could be traced?

Tracy immediately stepped to her desk, lifted her hat from the neat surface and placed it on her head, tucking the shiny blond braid out of sight. "Let's go, Ana. I want you with me when we talk to her to get her reaction." Turning to Bob, she said, "Good work."

She accepted a printed sheet he handed her and we went outside together. In the parking lot, I assumed I'd follow her and headed for my Jeep, but she pointed at the police cruiser. "It will have more clout if you arrive in an official car," she said.

I didn't even know where the Fannings lived, but soon learned that it wasn't far. Theirs was another large Victorian mansion, not on Cherry, but one block west on Peach. It filled an impressive corner lot at the intersection with Taylor, just two blocks from the much-desired school building. And, I realized, just three or four blocks from Jerry's. She could have easily driven or walked by and slipped the note into my car without seeming out of place on that street.

We climbed five steps to the large porch that wrapped around the corner of the house. The Fannings' front door was solid oak with an oval of beveled and frosted glass decorated in geometric etchings. It looked original to the house, but professionally refinished. The varnish wasn't cracked or dirty. Tracy rang the doorbell. Three times.

After we had waited several minutes, Mavis Fanning herself opened the door. I wondered if she always did so, or if there was a servant somewhere who was supposed to attend to such trivial matters. A small dog was yapping from a far room. Mavis didn't look happy. I wasn't sure if it was because she had to answer the bell herself or if we personally were the cause of her obvious displeasure.

"Miss Jarvi. Ms. Raven. How can I help you?" From her tone we could tell she wasn't going to offer us tea and cookies.

Tracy cleared her throat. "That's Chief Jarvi, ma'am. May we come in?"

"Certainly." But she still didn't sound pleased. Mavis was dressed as if she were planning to go out. She wore a knit suit in a deep blue-green. The slim skirt hugged her boyish hips suggestively. A long silk scarf with a multi-color abstract design was wrapped elegantly around her neck and one end was pinned to her right shoulder with a large gold broach. The rich colors enhanced her dark auburn hair and flashing green eyes. I detected a subtle scent of White Diamonds perfume. In heels, Mavis Fanning was nearly six feet tall. And in one word, she was stunning.

She led us to the formal sitting room and motioned for us to sit down. The antique furniture was beautiful, but it was obvious this was the room where she entertained unwelcome guests. The horsehair upholstery was prickly and uninviting. Mavis glowed in the dark setting like a jewel. Tracy's navy uniform and my blue jeans and sweatshirt seemed to make us disappear like specks of dust in a velvet jewelry box.

Tracy, however, was up to the challenge. She declined the offer to sit although I perched on the edge of a delicate-looking carved chair.

"Well, Chief," Mavis began, emphasizing the word "chief" with a slight grimace, apparently not wanting Tracy to have the verbal advantage, "what have I done to prompt what appears to be an official visit? And why is Ms. Raven here?"

Tracy didn't blink or hesitate a moment. "Ms. Raven has received a threatening phone call from your phone, Mrs. Fanning."

Mavis came right back at her. "What? Impossible. I'll show you." She reached around the corner to a table in the entry hall and grabbed her purse. She pulled out an expensive smart phone, pushed some buttons and thrust it at Tracy. "Here are all my recent calls. Check them yourself."

Tracy took the phone and swiped at the screen for a few seconds. "Thank you," she said. "The call wasn't made from this phone. Is this the only one you own?"

"Yes it is. Harold and I exclusively use smart phones now. Land lines are so limiting. We even bought a cell for the cook to place orders with."

"Is that a disposable phone by any chance?" Tracy asked.

"No, of course not. It's just like this one. It was a package deal, under one bill." Mavis' lip was practically curling now.

Tracy continued, unruffled. "Have you ever purchased a disposable phone?"

"Ever? Probably. What difference does it make?"

"Ana received a threatening phone call from a woman on Friday. It came from a disposable cell phone that was charged two years ago to your personal credit card."

Mavis looked as if she was thinking hard. Was she honestly trying to remember, or was she busy thinking up a good lie?

Tracy kept looking directly at Mavis. "I have a copy of the receipt right here, if it would help to refresh your memory."

Mavis blinked slowly. "Yes, it might. Two years is an eternity ago." She took the paper from Tracy and appeared to study it carefully. Maybe she was just using the time to polish a plausible story.

Mavis looked up. She smiled at me. It was a cold smile, as if I were some sort of small unpleasant reptile she was about to crush. "I do remember this phone. It was one of those random purchases one makes in a hurry. Our younger daughter, Claire, was just starting college. She had lost her cell, and we bought this in Madison— University of Wisconsin, you know— as you can clearly see, so she'd have something to use until we could find her regular phone."

"Where is this phone now?" Tracy asked.

"I have no idea. She probably lost that one too. I can't tell you how many phones that girl has lost. Ask her."

Tracy continued to look at Mavis, but her next question was directed at me, "Ana, you've been listening to Mrs. Fanning for quite a few minutes now. Is this the woman who called you?"

The voice on the phone had been harsh. The tones I was listening to this morning were tense but melodious, cultured. I had seen Mavis Fanning around town a few times, but had never been face to face with her. Despite her height, and ostentatious manner, I wasn't about to be intimidated. I stood up and raised my eyes to hers.

21

"Where did you grow up, Mrs. Fanning?" I asked. From the corner of my eye I could see Tracy blink slowly in reaction to the unexpected question.

Mavis shot back, "I don't see how that's any of your business, but if you must know, Indiana. Not my favorite state by any stretch of the imagination, but we can't help our roots, can we? Is this a get-to-know-you exercise? Where did *you* grow up?"

"I'm from Chicago, born and bred there. Possibly you can tell by my shifted vowels, a and o in particular. It's how Cherry Hill folks figured out right away I was from that city."

"So?" Mavis demanded.

"I used to teach literature. One side aspect of that is studying dialects, how to hear them, how and when to try to write them. The person who spoke to me on the phone was angry. A person's natural speech patterns usually come out when emotions run high."

"I can imagine that if someone was threatening you they might be angry, but is there a point to this fascinating topic?" The dripping sarcasm was gathering into a river of animosity.

"The person who called me definitely had an Appalachian twang and patterns of sentence structure. That would be true of some places in Indiana."

"I doubt that," Mavis said.

"Oh, it's real enough. Well documented in speech studies. The caller's voice was rough, but that could have been a deliberate attempt to disguise the sound. I can't say for sure that you were the person who called me, but I'm not going to tell Chief Jarvi it wasn't you."

Tracy nodded. "That's fair enough. I also need to ask you if you were on Cherry Street Friday morning."

"Probably," Mavis shot back. I walk the dog every day. Our route often includes Cherry. So what?"

Tracy sighed, "We do need to track down that phone. Could you call your daughter, Mrs. Fanning?"

"It's Monday morning. She's probably in class or asleep. And I have an appointment. Can't it wait?"

"One call shouldn't take long," Tracy continued. "Let's try to clear this up."

"Oh, all right," Mavis said with a slight movement that was almost a petulant flounce.

She'd been holding her smart phone all the while we talked, and she quickly poked the black glass once. Claire must have been on her speed dial. She poked it again, and the sound of a ringing phone came over the speaker. If Mavis were trying to hide something or give Claire some sort of signal as to what to say, it wasn't going to be easy with all of us listening.

The phone rang a number of times. I forgot to count because I was busy watching Mavis' face, but she exhibited no emotion except irritation. I thought the call was going to go to voice mail, but at last a sleepy voice came from the phone.

"Yeah, Moms? Wha d'ya want?" Despite the electronic buzz and echo, it was obviously a young girl. "Moms" seemed to prove it was Claire.

"Honey, wake up. There is a policewoman here who has a question for you."

"Police? Moms, what's happening?" Claire sounded wide awake now.

Mavis' tone changed to flippant. "Oh, there's some mix-up about that old disposable phone we bought for you when you first went to the university."

"Oh. What about it?"

"Do you know what happened to it, honey?"

It didn't seem to me that there was going to be any opportunity for the policewoman to ask any question. Mavis was dominating the conversation.

Claire's voice came from the metallic black box. Mavis gripped the edges, and held it up so we could all hear the answer. Her long manicured nails shone with pearly polish. She seemed perfectly confident that Claire wasn't going to say something that would be problematic.

"Let me think. That was a long time ago. Two phones ago, maybe. I loaned it to Paulo Marino for a while. He's that guy Jessica was dating, the one from Italy whose major is chemistry. He's so divine, but Jessica dumped him for Bill somebody. He was always telling her what things were made of and reading lists of ingredients out loud. She said the names sounded gross, even with an Italian accent."

Mavis interrupted. "The phone, honey, the phone."

"I'm telling you. That's why Jessica got the phone back from Paulo, and I know she had it for a while, because I kept asking her about it, and she kept forgetting to give it to me, and I thought maybe she gave it to someone else. But I think she did eventually."

"Did what?"

"Give it back. Gees, Moms. Pay attention."

Mavis rolled her eyes and looked at me. I might have been the enemy in one respect, but mothers of students always empathize with others of their kind.

Tracy interjected a question. "Claire, this is Tracy Jarvis, Chief of Police here in Cherry Hill. That phone was used to place a threatening call. Please try hard to remember if your friend returned it."

"Wow, the police really are there? I'll bet Moms is mad as a hornet. She's so uptight."

Mavis cut in. "You're on speaker, Claire."

"Oh. Sorry Moms. But you are. OK, the phone. Well, I wanted it back to loan to Kerri to make calls for the sorority Christmas party. That was such a blast. We invited a whole bunch of people anonymously, that's why we needed the disposable phone, so Jessica must have given it back, and then when they showed up we let them in the door based on their answers to ten questions. At least that's what we told them, but really anyone who was wearing something blue got in. Some people snuck in the windows anyway, and we all had too much to drink and..."

"Claire! Can you focus on the phone for a minute?" Mavis was getting annoyed.

"I am. That's when I found it, when we cleaned up the mess the next day. It was under the couch cushions, and it showed up when we rolled Margo Thompson off onto the floor. She's fat, and not so pretty when she's sleeping off a drunk. The phone just bounced onto her boobs and sat there, you know, in between." Claire paused and giggled. The mental image was admittedly funny.

"Miss Fanning, do you know where the phone is now?" Tracy wasn't giggling.

"Sure. Why didn't you say so? It's in my underwear drawer."

"Would you go check, please?" Tracy asked, but it was more of a command than a request.

We could hear bare feet hitting a floor and a few quick steps then the squeak of wood against wood and some scratching noises. The drawer thumped shut and there were more squeaks, thumps and rustlings.

At a distance from Claire's phone we faintly heard, "It's not here, Moms. I don't know where it is. I'm sure that's where I put it."

"All right, honey. Thanks for looking." Mavis was about to poke the phone and break the connection.

Tracy held up her hand as at a traffic stop. "This is Chief Jarvi, again. Is that phone still activated? Who would have put minutes on it?"

"It was working last December. A couple of us chipped in to add time. All it takes is a little cash."

"Please keep looking and thinking about where that phone might be. It's very important," Tracy said.

"That's where it was, last time I saw it. Honest."

"When was that?" Tracy asked.

"Maybe a few months ago. I don't know, really."

Tracy continued, "Who has access to your room? Do you have a roommate?"

"There are six of us who share an apartment. We all have friends and boyfriends, and parties. This is college, you know?"

Tracy sighed again. "Thank you for your time, Miss Fanning. If you have any other ideas of where that phone might be, please contact me. Just call the Cherry Hill police."

"OK by me. I better get ready for class. I didn't realize what time it is."

"Goodbye, honey. Your father and I might come see you at Thanksgiving." Mavis waited for a response, but the connection had already been broken. A brief expression of annoyance crossed her face, but she covered it well as she set the phone down on an end table. "See, I told you she'd probably lost it."

"Have you put more time on that phone lately?"

"Of course not. I don't have it," Mavis snapped.

Tracy turned to me and shrugged her shoulders. "I guess there's nothing more for us to learn here, right now," she said.

Mavis motioned us toward the door. "It would be good if we could wrap this up. I'm going to be late for an appointment." She no longer sounded so belligerent, but still acted as if we, and our questions, were of no consequence.

The appointment explained why she was dressed up, but it must have been something important for her to be wearing such a classy outfit, unless she was one of those people who always overdressed. I could believe that was a possibility.

As we left, Tracy asked Mavis what Claire was studying.

"Her major is Human Resource Management," Mavis told us with a touch of pride. "She's very good with people, but she'll need a secretary to keep her from losing every pen or piece of paper she touches."

22

I wasn't sure I was looking forward to spending time with Cora on Tuesday. She had seemed interested in the plan to reenact the Judge's murder, but would she be willing to attend a busy social event planned by the man she seemed to hate most in the world? I expected she'd be at least a little bit crabby.

Nevertheless, at nine in the morning I turned the Jeep into Brown Trout Lane and pulled to a stop beneath a maple whose yellow leaves were beginning to fall gently into Cora's yard, and float on the smooth surface of the Pottawatomi River. The little brown frame house, with a porch that faced the curve of the river, seemed snuggled into a comforter of golden trees. Although the fall color had not yet reached its peak, it was obvious that cooler weather was here, and we had an awful lot to accomplish to make this Harvest Ball a reality. *Invitations*, I thought, *is Jerry going to just put something in the paper and make posters, or is he going to try to do something personal? Would there be snob value in sending some private notes? Maybe he could raise some money to renovate the building by offering tickets with perks- a special tour or early wine tasting, or something.*

Before I had time to contemplate whether this was important, Cora opened the door of her pole barn museum and beckoned eagerly to me.

As I slipped out of my jacket and placed it on the back of a chair in the small office, she asked, "What were you doing just sitting in your car? Gathering wool? I'm so excited! I can't believe people really want to learn something about our most famous local crime."

"I'm not exactly sure that the general population requested..."

But Cora was off and running with enthusiasm. "Come see what I dug out. Actually it wasn't difficult. Because this story was so important, I had carefully labeled these items and knew right where they were."

This explanation was superfluous. Cora carefully labeled and documented every single box of items that came into her possession, as fast as she could. This obsession was why I was now spending time each week entering a record of every artifact, news article, and knick-knack into a database that could be cross-referenced with locations and people and families and dates. Cora was a senior citizen, but she was no techno-phobe. She'd designed the data base herself.

The diminutive woman's face was rosy. The light blue blouse and faded denim overalls she wore highlighted her pink coloring. Wisps of white hair escaped from the braids she had wound tightly around her head. It looked like she'd been working hard already this morning. What was it my mother had said? "Men sweat, but women glow." Cora certainly was glowing.

"What all have you got?" I asked.

"Well. Hmm. What haven't I got?" she questioned coyly. I could see the young, teasing Cora behind the white hair and wrinkles.

I laughed. "Let's see your loot."

Of course, the first thing she did was open a scrapbook containing a photocopy of a news article. This was a summary after the fact, highlighting the effect of the Judge's murder on Cherry Hill. She'd told me the basic details of the case in the spring, and as I scanned the report, I was reminded of what had happened. Zeke Bradley's wife, Nora, had always had light fingers. She would sneak a few penny candies into her shopping basket even though she paid for the rest of her goods. Hoyt O'Rourke accused her of pocketing an extra egg, one she hadn't purchased, from his chicken coop. But no one wanted to start a ruckus. She didn't take very much at one time, and everyone liked Zeke. He worked at the local service station and could keep old Fords running like nobody's business. It wasn't going to be a good idea to antagonize him.

"I didn't realize Zeke was a respected man," I commented. "It seems out of character with what he finally did."

"There's no accounting for the wickedness that lurks below the surface in some people," Cora said, shaking her head.

I read on, out loud now.

On August 25, 1924, Nora Bradley was apprehended by Dieter Volger, of Volger's General Store, as she exited via the alley door carrying a large ham for which she had not paid. This crime was too much to overlook, and Dieter pressed charges. Nora was sentenced to thirty days in the county jail, which she served without incident. After her release on October 6th, she returned to her home behind Keto Brothers Oil and Service, where she resided with her husband, Ezekiel Bradley.

Cora interrupted. "Keto Brothers is now Aho's. John's grandfather, Miko, bought it around 1950." For a few moments the room was quiet as I assimilated this information. The large gas heater kicked on, ending the silence. "Keep going," Cora urged.

Only six weeks later, on October 8th, appearing to shop as usual at Volger's, after Nora had paid for a few sewing notions, Dieter Volger demanded to inspect her basket which was lined with a gingham cloth. Beneath the cloth he found a set of fine linen napkins, a tin of tooth powder, sheet music for "I'm Always Chasing Rainbows," and several handfuls of loose horehound candies. He also uncovered a gold brooch which had been traded for goods the previous day, and which he had not yet placed in the safe. Dieter declined to say who had surrendered the valuable trinket in exchange for sundries. He valued the items at a total of $31.87. "Those napkins were made by Mrs. Ethel Radcliffe, and were worth a dollar a piece,"

Volger explained to the *Herald*. "*Ja*, that is what makes it so much provoking. Ethel does not make those fine linens for my store, but once in a while."

Cora interrupted again. "Ethel's granddaughter claims to have those exact napkins. I have my mind made up that they will be part of my collection one of these days."

I was sure they would be. I read on.

The Sheriff was summoned via telephone, and Nora was then escorted in handcuffs to the county jail. Ezekiel was informed of his wife's misdeed, and he visited her nightly until her appearance before Circuit Court Judge Reuben Pierce Oldfield on November 7th. She pled guilty, on the advice of Arnold Schoenbrunn, Esq. who was appointed to represent Mrs. Bradley. He recommended a light sentence, and required visits with a specialist doctor in Emily City.

However, when court next convened on November 21st, and sentence was passed, Judge Oldfield stated that the recurring nature of Nora's crimes caused her to be a public menace, especially due to the escalating value of the thefts. Surprisingly, he handed down the maximum sentence, one year in the state prison.

On Sunday morning, just two days later, the Honorable Judge Reuben Pierce Oldfield was asleep in his bed at the family home on Peach Street, his wife having already arisen to fix breakfast, as it was the servant's day off. Suddenly, Ezekiel Bradley crashed through the window of the ground floor room and waved a pistol in the air. Shouting like a madman, Zeke declared that if his wife was going to prison he'd go there with her as she was the best dad-gummed cook he'd ever lived with. Upon making this statement, he leveled the pistol at the Judge, and shot him through the breast. The Judge lived but a few moments more, and uttered no dying words, according to Bradley. He was the only other person in the room when the Judge expired, and we may assume his account may not be entirely trustworthy.

"Ezekiel perhaps wasn't the brightest man in the world, but he certainly loved that woman," Cora said.

"This must have been very upsetting in such a small town," I commented.

Cora pointed at the printed page. "Read the ending. It's something of an editorial."

It is a sad commentary on the state of the human condition, that in a village as close-knit as Cherry Hill that in one rash act we have lost more than one good citizen. The loss of Judge Oldfield, of course, can hardly be measured. But yet, who can place a value on someone who knew every motorcar on the local streets, inside the engine compartment, as well as by make and color, and kept them running smoothly. Zeke Bradley's skills will be missed. Nora, despite her attraction to trinkets and candies, was always cheerful, and a staunch member of the Ladies Aid Society. Dieter Volger, our own merchant extraordinaire, is less likely to be as trusting and open as on previous occasions. And all these troubles because a woman was possibly in need of a special sort of treatment from a doctor not found in our small city.

"For want of a nail the shoe was lost. For want of a shoe the horse was lost. For want of a horse the rider was lost. For want of a rider the battle was lost. For want of a battle the kingdom was lost. And all for the want of a horseshoe nail."

I laid the scrapbook on the table and looked at Cora. "Rather melodramatic writing, isn't it?"

"Those were the customs of the times," she said.

"I know you have the actual furniture set up in the corner over there. The judge's bed and all."

"Yes, that's a permanent display. But look what else is on the table. I have the pistol Zeke used, the bloody nightshirt..."

"That's a bit gory," I protested.

"Probably for use in the play, but what an artifact to have! When the Schoenbrunn law offices closed, I convinced them to give me everything they had on the case, and it turned out they had all the evidence. Who knows why? It should have been in the District Attorney's files. But I'm thrilled!" Cora smiled and softly stroked an unstained portion of the yellowed, striped flannel.

"What are these pictures?" I asked, flipping to the next page of the archival scrapbook.

"Take a look. I got the book out just for you."

The first picture was a funeral procession. "For Judge Oldfield?" I asked.

"Yes, that's on East Liberty, right at the bend where it becomes Cemetery Road."

A hearse was drawn by six black horses. Behind the dark wagon could be seen a long line of automobiles, followed by carriages, curving away between fields of corn shocks. On the next page was an image of a man in chains. His eyes were sunken and he looked defeated and lost.

"Zeke Bradley, after his trial." Cora said. "He found out men went to a different prison from the women. And he got sent up for life. No more good cooking for him."

The next picture was a posed family portrait. There was a pleasant, round-faced young woman, seated and holding a baby on her knee. Behind her stood a slim man with a mustache. Although they were dressed nicely, neither of them looked particularly comfortable. Beside the picture was mounted a photocopy of some spidery writing, I assumed from the back of the photo: "Ezekiel and Nora Bradley, Elizabeth, 1913."

"What happened to Elizabeth?" I asked. "She would have been just eleven or twelve when this all happened."

"Died in the great influenza epidemic of 1918. She was gone before this happened. They left no heirs."

I turned to Cora. "This is great stuff. Can we scan the pictures and article and send them to Chad's friend who wants to write the skit? We can take a new photo of the furniture."

"Certainly. I was hoping you'd want to do that. How do you think she'll end it? At the shooting or with Zeke in chains?"

"Chains will probably appeal to the young people, and it's perfect for the Halloween season. Maybe Zeke can appear out of the basement at the end and give everyone a good scare." I paused and looked directly at my friend. "Cora, you'll come to the Harvest Ball, won't you? You don't want to miss this."

Cora glanced sideways toward the door. "I might," she said with a little smile. "Can't let my museum pieces go unescorted, can I?"

23

I stayed at Cora's a few more hours, trying to concentrate on the database, but my mind kept drifting away to invent scenes for the skit. It was going to be difficult to leave the creative process to the kids.

Cora copied pages from the scrapbooks and newspaper stories. She also took pictures of the furniture, pistol and nightshirt. Compared to her usual quiet self, she was positively chatty, continually explaining connections with the people and places from the Judge's story to current Cherry Hill residents and locations. By noon I was brain-weary and hungry. I collected all the newly digitized information into one folder and emailed it piecemeal to Chad. That took several tries. Internet connections in the back corners of Forest County are not known for their speed. Then I headed for town.

By that time it was past one o'clock, and I thought I'd grab a bite to eat and drop in on Detective Milford. Being at Cora's had reminded me of the package that had begun this long, strange sequence of events. I wanted to know if there was any more information about where it came from. I wasn't sure he'd tell me, but I was going to ask, just as soon as I got something in my stomach.

I did forget that the Pine Tree Diner was closed. And that was another of the goofy things that had happened since this— whatever it was— all began. What had made Jack Panther suddenly lock his doors and take off? Where had he gone? Wasn't anyone interested in finding out why he had disappeared on the same day the actual crime scene was located? There were a lot of unexplained coincidences swirling around like the golden leaves in the breeze. It seemed as impossible to put the pieces of the story together as it would be to try to restore the leaves to the correct branches.

Since I was on a focused mission, I didn't want to spend an hour chatting with Adele at the grocery. Instead of turning right, I pulled the wheel left onto Main Street and parked in front of the small drugstore. I had no idea how it managed to remain open, but in addition to pills and bandages, toiletries and small discounted novelties, they sold candy bars and single bottles of soda pop. It wasn't a lunch to brag about, but it would have to do. The sugar set my teeth on edge, and I chastised myself for thinking this was better than a tub of coleslaw, even if I would have had to visit with Adele for a while.

By the time I had finished my snack and thought this through, I was already at the Sheriff's Department. I entered the plain building and asked to speak to Detective Milford. I didn't have too much confidence that he would talk to me, but it was worth a try. The deputy at the desk made a call in response to my request, and in just a few seconds he was leading me back through the cold, dreary block hallways to Milford's office.

The detective was waiting for me, standing behind his desk. "Have a seat, Ms. Raven. Do you have some new information for me? Maybe another strange event to report?" He pointed at the plain unoccupied metal chair and sat down in his more comfortable, but worn, padded one.

"No, no. Nothing new," I said. "I think we have enough mysteries going on already, don't you?"

"Yes, I do."

"Are you having any luck tracking our hatchet in a carton?" I tried to sound lighthearted.

"*Our* hatchet? You feel some ownership of it? Now, I find that extremely interesting, considering where it came from." He leaned forward.

"Oh! You've tracked down the sender. That's great. Can you tell me who it is?"

"Maybe it was you." Milford cocked his head to the side and scratched the coarse gray hair behind his right ear.

"What? I didn't send that box. I found it in Cora's office," I protested.

"Did you?"

"Of course I did. She told you herself it came in the mail."

"Now there's the problem, Ms. Raven. We don't actually know where it came from, but it didn't come in the mail."

"But..."

"There are really several problems with it. One of them was obvious right away to anyone who lives here."

"Cora didn't seem to notice anything amiss." I could hear a slight whine creep into my tone.

"Yes, and I find that odd, too." He paused and his eyes bored into mine, as if searching for pieces that were out of place.

"So, what's wrong with it?"

"Most telling is that the address is all wrong."

"Because there is no actual Historical Society? That was part of the address, right? But everyone knows that's just Cora."

"They do, for a fact. But Cora doesn't live in Cherry Hill."

"I don't understand."

"She lives at least ten miles south of town, as the crow flies, even longer by road. Her actual post office address is Thorpe."

"Oh." I thought a minute. "But wouldn't a small town postal service just deliver it anyway?"

"Cherry Hill rural routes don't go that far out. Perhaps some individual might have recognized where it went and been kind enough to take it out there."

I brightened and held out a hand. "That must be what happened."

"But it didn't. No one who works for the Cherry Hill Post Office has ever seen that box."

"It had a postmark, though. Chicago. I saw that myself. But the date was smudged. Didn't you send it to a lab or some place where they could clean it up and read it? Then you'd know where it was mailed." This seemed like preaching to the choir, but I'd seen the evidence of a mailing with my own eyes.

Milford pushed his chair back and put his hands behind his head, see-sawing on the back legs. "Now that's another interesting thing."

I continued to gaze at him. He didn't say anything, so I raised an eyebrow and opened my eyes wide. "Well?"

The chair crashed back to the hard floor. "It did have a Chicago postmark," he admitted.

"I knew it!" I gloated.

He leaned toward me slightly, matching my pop-eyed gaze. "From 1998."

"1998?"

Detective Milford positively smirked. "The wrapping paper was re-used from some earlier mailing, and we haven't found the information on it to be very helpful. If you see what I mean."

"There was no address under the label with Cora's name?"

"It had been cut out. Didn't notice that did you, Miss Amateur Detective?" he said sarcastically.

"So, somebody left that package by the mailbox." I jerked upright with the realization. "That's a little scary. They were right there near her house. The person that killed Jared Canfield... no, wait. That wasn't the same hatchet."

"You begin to see why we are finding this case, if it's only one case, difficult to solve," Milford drawled.

24

I needed time to think. There were basically two locales involved in the murder of Jared Canfield if you left out the hatchet sent to Cora that apparently wasn't connected to the crime at all, except perhaps by implication. They were Jalmari and the old school, connected by the Petite Sauble River, in which Canfield's body had been found.

Leaving the Sheriff's office, almost without thinking I turned west and followed US 10 until I reached Jalmari Road, which I took and headed straight north to the river, and to what was left of the small town. There was no longer any village limit sign at all, just a billboard advertising the Jalmari Canoe Livery, which was almost the only remaining business. The gas station and pizza parlor were across the river, nearly out of sight behind trees which lined the banks. I pulled into a deserted strip parking lot in front of the log-faced livery. Multi-colored kayaks had been leaned against the logs, creating an appealing storefront. Maybe they were already closed for the season, but I thought I saw lights on inside. The front door opened inward when I turned the knob, and a bell jingled— a cheerful tinkle.

As I surveyed the inside of the building, I realized this was much more than just a place to rent canoes. It appeared to be a full outfitter, with kayaks, canoes, tents, gear, and clothing for sale. I was surprised to find such a going establishment in a locale that was so out of the way. I'd learned in July that there was a large lake on the other side of Cherry Hill, known as Turtle Lake, where water sports were popular, and it seemed to me this business would have been more likely to succeed over there.

A young woman approached me. "May I help you?" she asked pleasantly.

"I'm not sure," I admitted. "I thought you just rented canoes and had no idea you sold a full line of outdoor gear. I'm very surprised."

The girl smiled. She looked young enough to be a college student. "Yes, we have some advertising issues. Actually, we expanded this summer. My husband and I bought the livery business, and hope to capitalize on the proximity of the Thousand Lakes State Forest. Are you into quiet outdoor sports? Maybe we have something you could use."

"I might be interested in making a purchase some other time," I offered hesitantly. "I really just have a few questions, if you don't mind."

"Sure," the girl said.

She didn't sound annoyed, so I was encouraged. "My name is Ana Raven. I live over on East South River Road." I paused, knowing my thoughts weren't too tactful, but wanting answers. "Actually, I would think a sports business would do better over there, near Turtle Lake, if I'm not being too pushy."

She laughed. "We think so too. But Shane and I just bought the livery this spring, and this is where it is. We hope to eventually have two locations. By the way, I'm Alex. Our last name is Clarkson." She held out her hand.

Her grip was firm but not forceful. I liked her instantly. Encouraged, I continued, "I know you can paddle down the river from the lake for some distance, but I haven't tried to make it all the way to my property. Someone at the lake told me the river might be clogged with snags. Do you know anything about how far it's clear?"

"We've been too busy to explore upstream from Cherry Hill this summer. But we've paddled on the downstream side quite a bit."

Questions suddenly jumped into my mind. "I guess you can't take a boat through town, though? There's the mill race."

"Just a couple of blocks portage can get you around the race," Alex said, "but the water is real shallow after that for a mile or so. In mid-summer the river is very low."

My other question was the important one. "I'm very curious

about the body that washed up here. If the water was low, how could it have been carried very far?"

Alex wrinkled her nose. "That wasn't much fun. We had to stay closed for three days right at the end of the season while the police did whatever it is they do."

"I know," I commiserated. "I was here the day they were diving for evidence. I saw all that 'police line' yellow tape."

"We lost a lot of business that week from summer people who wanted a final adventure while closing up their cottages. To answer your question, the water is higher now. We had some good rain early in the month. I'm not sure how far upstream a body could have come from. At least a few miles if it didn't catch on branches or get caught in an eddy and pushed to the outer bank of a bend."

"Why did they find the body here?" I asked. "I mean, if there are so many places it could get hung up?"

"Probably two reasons," Alex speculated. "The river widens out, so the current does diminish. I've been told that's why the town was built here in the first place. The river could be forded before there was a bridge; now it's been dredged for boats to pass through. But also, there are people here. We saw it and called the police. The body was snagged on that tree near the public access. Shane actually pulled it, him, ashore." Alex stared into the distance with the corners of her mouth drawn down, obviously recalling the unpleasant experience.

"That makes sense," I agreed.

"Although there are cottages along the river, most of them are only occupied in the summer. I suppose some paddler might have spotted the body, but I guess no one did. It was mid-week, after all," Alex pointed out. "Did you know him?"

"Oh, no," I quickly answered, shaking my head. "But I've gotten connected to the whole mess through a strange set of coincidences. Jerry Caulfield— he owns the newspaper— and I found the crime scene." Now it was my turn to shudder with a gruesome memory.

"At the old school building, right?" Alex asked, suddenly curious.

"Yes. Are you from the area? Do you know where it is?"

"Only sort of. On the edge of town, I think. Shane and I are from Sault Ste. Marie. But we wanted to go into business promoting quiet sports, and there are so many rivers here and the state forest. When we saw that this livery was for sale, it really seemed like the perfect place to begin."

"I hope you do well," I offered with a smile. "I didn't realize this was such a popular area for recreation."

"It's trending. We've got a Facebook page, and lots of people from the city come here in the summer. We just need to tap into that potential business. Convince them they can get high-quality goods right here. The area needs some other businesses that cater to tourism, though."

"There isn't much," I agreed, thinking about the current dearth of restaurants. "Are you going to stay open all winter? There can't be much traffic here now."

Alex glanced at the closed entry door. "We think we might as well stay open. Shane and I made a small apartment in the rear. We have to keep the electric on and part of the building heated anyway. We'll hold out till Christmas for sure. An order of cross-country skis should be arriving this week, and some sweaters and parkas, stuff like that."

"Skis? That sounds like fun. I've never tried it." I mused aloud.

"Oh! We can teach you." Alex clapped her hands like a child. "Classes. I hadn't thought of that. I'll talk to Shane. Would you pay for something like that?"

"I think I would," I said, picturing the trail through the swamp and the extension of the road past my house that I knew wouldn't be plowed in the winter.

"There are trails through Thousand Lakes. I wonder if local people use them in the winter," Alex said.

"I don't know," I admitted. "I just moved here in the spring myself."

Alex ducked her head sheepishly. "I know," she said. "Your name has been in the paper a couple of times. I recognized it when you introduced yourself. I should have told you."

I laughed. "It's OK. I'm infamous, but not by choice. I really would like to live a quiet, private life. Have you heard about the Harvest Ball Jerry is planning?"

"No," she said.

"It's going to be in the middle of October, but not in conflict with Halloween— the kids' Trick or Treating, you know. We really have to set the actual date soon."

"We?"

"Oh, well, Jerry has me pretty thoroughly wrapped up in helping with the plans." The secret motive to surprise Cora flitted through my mind. "It'll be open to everyone. Come! The more people you meet, the more business you're sure to get."

"I'll tell Shane, and we'll be there." Alex said.

After looking around at the goods for sale and taking a business card, I promised Alex I'd be back to do some Christmas shopping. For one thing, there were clothes I knew would appeal to Chad. I gave her my phone number and asked her to call me when the skis came in; she eagerly promised to let me know as soon as they were ready.

From Jalmari, I drove slowly along the winding West South River Road back toward Cherry Hill. It was the route Chad and I had taken in the opposite direction the day after Jared Canfield's body was discovered. I passed the driveway leading to the large, white and green cottage that was for sale. Virginia Holiday's Realty sign was still at the corner, although it had been knocked slightly askew. That was a beautiful summer house, I recalled. I wanted to see the inside.

Within a quarter hour, even driving at a casual pace, I reached Cherry Hill. As I passed the old school, it was obvious that Jerry had summoned teams of workers to the site. The place was swarming with vans displaying logos of various construction firms. Two men in hardhats and coveralls were carrying a large pane of taped glass toward some scaffolding. There was such a loud banging noise coming from the building, I could hear it even with my car windows closed.

I smiled, partly at the unlikely success of Jerry's plan to win Cora back, and partly at the amount of effort and money he was pouring into the project. He was getting things done. I'd give him that.

Without stopping in town, I arrived at my house just after four p.m. I was looking forward to a cozy evening with a good book.

25

The minute I pulled into my driveway, a thin young man wearing a hooded sweatshirt and jeans jumped out from behind the large maple tree near the road and raised his arms. I was more than a little startled and stamped on the Jeep's brakes, causing the metal to squeal and the tires to send a small cloud of fine brown dirt flying. The boy was grinning from ear to ear. After a moment my heart stopped pounding; I recognized the intruder as Jimmie Mosher. He was as skinny as when I had met him in May, but perhaps not quite so gaunt-looking. And I was sure he was taller.

His bicycle was leaning against the support post for the upstairs porch, which explained how he had gotten to my house. He immediately ran to the driver's side door and wrenched it open. He grabbed the frame and leaned into the car, peering right into my face. This certainly wasn't the almost shy boy I'd gotten to know earlier in the year.

"Ana! You won't believe what Mrs. Volger and Mrs. Preston are doing!" He was practically yelling.

"Hi, Jimmie," I said, leaning back a bit just because he was so close. He smelled like mint. "It's nice to see you. It must be something incredibly exciting. You caught me by surprise; a little too much surprise, maybe."

"Oh. Sorry 'bout that." He hung his head; but only for a moment. "But, honest, you'll never believe it."

"I might, if you tell me what 'it' is. Come inside and I'll see if we can scare up some sandwiches. I'm starved. I only had a candy bar for lunch."

"Gees, that's not so good, Ana. I'm learning all about nutrition in my Health class. You shouldn't do that."

He looked deadly serious, and I couldn't help but laugh. "You are so right," I agreed. "And my stomach isn't very happy with me. How about a salad? I think I actually have a full refrigerator for a change."

"Sure. Let me fix it, OK? Hey, I found some spearmint at the edge of your yard. I'm learning about wild edibles. We can garnish the salad with it."

He abruptly ran off toward the fenceline to the west. I shook my head. Apparently, Jimmie hadn't wasted any time beginning to educate himself about food. His dream was to buy and re-open the Cherry Blossom Restaurant previously owned by his grandfather Jimmie, for whom he was named, and then by his father. The building had stood empty for years, just west of town. I'd been told it was, back then, the nicest eatery in the county, known for excellent food and atmosphere, yet affordable. But that was long before I moved to Cherry Hill.

Jimmie dashed back toward the house, his left hand filled with aromatic greens. I held the front door open, and he headed for the kitchen. The rooms were familiar to him for two reasons. We had become friends, and he'd spent time with me in May at the end of the school year. But he'd known every nook and cranny of the building before that. His grandfather had grown up in this house, and as a youngster he'd explored the empty and neglected family home.

I was still taking off my jacket and making sure I put the keys in the basket on the counter when I heard the refrigerator door open. Jimmie called, "Really, I can make the salad, right?"

"Sure thing," I called back, grinning at his enthusiasm. "I'll get out the sandwich things."

Jimmie was definitely taller than when I'd last seen him; he could now almost look me directly in the eye. He had pale skin and straight black hair. His hair wasn't really long, but the forelock always seemed to hang in his eyes. And even after an entire summer he didn't look tanned, but he certainly looked healthy.

"Tell me how you've been," I commanded, as I entered the kitchen. "I don't know how your mom is, or what you did all summer, or anything." A lot of my summer had been occupied with the addition to my house and an adventure involving two girls from Hammer Bridge Town. I hadn't seen Jimmie in several months.

"I'm in eighth grade this year. Next year will be high school. I don't want to waste any time. The Cherry Blossom is going to be mine, and I don't want to take a chance someone else might buy the building."

It seemed unlikely to me that anyone was interested. Cherry Hill was a dormant town, with very few needs for expensive services. And yet, Alex and Shane had speculated, even gambled on the notion that there were serious tourist dollars in the area waiting to be harvested by those with business acumen.

"How can you get enough money to buy and repair a large building?" I asked. "And you'll have to be at least eighteen to own it, won't you?"

"Oh, those are minor problems," he glibly replied, shooting me a glance and a grin. "I just want to be sure I know how to handle it all. They won't let me take any business classes till next year, but I found some basic courses on line. I had to fib a little bit about my age, but I figure they will give me a head start on the real thing."

I shook my head. "You are something else, Jimmie Mosher!"

"And I'm learning how to cook. Mom likes that I can make good meals that don't have ingredients that interfere with her medicine."

"How is she?" I asked tentatively. Jimmie's mom, Dee, was obese, partly from an undiagnosed condition of hypothyroidism. She'd also been abused, and had low self-esteem with little motivation to eat right. Conditions were vastly improved now for Dee and Jimmie.

"She's doing great! She's lost thirty pounds. It's not enough, but she's getting there, and now that we live in town she walks a bit every day. That helps."

I thought the loss of thirty pounds in four months was a serious accomplishment.

He switched to financial topics. "We have the Social Security money from when Dad was killed, and Mom is writing things for some on-line web site. It brings in a little extra money. And the new house is great."

I knew that although they had to make a small payment each month, the house Habitat for Humanity had fixed for them was affordable and clean.

Jimmie continued. "I can get a real job next year when I turn fourteen, but I'm still picking up scrap metal for cash too. Oh, and I've started tracking down parts for antique cars for customers at Harold's. They pay me a fee if I connect a potential buyer with someone who owns a junker with good stuff in it. I've learned where a lot of old cars in the county are stashed from biking all the back roads."

Harold's was the scrap metal yard on the north edge of town. Jimmie used to go there nearly every day with metal to redeem for cash.

For several minutes we worked quietly. Jimmie chopped vegetables, while I placed dishes, deli meat, cheese, bread, and condiments on the table.

Jimmie laid down the knife, and began to toss the salad. "I like cooking, but I think I'll be better at running the business. I can always hire a chef."

"So, what's your exciting news?" I asked. I'd made him delay his story to bring me up to date.

"Mrs. Volger is the best!" Jimmie enthused. "She's always been so nice to me. Even before, you know... Anyway, they need food for this big Harvest Ball. I guess you know about that, too. She says you and Mr. Caulfield are planning it."

"We are," I said, although I knew Jerry and I had to get down to deciding more details really soon.

"With the Pine Tree closed, Mrs. Volger called Mrs. Preston. Then she thought of me. I'm going to go to Preston's every day after school and on Saturdays. We'll start this weekend. We're going to make hundreds of little tart shells, and pulled bar-be-que pork, and slider buns. That can all be made ahead of time and frozen. Then at the last minute there will be vegetable trays to make and we'll fill the tarts with pumpkin and apple. Maybe chocolate, too."

"That sounds amazing," I said. I didn't have to fake that sentiment.

"Mrs. Preston said the newspaper is paying for it all. A community support thing. She thinks the bank and Sorenson's Implements have been asked to chip in. Those are the richest businesses in town. Volger's is donating a lot of the ingredients. I'm volunteering my time, like everyone else, but I'm going to learn *so* much."

"A public relations coup," I agreed. "Sounds like Jerry, Mr. Caulfield, is right on top of it, getting more local involvement." I wasn't surprised.

We sat down at the table and concentrated on food for the next few minutes. Jimmie had added mint leaves to the salad, and the tangy flavor perked up the lettuce, while the aroma freshened the entire kitchen.

Once the edge was off our initial hunger, we chatted about other personal matters. His half-sisters had been allowed to visit for a week over the summer, and he'd been thrilled to spend time with them. I told him about the visit from my son and assured him he'd get to meet Chad at the Ball.

He countered with stories Cora hadn't shared with me of time spent at her house, learning more about his family history. He'd begun calling her Nana almost as soon as they'd met, developing an instant bond with the woman who was almost his grandmother. I told him about the old cabin foundation in the woods near the river, the island, and Chad's possible plans to rebuild the cabin and a dock. The idea of paddling a hidden stretch of the river made the boy's eyes light up.

Several hours later, the sun was low in the sky, and Jimmie realized he needed to head home, since he didn't want to bicycle after dark. Much to my amazement, he gave me a warm hug as we stood at the front door saying our goodbyes.

"You rescued my mom and me, Ana. I won't forget. You will be my first guest when I open the Cherry Blossom." Then his cheeks reddened, and he rushed out the door, jumped off the terrace and grabbed his bike.

26

On Wednesday I puttered around the house doing chores. When one lives alone, the laundry and cleaning don't happen unless you do them yourself. But I didn't mind. At least I wasn't expected to do them for someone who clearly didn't appreciate me as a person. In fact, I thought very little about my ex, Roger, any more. I figured that was a good thing. I'd made so many friends here in Forest County. I wasn't nearly as angry as I'd been in April, and I'd learned that I wasn't looking for a new mate. All this recent self-knowledge made me feel confident. The golden glow of sunlight filtering through the maple leaves and shining in the southern windows mellowed my mood even more.

As I ran the vacuum and sorted stacks of junk mail, I also thought about the logistics of the Canfield murder and made a plan for the next day. I had to be in town anyway for the Family Friends Committee meeting at church.

The meeting was brief, with no new business, for which I was thankful. Before eleven o'clock, I wolfed down a sandwich I'd packed in a small cooler, and was facing the entrance to the old school building. A small backpack hung from my shoulders, containing a few things I thought I might need. Even though it was September, the mid-day sun was intense and hot, and it made the bricks glow with a lovely red-gold patina.

Only two vehicles were parked outside. One was a battered pickup that had the faded and scratched words, "Ringman and Son Heating and Plumbing," hand painted on the cab door. The other was the large truck I'd seen on Tuesday that was specially designed to transport sheets of glass. A look to my right confirmed that the window crew was busy moving scaffolding to give them access to another broken pane that needed replacing.

I climbed the ten broad concrete steps and tried the front door.

It was unlocked. Part of my intent was to check on the condition of the auditorium. I remembered it as being rather dingy, but not in too much disrepair. Walking across the entrance hall, I smiled again at the Cherry Hill Bomber's tiled emblem in the floor. The auditorium door was propped open and the lights were on, but there was no one in the room. As I entered the large multi-purpose space, a familiar banging sound assaulted my ears. It was the same tone I'd heard on Tuesday, but much louder inside the building. I assumed it was Todd Ringman, working on the boiler. The fact that there were plumbing tools scattered around on blankets laid on the floor in the vicinity of the uncovered radiators seemed to support that theory. I cupped my hands over my ears and studied the layout of the room.

The musty maroon curtain that had previously closed off the raised platform had been removed. I wondered if it was being cleaned or replaced. Its absence allowed me to see into the depths of the stage. Steps on each end of this space made access easy. The food tables could be placed here. *No*, I thought. The band should be here. We can put the food service, and small bistro tables in the halls. That will keep all that mess out of this room and give people lots of space in here for dancing. This floor is still in good condition. It doesn't really need anything at all except cleaning. Thankfully, the banging suddenly stopped, and I uncovered my ears.

The ceiling was two stories high. In fact, across the long side of the room opposite the stage, the side that abutted the hallway, there was a narrow balcony with four rows of seats. I could see two access doors that must open onto the upstairs hall. Any decorations we wanted overhead would be difficult to hang, except at the edge of the balcony.

Most of the wall space was bare, painted in some non-descript color that looked grayish-brown in the dim light. That made me realize several of the fluorescent tubes needed to be replaced. *Well, maybe not.* We'd want low light for the Ball anyway. Maybe we could just enhance some areas with plug-in mood lights.

I was visualizing corn shocks and garlands of colored leaves and scarecrows, when an older man in greasy coveralls with a large wet spot on one hip entered the room from the stage area. He didn't look up until he had come down the steps. He jumped back when he saw me.

"Hey there, Missy," he said in surprise.

"Hey, yourself," I answered. "I didn't mean to scare you. I'm Ana Raven. Just trying to get an idea of how we can decorate for the Ball."

"Todd Ringman. Pleased to meetcha." He held out a blackened hand, then quickly withdrew it and wiped the palm on his wet hip. "Ah, well, let's shake another time." He stuck his hands in his pockets.

"I take it you're trying to get the heating system to work," I said, nodding.

"Jest about got 'er. I jest hafta open this line and I'm gonna fire 'er up." He knelt on the blanket with his tools and twisted a valve on the side of the radiator. "I'm happy t' have someone else here," he continued, standing and turning to face me. "These old pipes ain't been pressurized for forty years. Might not be so good, if you catch my meanin'. Would you watch for leaks and holler down if she starts sprayin' water all over?"

"I can do that. Did you come from the basement? I saw you step off the stage." I was a bit confused.

"Yup. There's a door and staircase way t' the back. Leads right down to the boiler room. We'll prop 'er open and you can watch from the stage. I should be able t' hear you holler if you see anything amiss."

I nodded and took my place on the edge of the stage while Todd pushed a chair hard under the doorknob of a metal door in the far back corner, stage left, to hold it open. Then I waited.

Todd's voice floated up the stairs, "I'm openin' the valves down here. Won't be long now."

Horrible clanking noises began, and while I watched the old radiator actually jumped and rattled as air and water surged through the piping. I smelled that peculiar mix of water and metal and dust that always signaled the start-up of a hot water heating line. But nothing that I could see was leaking. However, the noise in the pipes persisted.

Todd reappeared. He grabbed an adjustable wrench and fiddled with something on the side of the radiator. A hissing noise was added to the medley, but the banging subsided. "Got t' bleed the air outa them pipes," he explained. "We aren't takin' any chances on firin' up too many lines. Just this room and the front, before your big shindig.

My idea for tables in the front hall required heating. "Will that include most of the front hallway?" I asked.

"Yup. Whole first floor hall is on one line. The side halls? That's a different story. Willya be needin' them?"

"I don't think so, Todd. This is great. Really, you're doing a tremendous job."

"Use t' *be* our job, me 'n' my dad. He's gone now. I knowed this system like the backa my hand. Not too much trouble t' recollect how it works. Thank the good Lord I had some spare fittin's in the barn. Jest hope these old pipes hold."

"I do too," I agreed. "Do you need me for anything else?"

"Nope, that should do 'er. I'll hang around awhile and make sure things are stable-like."

"I'm going to poke around outside a bit. Take care now," I said. I smiled at Todd and he smiled back, revealing a missing tooth. I wondered if he had steady work, since few buildings still used antique boiler systems for heat.

27

Now that I'd gotten a pretty good idea of how we'd have to do decorations for the Harvest Ball, my thoughts turned to the other part of my day's plan.

I circled the school building, being careful to watch for any boards with nails in them. I was only wearing sneakers, and a puncture wound in the foot wasn't on my agenda. Fortunately, the work crews had thoroughly cleaned up after themselves. The yard was tidy, and even mowed, although lots of weeds were mixed with the grass.

As I'd remembered, there was a chain-link fence close behind the building, with a messy hedgerow of sumac trees, grape vines and alien honeysuckle grown up, through and over the wire barrier between the school and the river. The space between the fence and school was wide enough to drive a vehicle around the back of the building, but without much room left over. It would be a great place to accomplish something surreptitious, such as load a body into a vehicle. There were plenty of tracks through the weeds and fallen leaves, proving that any number of cars and trucks had driven through there this fall. This section had not been mowed.

Or, a body might have been dragged to the river right here, if there was a break in the fence. I was sure the police had thought of all these things, but I wanted to see for myself what was possible.

As I walked farther I discovered there was a sort of three-sided courtyard in the center rear of the building, enclosed by the brick wings. But the door that I knew the drag marks in the basement had led to was in the rear of the western wing.

Sure enough, right in back of the building, completely out of sight from the street, one panel of the chain mesh was hanging askew from the top rail. It wasn't fastened at the right side or the bottom at all. I pushed on the wire, and it flapped like a crooked door, squealing as metal grated against metal. My backpack contained pliers and a fencing tool, but I wouldn't need them to get through the fence.

Here in the perpetual shade on the north side of the building, the air was chilly, the light dim and the vines and scraggly branches oppressive. A workman on the other side of the building shouted something. I was glad for the reminder I wasn't really alone on the property.

Without any trouble at all, I ducked a little and stepped through to the river side of the fence. The shrubs and vines had been cleared here; there was an obvious path to the water. I supposed children found this an appealing place to play. The bank wasn't steep, and it angled gently down to a fairly straight section of the waterway. I walked to the edge of the low bank.

The next part of my plan was to assess how deep the water was. Laying the backpack on the ground I pulled out a small folding saw, opened and locked the blade. There weren't any loose sticks of a good length on the riverbank, so I stepped back up to the hedge and sawed through a honeysuckle branch that was about an inch in diameter. One more cut removed the branches splayed from the top end. It was rough and gnarly, but I now had a staff about four feet long.

I sat down and removed my shoes and socks. Then I stepped out of the sweatpants I'd worn over a pair of shorts. I put the clothing and the saw in the pack and took out a pair of rubber sandals, which I slipped on my feet. I could see that the water by the bank was shallow, but small ripples farther out prevented me from judging the depth accurately.

Standing up, I planted the stick in the river bed and learned that it was sandy but seemed quite solid. I stepped off the bank. The water was chilly, but not frigid. I gritted my teeth and shivered, glad that I had an extra sweatshirt in the car. Feeling ahead of me with the stick, I headed for the opposite bank, about fifteen feet distant.

Walking slowly, and checking each step with the stick, I

crossed the entire river. The water wasn't deeper than mid-calf anywhere, and the current didn't tug at my legs. At this point, at this time— we hadn't had any rain for over a week— only a lightly-laden kayak would have floated downstream easily.

More confident now, I walked up and down stream a bit. By poking carefully with my makeshift walking stick and paying more attention to the looks of the riverbed, I did find a couple of deeper holes, which I managed to avoid falling into, but generally, the river here was very shallow. I decided to look online and see if I could find water level recordings for the Petite Sauble. I could do it from Cora's computer, since I didn't have internet service.

Convinced that it was unlikely the body had been put in the river here, I headed for my car. The fleece sweatshirt was welcome after the chilling effect of wading in the cold water. I toweled my feet and put my sweatpants, socks, and sneakers back on, wishing for a cup of hot coffee.

28

My next stop was downtown. I turned right off Liberty, crossed the bridge on Mill Street, and parked in front of the one small building in the newspaper block that Jerry didn't own, Holiday Realty. *Kind of a cutesy name*, I thought, but then remembered the realtor's name was Virginia Holiday. *That sounds a bit fake too.* But I supposed she couldn't help that. After all, I knew people with much goofier names, Ted Bear, Brook Trout. That one always made me guffaw. *Why did people give their children names that were sure to invite teasing?*

I locked the car, having learned my lesson too many times this summer, and approached the block structure which had been modernized with a slanting shake gable on the two sides which faced streets. Pictures of houses and cottages with lists of amenities were taped in the windows. I wasn't even sure Ms. Holiday would be there, but the door was unlocked.

When I entered, I swept my eyes around the empty room. The desk and customer chair were strewn with papers, but there was a doorbell mounted on the countertop and a hand-painted sign "ring for service." I pushed the buzzer and waited what seemed like forever, then rang again.

Faintly, a voice floated through a cold-air register. "Coming. Hold on."

In a few minutes, I heard ascending steps, and Virginia Holiday emerged from a door across the room. She was straightening her skirt. She tried to wipe a spot of dirt from her face, but only succeeded in smearing it.

She lit a cigarette and let it dangle from her lip. "I was looking up some things in the files. That basement is filthy," she commented, pulling the cigarette from her mouth with long fingers adorned with many rings. Bracelets clinked, and her office chair squeaked as she sat down.

"Hello," I said in greeting. "I wasn't sure I'd find you here." The stench of the smoke was difficult to handle, but I wanted to talk to this woman.

"Hello, yourself," Virginia answered in her deep voice. "What can I help you with?" She placed the cigarette in an ashtray filled with butts.

Her taste in clothes ran to bold prints and loose peasant styles. This outfit was no exception. The tiered purple paisley skirt hung to her ankles, and she'd paired it with a silky lavender blouse. Over that she wore a purple fleece vest. Long earrings dangled near her shoulders, where they could be seen through long, nearly-straight dishwater hair parted in the middle. She wore slightly too much makeup, and I realized she must be older than I'd previously thought. Except for the makeup her style was very 1970s. Of course that look was back in vogue, if one could believe the magazines. For footwear, she'd chosen pink rubber clog sandals.

I glanced at the narrow shelf along the back wall. "For starters, may I bum a cup of coffee?" I asked.

"Sure. It's pretty fresh, I made it at lunchtime. Sugar and white stuff in the cupboard."

"I take it black, thanks," I responded.

While I filled a foam cup with the hot brown liquid, Virginia cleared the extra chair, moved it back to the front side of her desk, and made some effort to straighten the papers that lay at every angle on its surface. I sat down, and she returned to her desk chair. It squeaked again.

"How are you liking Cherry Hill?" I asked. "I think you may be the only person in town who's lived here for a shorter time than I have."

"I'll admit, I'm not a small town girl," she said with a rough chuckle. "Of course, I'm trying hard to convince people to move here. I'll never be able to stay if I don't sell some properties."

"What made you come here, if you don't mind me asking?" I was sipping the hot coffee, and it was most welcome.

"Oh, I had some relatives from this area a long time ago. I'm tracking down some of their history," she answered vaguely. "How about you?"

I laughed. "I was looking for something completely different, someplace I could hide from a relationship that went bad. I've made a lot of good friends here, now. People are very nice once you get to know them."

"I suppose so," she said. "I've been busy. Summer people seem to trade houses and cottages quite often even if the locals don't."

"Have you heard about the Harvest Ball we're putting on in October?" I asked.

"No, I don't think so."

"That's why Jerry Caulfield is fixing up the old school building. You must know about that."

"Of course, I had the building in my listings for a while, but the time ran out, and it reverted to the city. He waited and bought it directly from them. I got no fee. What's that got to do with this Ball?" she asked, visibly irritated, probably at the lost fee.

"Jerry has this idea to bring the community together. Everyone is chipping in with food and décor. There will be live music, dancing, who knows what else. It's not completely planned." My stomach turned as I thought about how little was actually arranged. Having donated decorations was an outright fabrication. "Oh. And it's being held in the old school auditorium." I lifted the cup to my lips to cover my discomfort with the white lies that were piling up.

"That's pretty short term. What does he want with the building after that?"

"I'm not sure," I lied again. "He has some ideas about a community center, or a conference center, or something."

"In this backwater," she scoffed. Her attitude didn't bode well for building trust with the residents. It didn't sound to me as if Virginia Holiday was falling in love with Forest County.

"Some people seem to think things might be turning around," I said defensively, recalling Alex's optimism.

"I don't think anyone is going to travel here for a conference, and neither does Jerry Caulfield," she said, picking up her half-smoked cigarette. She looked at it, sighed, and placed it back in the saucer. "That man is devious."

I attempted not to fidget, and countered. "Well, I don't know about that. But we certainly want you to know that you're invited to the Harvest Ball. It will be a lot of fun. Watch for ads in the newspaper. Or posters."

"I'm not much of a dancer," she said. "Too awkward. Big feet."

"Not a problem," I promised. "I suspect a lot of people will simply be chatting and enjoying the music. And eating. Janice Preston is taking the lead on the food preparation. Do you know her?"

"Haven't met her," Virginia said, taking another drag on her cigarette.

She seemed to be cutting responses short, as if she wanted to end our conversation. I knew it was time to get to the real reason for my visit to the office.

I changed the subject abruptly. "My son, Chad, was here earlier this month."

"Oh?" she said with interest, as if sensing new blood.

"We drove west on South River Road, and took a quick look at that large cottage with the green trim. 'Chippewa Lodge,' I think it was called. He liked it a lot." I didn't tell her that Chad was still in college, and certainly wasn't going to buy a huge summer home.

"That's one of my especially nice places. It's vintage turn of the century—twentieth century. Stone fireplace, screen porch, boathouse. All kept up very well. Quite high-priced though. Unless the owners decide to come down." Virginia was all business now.

"Virginia... may I call you Virginia?"

"Of course."

I hesitated. Lying wasn't one of my best talents, but I'd been fudging almost everything for the past half hour. "Chad really liked that place. He asked me to find out more about it. Do you think I'd be able to see the inside?"

29

The realtor stood, her abundant jewelry clinking against her thin bony wrists and fingers. She stubbed out the cigarette and picked up a leather slouch purse. "Are you free right now?"

This was exactly what I'd been hoping for. I wasn't sure why, but the hundred-year old cottage fascinated me, and its location was intriguing too, conveniently situated downriver, where the water was deep, toward Jalmari. And empty. River access with no one nearby.

"I am. Do you want to ride with me?" I offered.

"No thanks. I'll drive myself. You can follow me."

I agreed, and we walked to our cars. She told me hers was over on Cherry Street since the office building didn't have an associated parking lot. This explained why she'd been walking through between Jerry's house and his cousin Karen's the other day. She'd been walking on Cherry and also had access to the school, but Mavis might have walked her dog on that same street, and she could have gotten keys to the school through Harold. Either of these women could have seen my car parked there and returned to slip the printed note through the window. But I knew of no reason for either of them to have that much personal interest in the old brick building.

Virginia said she'd wait for me to pull up behind her. By the time I did so, she already had another cigarette lit and was tapping ash out the slightly opened window.

The drive to Chippewa Lodge took only seven minutes when one wasn't sight-seeing. It was closer to town than my place. It was probably only five minutes from the school. A very fast drive for someone who needed to dispose of a body. Of course, that person would have to have known about the empty cottage, but any number of people might have seen the "For Sale" sign and explored the property, just as Chad and I had. And what about Virginia herself, the previous owners, anyone who had legitimately considered buying the cottage, guests of the owners, possibly even renters? And there were certainly other vacant properties along the river. I decided my bright idea didn't narrow the possibilities very much.

We turned off the paved road, and wound our way toward the river through the forest of mixed hardwoods and conifers, mostly white pine, I thought. We reached the end of the road and parked.

Virginia opened her car door and swung her long legs out. Smoke was escaping her nostrils, but I was glad to see she left the cigarette in the car.

She reached into her purse and drew out a large wad of keys, then headed for the wide green wooden steps that led to the white clapboard cottage. I looked around. I'd forgotten there were two other homes located down this same road. One of them was also for sale, but the other one wasn't. It might have been occupied into early September, although it looked closed-up now, with wooden storm shutters tightly fastened over the windows and tarps tied over amorphous shapes in the yard.

"Are you coming?" Virginia asked impatiently.

"Yes, of course," I answered, following her up the steps to a narrow porch that encircled the landward sides of the cottage. The rustic sign, "Chippewa Lodge," hung from the green eave, and enhanced the aura of Romantic Era authenticity. She already had the door unlocked, and we stepped into a room that seemed smaller than I had imagined it would be. Virginia plopped her purse on a small table beside the door. It was the only piece of furniture in the room, but I could picture a chintz-covered daybed against the far wall.

It was apparently sort of an entry hall, open two stories, clear to the roof. Once my eyes adjusted to the dim light, I realized there was a stairway built against the outside wall with a landing at the corner where it turned and continued to climb to the second floor. The other end of the room had built-in bookcases. All the woodwork had the original dark varnish. The walls had been re-papered recently, but the patterns selected matched the style of the house. Beneath the upper portion of the stairs, to our left, a door led to a larger room, which we entered.

"These rooms seem to defy standard names," Virginia said. "This is sort of a summer living room, and yet the fireplace is in here."

The fireplace was enormous, built of large field stones, with a herringbone brick hearth. It looked as if it were still functional.

"Summer evenings in the woods can be chilly. This place is really beautiful," I said, and I meant it.

We continued through the house. The largest room on the main floor was in the center, sort of an all-purpose great room, although it certainly wouldn't have been called that in 1900. The kitchen was located on the landward side of that room, separated only by a counter. The kitchen had been modernized, but not to the extent that it detracted from the style of the house. On the river side, a huge screen porch was supported on piers as the ground fell away sharply beneath it.

The upstairs was divided into three bedrooms. An addition to the house had been built which provided for a bathroom on each floor, all fitted with modern fixtures, but in Victorian style.

Returning to the great room, we descended to a large unfinished, but clean, basement that looked as if it had been added later. This room was largest of all and except for support posts, was undivided. At the back wall was another bathroom, directly below the other two.

"What are the owners asking for this?" I ventured.

"Three-hundred sixty-five thousand," Virginia said, without blinking an eye.

I gulped. "That's pretty steep, isn't it?"

"Classic and modern at the same time, twenty-five hundred square feet, navigable river frontage, boathouse... it's worth it," she said with a shrug.

I suddenly realized that the summer people who lived in the area for part of each year certainly had enough money to raise the standard of living in Forest County if the local businesses could provide goods and services these people wanted.

She continued, "I'll show you the boathouse. It's very nice, and a bit unusual to find on the river."

We returned to the front door. As Virginia reached toward the table to retrieve her purse, one of her many bracelets snagged on the strap hardware. Myriad typical female objects spilled across the bare pine floorboards. She immediately bent down to gather a small wallet, comb, a nail polish bottle, loose change, and miscellaneous office supplies, which she stuffed back in the bag. I chased a bottle which had rolled toward the far corner and picked it up.

Virginia gave me an unpleasant look and snatched the bottle from my hand. "Here, give me that," she said roughly, enclosing the label quickly with her fingers.

But I'd already read the lettering; "Cenestin."

I wouldn't have had another thought about the bottle if the realtor hadn't seemed so upset, but she immediately hustled me out the door and locked it behind her.

"Take those steps," she said, pointing toward a long flight that zig-zagged down the steep bluff and led to the green and white boathouse. The stairs were also green, making it obvious they belonged to this cottage.

Soon I heard Virginia's rubber clogs thumping down the steps behind me, and we reached water level. A cleared area on the bank had been fitted with a fire ring in the center of a cultured stone patio. This was set back from the water enough that it hadn't been visible from above. I looked back up the bank. I hadn't counted, but there must be over a hundred steps in the descent. And the ascent, which we had yet to do.

"The river floods in the spring, so I've been told," Virginia stated. "That's why the fire pit is so far back from the water."

"Makes sense," I commented.

She pulled out her keys once more, but she was now holding the purse carefully, as if wary of spilling the contents again. She unlocked the rear door of the boathouse, and reached in, flipping a switch. The dark interior was flooded with light. She stepped back, and I peered in. There was the usual dock/walkway around the edges, and a sliding door facing the water, which was closed and secured with a padlock through a hasp at one side.

Much to my surprise, there was a small motorboat suspended in a hoist within the gabled building.

"They didn't take their boat with them?" I asked.

"It goes with the property. I forgot to mention that. The owners bought a bigger one, and this boat is the largest that will fit entirely within the boathouse. As you can see, it's all prepped for winter."

"Very impressive. So the river is deep enough here for motor boats?" I asked.

"Absolutely. Lots of good fishing holes in this section. In the summer, the stream is filled with boaters. But very few river cottages have an actual boathouse, which is another nice feature of this one. It's more common on lakes."

"Where do cottagers keep their motor boats?"

"Most people just store them on the trailers, up at road level. Then they drive to a public access to put them in. Of course, small boats like rowboats and canoes can be gotten down to the water and just left on the bank. Above high water level, of course."

"Of course," I echoed. All sorts of possibilities for moving a body now coursed through my brain. Where were the public access points, in addition to Jalmari? Wouldn't someone be more likely to take a body to one of them, instead of dragging or carrying it down all these stairs? Or would the stairs be an acceptable trade off for a higher guarantee of privacy? Keeping a body in this locked boathouse for a few days could explain why it hadn't been found immediately, but that meant the murderer would have had keys. I glanced at Virginia and found her staring directly into my eyes.

"Time to go," she said. "I've got another showing at three. And you can stop playing games. I know you and your son have no intention of buying this place."

We began the long climb back to the top of the bluff.

30

Back in town, I stopped at Volger's Grocery. It seemed more likely to me that Adele would know what kind of medication Cenestin was, rather than Cora. Virginia Holiday's attitude had made me suspicious. Almost every woman has some sort of medication they are taking, or some bottle of an outdated prescription lingering in a purse. Why did the realtor seem upset that I had seen this particular one?

There were no customers in the store, but Suzi Preston was rearranging small items near the checkout lane. She looked up and greeted me. Since she was wearing a green apron with "Volger's" embroidered on it, I gathered that Adele had hired her after the Pine Tree closed so abruptly.

I found Adele standing in the office, holding a pile of printed sheets of paper in her left hand and slowly checking off items on another paper with a sparkly purple pencil. She looked up when I knocked on the door frame and smiled.

"Ana! How nice to see you!" She exclaimed. She laid the pencil and papers down, and sat heavily in her chair. Although Adele wasn't really fat, she was certainly matronly with a generous middle-age spread. She pointed at a tall stool by the door. "Take a load off your feet."

"Thanks. I think I will." I sat.

"You look like you've been up to something," Adele suggested, squinting at me.

I never understood how this woman managed to take one look at people and figure out what was going on inside their heads. And then, she usually managed to verify her suspicions by convincing them to reveal specific details. Sometimes it put me off, even though I liked Adele. But today, I was more than willing to discuss my adventures with her.

"Hmmm," I pondered aloud. "Where shall I begin? I've been snooping around a bit. I'll admit it."

"Do tell," Adele said, with a conspiratorial lift of both an eyebrow and her voice at the end of the phrase.

For the better part of an hour I explained how I'd just spent the day. We talked about the possible ways to spirit a body out of town. It was common knowledge by now that it had probably been dragged down the basement hallway on a large piece of cardboard that was left by the door, but then what?

We agreed that it would take someone quite strong, or else two people, to pull a body up the stairs and load it in a vehicle. It must have been transported; the river just wasn't deep enough behind the school. We searched on her office computer for river level monitoring station data, and learned that at all three locations closest to Cherry Hill— Centerline Road, just upstream from the mill race, and Jalmari— the river was shallow, rarely exceeding two feet even during spring floods. The school was between the old mill site and Jalmari, but not far from the race. But the river between Cherry Hill and Jalmari at Chippewa Lodge had to be much deeper for frequent use by power boats. Technology didn't seem to be much help in answering our questions.

If someone had dragged a body through the loose fence section it also seemed likely some fibers, or flesh, or something would have caught on the rough and rusty wire. Surely the crime techs would have checked for that.

And with the amount of blood involved, the corpse must have been wrapped in something, since no blood had been found anywhere except the school basement. At least not that we'd heard about. Since Adele kept one ear glued to the police scanner, as did many other townspeople, unless law enforcement people were extremely tight with their facts most details made it into public consciousness.

I began to tell Adele about the beautiful Chippewa Lodge, but she cut me off.

"Isn't that quite the place?" she interrupted. "It was built by Tor Pedersen, before 1900. Opa, Henry's *großvater*, used to talk about playing there with the Pedersen children." She looked at me closely. "They would swim there all summer, so I know the water is much deeper than two feet. Did you find something interesting?"

"Not really." I sighed. "But I didn't have time to look at anything closely. The boat was pulled up into the hoist. I couldn't see in it at all."

"That might be worth another look when you are alone," she urged.

"I don't see how. The boathouse is locked up tight. Listen, here's a question I bet you do have the answer to," I posed.

Adele perked right up. She liked having answers.

I told her about Virginia Holiday spilling her purse on the floor by accident, and the odd way she'd acted when I saw the medicine vial. "The label said 'Cenestin.' Does that mean anything to you?"

"Sure, but it's not very mysterious," Adele said. "It's estrogen. HRT—Hormone Replacement Therapy treatment."

"That's all?" I said. "Huh."

"Maybe she's embarrassed about it," Adele suggested. "She's not exactly a raving beauty. Kind of gaunt, you know."

"One thing's for sure. She's older than I realized. When I was close to her today that fact was obvious."

"That's got to be it. She's aging and doesn't like the process very much. Realtors have to sell themselves as well as houses."

"That reminds me," I added. "She said something about having relatives who lived here in the past. Do you know who that might be?"

"Now, that I find very interesting." Adele nodded vigorously. "I have no idea. There are no Holidays in the county that I know of. She must have come by that name through marriage somewhere."

I remembered something else I wanted to ask Adele. "I've been thinking about Mavis Fanning, what you said about her interest in the old school."

"And?"

"You know the crank call I got was made on a phone she

bought, right?" I asked.

"She's the person who called you?"

"Maybe. It didn't sound like her. Her daughter had the phone last, but no one knows were it is now. Anyway, I wondered if you knew any more about why she wanted that building."

Suzi stuck her head into the office. "May I leave early today?" she requested. "Things are really dead out here. I straightened stuff up, but I could use the time to study if there's nothing else."

"Sure, honey. Go ahead," Adele said. "Tomorrow's Friday. Come at nine; you don't have class on Friday, right? There will be steady traffic pretty much all day."

"No Friday classes; I can be here."

I was surprised. "I thought you graduated in June," I said.

"I did. Now I'm a freshman at Sturgeon Community College. It's the closest place," she added.

"What are you studying?" I asked.

"Just general stuff for right now, till I decide. Mom thinks we should expand the catering business, but I'm not sure I want to cook my whole life, and I'm no math whiz. She doesn't want me keeping the books; that's for sure," Suzi said with a light laugh.

"Good luck," I offered.

"Thanks."

Adele pointed at the wall. "Don't forget to check out."

Suzi turned and pulled a manila card from a rack on the wall. She picked up the purple pencil and began to write, but the lead broke. She stepped around the corner to use the sharpener that was mounted just outside the office door.

"I haven't been able to figure that out at all," Adele said over the grinding of the pencil sharpener, turning the conversation back to Mavis. "She's not really involved in real estate dealing."

Suzi came back in the office. "You're talking about Mrs. Fanning, right?" she asked.

"Yes, Mavis Fanning, Harold's wife," Adele said, in a tone designed to extract more information.

"She's really into fitness stuff."

"We know that, but lots of people exercise," Adele pointed out.

"True," Suzi agreed. "But she actually teaches Yoga classes at the college in the evenings, and does Reiki."

"You're not serious?" Adele said forcefully.

"I am. She wears all those fancy clothes in public, but the way she keeps that killer body is exercise. I think the classes are extra, like for the community, not part of the regular curriculum."

"Thank you for telling us," Adele said, as if this were some huge revelation.

"Sure," Suzi said with a shrug. "It's no big secret."

31

Adele treated us to cold bottles of pop and some sandwich cookies while we discussed the importance, if any, of Mavis' apparent obsession with health and physique. I remembered that Jerry had said something about Harold Fanning when he told me he'd bought the school building. Or did the name come up just because Harold was the city manager? I couldn't remember. Would the Fannings have any reason to want me to stay away from the building? Maybe they knew about the blood in the basement and wanted to forestall anyone else finding it for as long as possible. The longer one could keep a forensics team away from a crime scene, the less able they would be to pinpoint dates and times, we decided.

Although the call about the note in my car had come from a Fanning-owned phone, it wasn't clear at all where that phone was, and it didn't seem as if Mavis was the last one to have it in her possession.

And, as far as anyone knew, there was simply no connection between Jared Canfield and anyone from Cherry Hill, except a business card from Holiday Realty. He was probably thinking about buying a house, so what? Or, did he plan to move here, and someone needed to prevent that from happening so badly the only alternative was to kill him? Who was he?

Where did the hatchet sent, or not sent, to Cora fit in? It was a complete muddle of possibilities. Adele and I gave up trying to figure it out, and I headed for home when she closed the store at six.

One thing was certain; Jerry and I needed to get serious about making more plans for the Harvest Ball. As soon as I walked through my door, I called him. Since the *Cherry Hill Herald* came out on Wednesdays, he was usually less busy at the end of the week.

"Jerry, we have to talk. Soon," I blurted without any preliminaries.

"Great!" Jerry sounded upbeat and excited. "How about breakfast at my house tomorrow? Fairly early."

Early is not my time of day. "That soon?" I stammered.

"It will be perfect. We aren't doing anything at all toward the goal of making Cora jealous. We haven't had any dates, or been seen together enough. Breakfast is intimate. I'll make sure Tom sees you here. Other people should see you leave here after we're done, too."

It was probably true that if Tom saw me at Jerry's, Cora would hear about it. Tom wasn't a gossip, but he did visit with his mother regularly. She didn't drive, and he did most of her shopping. I agreed, groaning inwardly, to be at Jerry's house at six-thirty the next morning.

The sun wasn't yet coloring the horizon when I pulled out of my driveway. My eyes were sticky, despite the fact that I'd showered. This was going above and beyond for Cora's sake as far as I was concerned, and I didn't even know if it was going to work.

I arrived at Jerry's front door at the assigned hour. He was wearing pajamas with a rich, navy blue satin robe over them. He stepped out onto the porch, grasped my arms, leaned over and kissed me warmly, then pulled me into the house.

"Jerry! What are you doing?" I hissed.

"Plenty of neighbors are up getting ready for work. That should get some tongues wagging." He grinned sheepishly. "You didn't mind too much, did you?"

"I'm not sure. I don't want people thinking we're sleeping together."

"They'll think that anyway. Come have breakfast."

He led the way to his modern kitchen. Since I'd had several other opportunities to visit with Jerry in his home, I was no longer intimidated by the expensive décor and appliances. The custom, light wood cabinets with black trim, and gray granite countertops were spotless, as always. The programmable coffeepot had filled its carafe with hot brown liquid, and the smell alone made my head start to feel better. I pulled a stool out from beneath the edge of the center island and sat down, resting my face in my hands.

"I hope you appreciate this," I said.

"I do, believe me I do," Jerry responded, filling a large black mug with the coffee and placing it in front of me. Next he opened the refrigerator and pulled out a pitcher of orange juice and a carton of eggs. "Eggs, or French toast?" he asked.

"Oooh, French toast. I never bother to make that for myself," I admitted.

"I'll just get dressed and then be back to fix your meal," Jerry said.

After we ate, for the next three hours, Jerry and I discussed every aspect of the Harvest Ball we could think of. Perhaps most importantly, we decided on a firm date. It would be the second Saturday in October, leaving plenty of time for parents and schools to focus on Halloween after it was over. Jerry said he'd get posters printed immediately and start running an open invitation in the next week's paper.

He nixed the idea of sending private snob invitations because it was too much work, and it didn't really promote community unity.

As soon as businesses were opening for the day, he got on the phone, and quickly collected an impressive list of commitments for donations of decorating supplies, and loans of folding chairs and serving tables. Probably the greatest coup was Sherri Sorenson's promise of genuine wheat shocks, harvested with an antique reaper she'd found and had restored in the company shop.

I shared my idea about making the front hallway into a sidewalk café, and he liked the concept, but wasn't sure where we would find the tables and chairs to make it work. We agreed to keep the idea on the back burner, without abandoning it just yet.

The live music defaulted to bluegrass because the band was

available on that date, and Jerry convinced The Blue Grass to reduce their fee for performing. By virtue of his standing in the county and his authoritative voice, which seemed to make people want to agree with him, he accomplished incredible feats of persuasion.

While Jerry was doing all this, I tried to call Chad from my cell phone. All I got was his voice mail, but I asked him to let me know if Brittney was working on the skit, and I told him the date of the Ball.

About eight o'clock, there was a knock on the kitchen door. Just as Jerry had promised, Tom Baker arrived to witness Jerry and me *tête-à-tête*.

Tom yelled, "I'm stoppin' by like you asked. Don't you want the presses cleaned tomorrow?"

"I do. I do," Jerry answered him. "But I think I'm going to run some posters for this Ball later today. Do you want some extra hours helping with the set-up?"

"Sure thing. I finish at Sorenson's at four this afternoon. Sherri's doin' a great job managing the place and Cliff's brother Karl is moving here next year to help. I don't miss Kevin Teeter one little tiddly-wink. Will that be OK? I can be here by half past."

"Sounds great, Tom." He turned to me and winked. "Ana, don't you think something Art Deco with a gold border design would catch people's attention? Cora will like the look, too."

"Um, I guess. I'll leave that up to you," I said.

"You be sure to tell your mother that's what we're doing," Jerry told Tom, clapping him on the shoulder. "I'll save her a clean copy for her archives. This is going to be the event of the decade. See you at four-thirty."

By ten o'clock we'd accomplished so much my head was spinning. Jerry sent me on my way with two sandwiches, a plastic bag of potato chips, and a travel mug full of coffee. "It's nothing," he insisted. "Your participation is critical to make this work. I owe you way more than a box lunch."

At least he didn't feel the need to kiss me when I left.

32

Although the sun must have come up while I was inside Jerry's house, you couldn't prove it by sight. The day was nothing like Thursday, which had been sunny and cheerful. The day before, the light reflecting on fallen leaves had made it look as though the trees were casting golden shadows. Now, the sky was lead gray and bleak. There were no shadows, and everything looked flat. But the looks of the sky had no bearing on my plan for the next several hours. I drove directly to Chippewa Lodge.

Since the house was for sale, I had every right to be there, looking around outside. Whether Virginia Holiday believed me or not, I had told her Chad and I were interested in purchasing the property, and she couldn't prove otherwise, so there was no need to be furtive. I put my small glovebox flashlight in my jacket pocket, exited the Jeep and looked around. As I had hoped, no one else was there, at any of the three cottages.

My first priority was to study the stairway that led down to the water. It was old and made of wood, sure to have splits and rough places, even though it was nicely painted. Maybe there would be some fibers caught in a crack. If I could show Detective Milford a thread from a rug or a tarp he'd have to investigate further. Any blood would have washed away in the rain we'd had the week before, but I knew there was a way to make blood evidence visible, if one knew where to begin looking.

I'd also come prepared with my small digital camera. If I found anything I wouldn't move it, but would take pictures and document exactly where each item was. If someone drove in, I'd hear them long before they could see me, and it would be easy to quickly switch to taking pictures of the river scenery and forestall questions about what I was doing. Of course, a brighter day would have made that more believable, but I could always stick the camera in my pocket and pretend I was just checking out the river access.

The large number of steps made my task daunting. First I walked all the way down to the river, counting as I went. There were one-hundred twenty-two treads, including the landings. With a sigh, I began working my way back up toward the top of the bluff looking carefully at each step, particularly the edges, scanning the dimly illuminated sides with the flashlight. I kept telling myself if it were easy it wouldn't be worth doing.

By the time I got to step twenty-five I was feeling stiff from bending over. By step fifty, I felt cross-eyed from looking at every swirl and sliver in the wood grain. On step fifty-seven I found something. Caught in a crack at the edge of the step was a scrap of undyed burlap, like from a grain sack. It looked neither very old nor very new, but there was no way to be sure. I took a close-up picture of the fabric, then backed off and took one of the step. I went down a few levels and took another shot to show exactly where that section of staircase was in relation to the bank and the various landings. With two more photos, I was certain I could show anyone exactly where the small fragment was located.

Energized, I continued on to the top of the bluff, but I found nothing else of interest. Back at the parking area, I glanced around and realized there was a second set of steps to the narrow beach. Even though there were two other cottages, I only saw one other stairway. Perhaps the owners had agreed to share. But, I knew I had to look at all those surfaces too.

This staircase was unpainted, almost new, and made of treated wood. There weren't nearly so many cracks and places where something could catch, but the near-natural color made it harder to see anything that was a neutral tone.

Underneath one of the landings, someone had stuffed a green plastic tarp. I wasn't sure if I should move it, in case it turned out to be evidence, but if I didn't look at it, how would I know? After debating with myself a few minutes, I returned to the car and pulled out a pair of jersey work gloves that I kept in the back and put them on. Then I took pictures of the wadded up tarp from every angle I could manage on the steep slope. Pulling gently, I worked it out from beneath the wood platform and carried it to the parking area.

Very carefully, I unfolded the edges. As soon as I'd done so, I realized how foolish this was. I should have laid it on a piece of plastic to catch any flakes of—anything—that might fall off. I should have called Detective Milford. Too late now. And what would I have told him anyway? That I was looking for something that might not exist, on private property, without any good cause? He'd be sure to drive right out and help.

In a few seconds the tarp was spread flat on the ground, and it contained nothing. It wasn't even dirty. Folding it in half, then half again, I flipped it over, hopefully without dislodging anything stuck to the plastic, and opened it to view the other side. Still nothing. Although criss-crossed with fold lines from being wadded up, it appeared to be nothing but an extra tarp someone had stuck under the stairway for some unknown reason. Disappointed, I returned it to where I'd found it and began searching the rest of the treated steps.

With only about ten steps to go, the wind suddenly gusted, throwing musty leaves into my face and momentarily destroying my sense of balance. I grabbed at the railing, and was pushing hair out of my eyes when the rain began. Large droplets pelted me, so forceful they hurt where they hit bare skin. The sudden noise of the rain rattling the dead leaves caused me to realize how quiet and still the air had been moments before. Within seconds, the impact lessened, but the rain became a deluge, soaking me to the skin. I ran for the Jeep, opened the door and jumped in.

33

Reaching for the key, I was about to start the engine, crank up the heater and head for home. Then I thought about it. *It*. The boathouse. What a perfect place to temporarily keep a body, if one had the key. I didn't have a key, but I was already wet. What did I have to lose? However, I wanted to be more certain that I couldn't be discovered. I'd had enough confrontations with dangerous people already this year. Who would be the best person to help me?

It had to be someone who was already in town, which eliminated Cora, who would have been my first choice. Tracy? Nope. Couldn't call in the law to help do something illegal. Jerry? Also a no. He'd probably try to talk me out of it, or feel that he had to come help. It was going to have to be Adele. I'd have to trust that she could keep her mouth shut if the secret were important enough.

My cell phone was in my purse, and I fished it out and punched in the number for the grocery store.

"Volger's Grocery, Adele Volger speaking."

"Adele, it's Ana. Can you leave the store for a few minutes?"

"Maybe. Suzi is here. What do you need?" Adele responded hesitantly.

"I need you to see if Virginia Holiday is at her real estate office?"

"Whatever for? Where are you?" Adele barked.

"Adele! Keep your voice down," I pleaded. "I'm out here at Chippewa Lodge, and I want to look inside the boat house. But I don't want to get caught, and she's the most likely person to come out here unexpectedly. I got her to show me around yesterday, but she's suspicious.

"Suspicious of what?" Adele's voice dropped and became

conspiratorial. "What have you done?"

"Nothing yet, but she knows I'm not really a potential buyer. Please," I begged, "will you go watch her office and call me if she leaves?"

"You don't even know she's there, do you?" Adele pointed out.

"No, not really."

"OK," Adele said quietly, "I've got my cell phone with me. I'll go check her office and call you. Give me five minutes. Don't do anything stupid until you hear from me."

"I won't. I'll start being stupid after you call."

"Oh, for pity's sake, Ana," she groaned.

"Shhh. Don't say my name out loud."

"You're giving me the creeps. I'll call you as soon as I find Vir... her."

Adele hung up, and I sat in the car shivering. The air wasn't cold at all, but I was still wet and not moving enough to keep warm. I wrapped the blanket that was in the back around my shoulders and killed the time by eating a sandwich. Then I put my flashlight into the plastic zipper bag. Even though I expected the call, I jumped when the phone rang.

"Ana. She's at the office," Adele said with suppressed excitement. "I'm in the drugstore. I can see the lights in her building, and I can see if she leaves in her car. It's parked on Cherry Street, headed this way. She'll be sure to come through this corner."

"Are you sure she's there?"

"Yes, yes. I walked around the block and looked in the window."

I groaned. Adele taking a walk in the middle of the day, in the rain, was probably fairly odd. "Did she see you?"

"No. She was on the phone. I only glanced sideways from under my big umbrella. She didn't even see me."

"Won't it look strange for you to hang around at the drugstore?" I asked.

"They won't bother me for a while. I'm looking at paperback books. Reading a little. The rack is right by the front window. I can pretend I'm waiting out the rain. I can see everything that happens on this corner. Mavis Fanning just drove past going east. She's probably on her way to the Post Office."

"All right." It sounded fishy as all get-out, but I didn't have many choices. "I'm going down to the boathouse now. If Virginia goes anywhere in her car, call me. You have my cell number, right?"

"Yes, I just called you, remember? You're as nervous as a fly on a hot window."

I ignored the comparison, since flies on hot windows usually died. "Wish me luck. Maybe I'll find something interesting." I hung up before Adele had a chance to wish me that luck, or say anything else.

I shrugged off the blanket and slipped out of my jacket. Then I added the cell phone to the plastic bag and made sure the zip closure was sealed tight. Finally, I opened the car door and stood in the rain while I switched from sneakers to the rubber sandals that were also still in the Jeep.

Quickly, I ran down the stairs and into the river before I had time to think about changing my mind or how chilly I was. Hugging the shore, I worked my way left till I could touch the boathouse walls, then ventured into the deeper water. The current wasn't bad, but the riverbed quickly dropped off and within three steps I was holding tight to one of the boathouse pilings, and my feet barely touched bottom. Taking a deep breath, and clutching the plastic bag holding my electronics, I ducked under the edge of the wall and came up on the inside.

I hadn't considered how I would get up onto the walkway around the edge, and it was really dark in the boathouse. The two small windows in the landward door only let in a small amount of light. I tread water for a few minutes while my eyes adjusted, and realized before long there was a ladder out at the far edge, by the river door. I swam out there and climbed onto the wooden platform.

I was cold and didn't waste any time getting to the reason for my prowling. The rain was drumming on the metal roof, making a huge racket, and that certainly didn't help my nerves.

The large hand wheel on the side of the hoist obviously raised and lowered the boat, but I didn't know if there was a brake that had to be released. I set my plastic bag on the walkway, out of reach of a clumsy toe, and tentatively turned the wheel counterclockwise, the normal direction to loosen things. It moved easily, and soon the boat was descending slowly toward the water. When it was lowered far enough for me to see over the gunwales, I retrieved the baggie and removed my flashlight, replacing the bag on the walkway. I didn't want to turn on the boathouse light. That would be obvious evidence of an intruder to anyone looking down from above.

Switching on the narrow beam, I flashed it over the interior of the boat. There was nothing inside. More carefully, I began to move the beam across the edges and seats, places that would have been certain to catch dripping blood. Section by section I studied the boat, determined to look at every possible surface.

Almost obscured by the sound of the rain, I suddenly heard footsteps on the wooden stairway. The hair on the back of my neck prickled, and I shivered involuntarily. Switching off the light, I jumped in the direction of the door and crouched beneath the small windows, hopefully out of sight. Peering through a crack, I saw long slim legs clad in black slacks, with the feet incongruously encased in lime green wellingtons imprinted with daisies. Probably a woman. I wondered if there was a matching raincoat covering her top half. The person was obviously already looking in a window.

"Anastasia Raven, I know you're in there." The voice was Mavis Fanning's. My only hope was to remain quiet.

"What are you doing? Your car is in plain sight, you know?" she continued. "I see you've lowered the boat. Planning on taking a clandestine river cruise, are you? Tracy Jarvi may be very interested in that idea."

My heart sank at the prospect of facing Tracy, but I also wondered what Mavis was up to. She didn't seem like a person who simply enjoyed hiking in the rain.

From halfway down the walkway, my phone rang inside its plastic bag. Any chance of escaping detection had just been erased.

34

Mavis pounded on the wooden door, as the phone continued to ring, ten times. Eleven. I'd always been glad that it rang enough times to give me a chance to answer before going to voicemail. Right at the moment, I cursed that setting.

"You're in trouble now, Ana," she yelled. "I'm going to call the police."

Over the jangle of the phone, I heard her steps receding as she began climbing toward the parking area. The rain had let up, allowing me to hear more sounds outside the boathouse. The phone stopped its ringing, but my nerves were still buzzing.

I jumped to retrieve the phone, but before I called Adele back I wanted to get out of the boathouse. Fortunately, the lift mechanism was well greased, and the boat rose easily as I turned the wheel clockwise until it stopped at the maximum height. Jamming the flashlight back in the bag with the phone and hastily sealing it, I jumped in the water and ducked under the wall.

Just as I emerged from the water I heard car doors slamming at the top of the bluff. Doors, plural. How had Tracy, or maybe a Sheriff's Deputy, gotten here so quickly? I couldn't see any way to get out of facing the music. I was soaking wet— wetter than the rain could explain, and very cold. Mavis had heard a phone ring inside the boathouse, and my car was parked up above. Slowly I climbed toward certain chastisement, if not worse. I'd forgotten all about returning Adele's call.

As soon as I was able to peer over the edge of the high bank I was surprised to see, not a police car, but Virginia Holiday's sedan. She and Mavis were having a heated discussion. Mavis was red-faced and waving in the direction of the boathouse. Virginia stood, hands on hips, shaking her head. I was too chilled to care what they thought, and walked directly to my car, grabbing the blanket to wrap around my shoulders.

"Ask her yourself," Mavis insisted, now pointing at me. "She was in the boathouse. See if she denies it."

Virginia continued to shake her head. "So what?"

"So what?" Mavis was practically apoplectic. "She's a trespasser. A troublemaker."

I used the towel I also kept in the car to dry my hair and didn't say a word.

I had no idea why, but Virginia was coming to my defense. "She's been here before, with me, as a prospective buyer for this property. If she wants to look around, I don't mind."

"But, but..." Mavis sputtered.

Virginia glanced my way, as I continued to drip beside my Jeep. "Her methods may be unconventional, but there's nothing in the boathouse she could possibly steal. No one can get the boat out without opening the river doors. And I know there's nothing else of value inside."

Encouraged by Virginia's attitude, I turned my pockets inside out and showed them I had nothing but the cell phone and flashlight. I grinned, hoping I looked apologetic.

"I see no reason to call the police," the realtor said. "If you're interested in the property also, Ms. Fanning, I suggest we take a tour. I have the keys, though, so that will make it easier. Perhaps Ana just likes doing things the hard way."

Virginia took Mavis by the arm and forcefully marched her in the direction of the Lodge. She didn't look back. But Mavis shot me a menacing look over her shoulder.

I had no idea what had just happened, but it seemed good. I stepped into my Jeep and turned the heater to high as I pulled away from Chippewa Lodge.

The phone was no worse than damp and lit up normally when I opened it. I punched in Adele's number. She answered on the first ring.

"Ana, where are you? Are you all right?" She sounded frantic.

"I'm fine. I'm wet and cold. I have to go home and change. Then I'll fill you in."

"Come to my house as soon as you're done. I'll heat some soup. I called someone to help Suzi at the store," Adele said.

"That sounds good. Give me a half hour."

"I'll be waiting," I knew she was more than eager to hear all the juicy details.

35

By Monday morning I'd decided I should tell Detective Milford about the remnant of fabric I'd found on the stairs at Chippewa Lodge. *What's the worst he could do*, I thought, *yell at me?* I'd broken no laws. Well, not on the steps. Maybe I wouldn't have to tell him the rest of the story.

Once again, I was escorted to his office in the drab Sheriff's building. I asked him if he had any ideas about where the body of Jared Canfield had been put in the river, but he was not about to be so easily steered in the direction I wanted to go.

"It sounds to me as if you might have an idea of your own," he said shrewdly.

"I have been looking around," I admitted, letting my voice trail off.

Milford shifted his weight and sighed. "I assume you came here to tell me about it."

I pulled the small digital camera from my purse and turned it on. Pushing several buttons, I brought up on the small screen the macro picture of the rough fiber and handed it across the desk.

"And what am I looking at?" he asked, sounding perturbed.

"I was thinking about places one could get to the river without being detected. This is at a property that's for sale, west of town, downriver toward Jalmari. This bit of thread is caught in the edge of a step on some stairs that lead to the water."

"Why do you think a body would be taken there? Why not to one of the public access points?" He sounded interested, but I felt as if I were being interrogated.

"Public access sites are— well— public. Anyone dumping a body at one would be taking a chance on being seen, don't you think?" I tried to keep my tone conversational.

"True, but if there are a lot of steps, that wouldn't be very handy," he pointed out.

"I know. But I decided to look anyway, and I did find this. I didn't touch it," I added quickly. "I don't know what the body was wrapped in. Do you?"

Milford shifted again. "No, we don't. Did you form an opinion about the kind of fabric this is?"

"It looked like burlap to me. Scroll through the pictures." I stood up and pointed to a button on the camera. "You can see which step it's caught in."

The detective fiddled with the camera for a few minutes, while I resettled in my chair. "This is interesting," he admitted. "Just where is this place?"

"It's called Chippewa Lodge, and it's about a mile west of town on South River Road, where the water gets deeper."

He handed the camera back to me and almost smiled. "That's fairly good detecting," he admitted.

"Thank you. Will you follow up on this?" I asked.

"We might." He leaned forward and drummed his blunt fingers on the desk. Then apparently coming to some conclusion, he leaned back slightly and took a deep breath.

I held my breath. It seemed as if he was about to tell me something significant, and I was right.

"We are pretty sure Jared Canfield was put in the river right at Jalmari. It was awfully convenient that he was found snagged on a tree there, where people would see him."

"But he might have been carried by the current and just happened to get hung up there," I protested.

"Sure, but then where would be the value in using him as some sort of threat? This killer needed the body to be found and identified. Remember, if this is connected in some crazy way to the hatchet in a box, the similarity in names is part of the puzzle. Canfield's wallet was still in his pocket."

"But it was all water damaged."

"Not that badly. The canoe livery reported finding the body soon after sunrise. The lab is pretty sure he'd only been in the river about an hour, even though decomposition was farther along. That doesn't allow enough time for him to have been carried very far downstream."

"I suppose a body doesn't float as smoothly as a kayak," I admitted.

"No, it certainly doesn't," Milford said.

"Why are you giving me this information?" I asked.

"Why are you so curious about a murder you claim has nothing to do with you?" he countered.

"I... I feel involved, with the hatchet and finding the blood...the place where it happened, you know."

"Ms. Raven, Ana, you better hope you aren't involved. So far, not very much is making sense here. We have a few bizarre facts and a lot of speculation. If all these facts are connected, we may be dealing with someone who is not mentally stable."

"That's probably true of many killers, I expect," I said evenly.

"Yes, but if this is all one case, the perpetrator deals in riddles, uses chicken blood to try to frighten someone— through his ex-wife, and kills a person simply as a warning to someone else, this person is totally unpredictable. I am telling you to stop poking around and to be very careful."

Milford stood, and I realized I was being dismissed. The detective did summon a deputy to copy the photos from my SD card to a police computer, which helped me believe the time hadn't been a complete waste. However, I felt more like a suspect than a bystander caught in a set of strange inexplicable circumstances. At least I hadn't needed to confess about the boathouse.

36

The rest of the week flew by. I was overwhelmed with collecting and arranging items needed for the Harvest Ball. The drugstore supplied crepe paper, garlands of silk leaves in fall colors, and strings of lights. A group of homeschooled children made paper lanterns from orange, green and brown construction paper, to cover the lights for atmosphere. We had stuffed scarecrows to stand next to the lovely vintage wheat shocks that Sorenson's delivered to the school. Cliff's widow, Sherri, who had been awarded the implement company, seemed to have a knack for business, and a great sense of community as well. She also volunteered to provide horse-drawn wagon rides from downtown, so people could park in the paved lot by the courthouse and be delivered to the Ball.

Hay bales appeared beside the school steps with a note pinned to them "For the Ball." I had no idea where they came from, but I lugged them inside.

Jerry found a rental agency in Emily City that could supply a few wire tables and chairs to create the sidewalk café in the front hallway. We'd fill in with card tables and folding chairs. But someone, me, had to borrow those and pick them all up.

I was so busy I had to call Cora and beg off working on the database on Tuesday. She sounded put out when we talked.

"Well, I guess you're just too busy hustling around with Jerry Caulfield to bother with my insignificant needs," she huffed.

"Oh, Cora, it's only for one or two weeks," I protested. "Everyone is getting so excited. I think the Ball really is a knockout idea."

When I hung up, I was smiling. She was as green-eyed as Jerry had hoped. It was hard for me to understand why, since I was exhausted from phoning and hauling and making lists, but she apparently thought Jerry and I were having a ball of our own.

On the other hand, Adele was delighted to be in on what she thought were all the secrets. Of course, I'd told her about the strange confrontation between Mavis and Virginia, and how Virginia excused my explorations without any further explanation. There hadn't been any repercussions from my adventure, except that it took me a whole day to warm up afterwards.

Many small businesses that couldn't afford large contributions offered goods or gift certificates for door prizes.

Adele donated all the tableware, and the foil tart pans which Janice and Jimmie were lining with crusts and loading into Janice's freezer. Jerry told me Adele also gave him a deep discount on the pork and other food ingredients. She was so enthusiastic about the Ball she couldn't stop suggesting new ideas. She cornered customers from the surrounding area and borrowed antique quilts their mothers and grandmothers had made, to hang on the walls. She got the 4-H kids to make luminaries to line the sidewalk and steps to the front door. We finally said "no" when Jerry overheard her trying to convince Peter Gebhardt to bring his two donkeys to town and tether them in the gym.

The posters had been an instant success. They featured gold and black woven line borders on two edges in an Art Deco style and 1920s lettering for the information. The opposite corner contained a spray of colorful autumn leaves and an apple-cheeked girl holding a basket of corn and squash. The balance between formal and rural seemed to appeal to everyone. Jerry hand-delivered the posters to every business in four counties, a monumental task. He also enclosed smaller black and white copies with the weekly paper. Spots were heard on the radio, and even though the nearest television station was seventy miles away, they mentioned the Harvest Ball on their evening news segment that highlighted small towns in the surrounding area. Everyone in Forest County, and beyond, was talking about the upcoming event.

Rev. Theo Dornbaugh, pastor of Crossroads Fellowship, announced it enthusiastically during Sunday services, and Adele assured me that the Lutherans and Catholics were endorsing it also. There didn't seem to be anyone who wasn't planning to attend. I began to secretly hope this wasn't true, or there would be no place to stand, and we'd run out of food.

Jerry worked out an agreement with O'Toole's Pub in Thorpe to cater the drinks, solving that problem. Coffee, water and cider would be provided, but anything stronger would be served from a cash bar.

Todd checked all the plumbing, and the bathroom fixtures, and declared them ready for use. He filled soap and towel dispensers, and stocked up on toilet paper.

We decided to put the food serving tables in a classroom to free up space in the auditorium for the skit and dancing. We picked a room that was in pretty good condition, at least none of the floor tiles were peeling. It was dingy and damp, and Todd Ringman spent more time banging and tinkering with pipes until the radiators in that room efficiently dispelled the musty air. One afternoon when I was decorating, Jerry appeared with cans of paint and four teenage boys in tow.

"These fine fellows have agreed to paint the food room," he announced.

"We traded this job for a week of detention," one of the boys stage-whispered to me as they walked by, carrying rollers, pans, plastic tarps, and brushes.

Suddenly, it was Saturday night, and I was exhausted. There was only one week remaining until the Harvest Ball. All I wanted to do was climb into a bathtub full of hot water and soak the aches out of my muscles. But, of course, the phone rang. It was Adele.

"I know you're tired, but come in and have a cup of tea and some cookies. We should talk about tablecloths, and trash bins, and volunteers to bus tables."

"Tonight?"

"Yes, tonight. We'll need to borrow some of those things from the churches, and if we get organized, we can call people and have them collect it all when they go to services tomorrow. And I'll bet some of the kids from youth group will help with the tables."

I groaned, but I knew she was right. "Why did we put this off till the last minute?" I questioned.

"No matter how much one gets done in a timely manner, something always is done last," Adele philosophized with a laugh. "Just come, the tea will help you relax."

"OK, I'll be there in fifteen minutes," I said.

I grabbed my purse and headed for the Jeep. In order to cross the river, I took East South River Road until it met Main Street and then jogged the few blocks west to use the bridge on Mill Street. This route took me past the Pine Tree Diner, which had remained dark and closed for weeks since Jack Panther's abrupt disappearance.

The front windows were covered with brown paper, but a yellow light glowed through in the dusk, and a huge placard was displayed between the paper and the glass, "Re-opening Soon."

Maybe Adele doesn't know yet, I speculated, grinning with unexpected pleasure at a possible gossip coup.

37

Indeed, Adele did not know the Pine Tree was ready to rejoin the active business community, and she insisted we go right over there. She bustled up the steps ahead of me and rattled the latch, which was locked. Undaunted, she rapped her knuckles with unnecessary fury on the glass, and tried to peer through a crack at the edge of the paper which obscured her view. When no one appeared within three seconds she knocked again, even louder.

Jack Panther, himself, appeared a few moments later. As he opened the door, his shoulders lifted and fell; he closed his eyes and shook his head.

"Ladies," he greeted us. "Come in, come in. I expected word to get around town quickly, but this is unprecedented. I've had the sign in the window for ten minutes."

Instead of his usual dark slacks and stained white apron, Jack wore coveralls, and a white t-shirt showed through where the front was unsnapped. Sawdust clung to his mustache and the hairs on the backs of his hands and seemed to glitter in the bright glow of the extra work light which had been hung from a tall step ladder. His black hair was mussed and his dark brown eyes snapped.

Adele plowed right into the meat of the matter. "Jack Panther, where have you been? Don't you know enough to let people know where you are? You're a lucky man the Sheriff hasn't hauled you back here in handcuffs for questioning."

Jack backed up a step and held up a hand. "Whoa. What are you talking about? I came by this money legally. Completely."

"What are *you* talking about?" Adele countered. "What were you thinking to leave town without a word on the very day the bloody site where that poor Mr. Canfield was hacked to death was discovered?"

The beleaguered man pointed to an open booth. "Sit down," he said. "You stay right there and wait for me. I'm going to make a pot of coffee. It's evening. Regular or decaf, ladies?" A restaurateur to the core.

"Decaf." I answered for us both. Adele and I slid into opposite sides of the booth.

As soon as Jack disappeared into the kitchen, Adele leaned across the table and whispered, "Regular or decaf, my left foot! He's out there thinking up a good story. As if he hasn't had three weeks to invent one." A look of sudden concern crossed her face. "Maybe we surprised him. I hope he doesn't have a gun back there."

"Don't be silly," I returned, without whispering. "Why would he come back and turn on all the lights after dark if he had something to hide?"

Her tight gray curls shook as she nodded her head, and her ample bosom heaved. "I suppose you're right, but his activity has been very suspicious. I'm sure the police have known where he was all along and didn't tell me."

I smiled at the improbability that the police would willingly keep Adele informed of everyone's movements.

"And money? Money! If Jack Panther had any money he'd fix this place up," she continued her rant.

I simply swept my hand outward to point out the obvious: a ladder, saws, lumber, boxes of tile stacked where a booth on the opposite side of the room had been pulled out.

Jack emerged from the kitchen with three mugs of coffee balanced on a tray, along with slices of a small packaged jelly roll. "Sorry I don't have any real food," he apologized. "I wasn't expecting company, but I suppose I should have known better." He slid in next to me.

"What money are you talking about?"

"Where was that man killed?" Adele and Jack said simultaneously.

They each opened and closed their mouths synchronously one

more time. The two had been friends for decades.

"Me first," Jack asserted. "What murder site, and what's it got to do with me?"

I let Adele fill him in with all we knew about the demise of Jared Canfield. Summed up, it wasn't much. Jack acknowledged that his leaving town on the same day as the gruesome basement discovery was an unfortunate coincidence. We both brought him up to date on Jerry Caulfield's purchase of the school building, and the plans for the Harvest Ball.

"Drat. They're coming Monday to rip the kitchen apart and bring in new appliances. I won't be able to be much help with the food," was his response.

"Janice Preston has things covered pretty well," I said. "Jimmie Mosher is helping her."

Jack chuckled. "That little smarty pants is going to be my competition in a few years."

"Now it's my turn," Adele announced firmly. "Where did you get this money you're boasting about, and how much?"

I nearly blushed at her demand for full disclosure, but Jack took it in stride.

"Dear Adele, I don't think you need to know the exact amount, but let's just say the Pine Tree will be a much nicer place to eat, very soon."

"No one gets huge amounts of money dropped on their doorstep." Adele tapped her index finger forcefully on the table top.

Jack leaned back and stretched his legs out straight, grinning from ear to ear. "Maybe not, but it's almost that simple." He let Adele simmer in the frustration of not knowing for just another minute.

She glared at him, willing him to tell the story.

Slowly, so slowly it had to be purposeful, he popped an entire slice of the jelly roll in his mouth and chewed. When that was gone, he took a long swallow of coffee, then reached across me and pulled a paper napkin from the holder. He wiped his fingers and mouth and smoothed his mustache. He was clearly enjoying the torture.

"Jack!" Adele pressed.

He grinned and began his tale. "Ana," he turned to me, "you may not know my family history."

I tried to recall what Jerry had told me. "I know you discovered you are part Native American, right?" I ventured.

"That is true." Jack said, nodding. "My father was killed in the canning factory explosion, and I didn't learn anything about his side of the family until much later. I was a baby, and I don't remember him at all. Turned out my great-grandmother was Pottawatomi."

"So?" Adele said. "Most of us know this already."

"So," Jack continued, shifting in his seat to lean toward her, "As a tribal member I'm entitled to casino profits. But I had to have a DNA test done. They're getting really fussy about payouts to impostors, people who can't really prove their ancestry. It turned out I'm actually a quarter Pottawatomi. Probably my great-grandfather was Indian too."

"And that kept you away for three weeks?" I asked.

"I'll admit I wanted a vacation. They gave me some of the money, outright, with a promise of more if the test was positive, so I got a room at the casino hotel and did a little gambling." His face lit up.

"That was foolish, don't you think?" Adele scolded.

"Perhaps." Jack admitted. "But it was recreation, and I know when to stop."

"That's what everyone says," Adele scoffed.

"True enough, but I really did stop."

I was beginning to get the picture. "How much did you win?" I exclaimed, not thinking how much I sounded like Adele, for asking.

"No, no. No actual numbers, my beautiful guests." Jack grinned and flashed his broad smile at us. "Let's just say I wouldn't have to work any more."

"Oh, Jack!" Adele reached across the table and touched his hand lightly, then withdrew it.

His pride deflated a little bit, perhaps as a touch of reality tempered his boast. "Well, I won't have to work as much," he admitted. "But I like what I do. I like the diner and talking to the regulars. I'm a good cook, and by golly, I contribute to this town. But the place isn't going to be such a dump, and I've made a down payment on the empty storefront next door. I'll have more tables, a handicap entrance and legal rest rooms. I should be open again before Christmas."

"That's really wonderful," I agreed.

"I'll donate a gift certificate for four meals for a door prize. How's that sound?" With that rhetorical question, he popped another piece of jelly roll in his mouth, nodded to each of us, then took his mug and walked to the table saw. We were clearly dismissed.

38

Adele was like a dog with a bone when it came to getting things organized for the Ball. She still insisted I come to her house after we left the Pine Tree. We made more lists and phoned people from all three churches. She extracted promises of tablecloths, more chairs, serving utensils, candle holders, trash cans and liners, and rolls of raffle tickets. People promised to deliver them to the school after their respective services the following day.

She boldly volunteered the Family Friends Committee to wash all the dishes. She did call the committee members to ask if they'd participate in the project, but each and every person she talked to knew that "no" was not going to be an acceptable answer. As I drove home, I made a mental note to ask Jerry if the sinks and hot water in the school kitchen were working.

The following morning, the Sunday worship service provided a much-needed uplift. For the past few months I'd been attending Crossroads Fellowship fairly regularly. I liked the mixture of hymns with modern praise songs. Dwight Morris kept the tempo up as he worked the organ with hands and feet, producing harmonious tones. Following the singing of the inspiring hymn, "Immortal, Invisible, God Only Wise," young men and women stepped to the podium and lifted guitars and a bass from their stands. A teenager slithered through the maze of electric cords and seated himself behind a drum set. He beat out a rousing paradiddle, and the worship team led us in "You Wear the Victor's Crown." The words to all the songs were displayed on a screen mounted at the front left of the church. Some people weren't as familiar with the newer songs, but they were undaunted and sang with fervor. The hymns had more complex words and music, but the newer tunes were easier for some people to sing. The variety of music was one of the things I liked best about the service.

Most everyone who attended this church was accepting, cheerful, and kind. Of course, every sort of organization has a few members who are more interested in their own agendas, but overall, this congregation made me feel that it stood for right and good but wasn't trying to beat up those who didn't agree with every detail of doctrine.

Following the opening songs, Rev. Dornbaugh began the announcements. I was distracted for a few minutes by a woman I didn't know, sitting several rows in front of me, who had shiny hot-pink hair. It looked synthetic, straight off a fashion doll. She turned around and discovered me looking at her. Grinning widely, she rotated her head quickly back and forth, making the straight shoulder-length strands swing. Then she raised her hands, palms up, and fluffed the ends, making the most of the encounter. I smiled back at her, and she laughed.

The pastor's voice broke into my thoughts as I heard the words "...Harvest Ball. We want to be sure to support this community effort, and I encourage everyone, of any age, who is able, to plan on attending. All the churches are lending a hand to make this the outstanding event of the year in Cherry Hill."

There was a smattering of applause. Adele was sitting behind me, and she leaned forward and tapped me on the shoulder. "We've got to get something organized for the children," she whispered urgently. "There's bound to be a hundred or more. See me afterwards."

"OK," I whispered as a new wave of panic washed over me, and then I turned back toward the front. The sermon began.

After every Sunday service Adele helped serve light refreshments in the Fellowship Hall, so it was easy to find her.

"You'd better head right over to the school," she admonished. "There are deliveries expected from all the churches. You've got a key, right?"

"I do," I verified, fishing in my purse to be sure it was there.

She grabbed Harvard Brown, the Sheriff's Deputy who attended our church. He was in civilian clothes today. "Harvey, can you go with Ana to the school to help unload chairs and other things folks are bringing over?"

"Sure," Harvey agreed, his toothy smile lighting up his dark face.

"And see if you can talk someone into planning games for the elementary school kids," Adele added to me, as if it were nothing monumental.

Frankly, I was feeling more than overwhelmed with the number of tasks that remained to be accomplished in one week's time. Nevertheless, as each car or truck pulled up, I asked the occupants for suggestions as to who might be a good person to organize games. A few names were tossed out. I then directed the vehicles to the rear where things could be unloaded without having to carry bulky loads up the long flight of front steps.

I was still there at one-fifteen. I hadn't eaten a thing, and had convinced exactly zero volunteers to take on the responsibility of herding excited children. At least I had a water bottle in my purse. It was turning into a hot, bright October day, and I would have been miserable without even a drink. It seemed as if the stream of deliveries was winding down, and I thought I'd run inside and see how Harvey was doing.

Just then, Adele pulled up in front of the school in her sturdy Ford, followed by Jerry in his shiny silver Sebring. Riding with Adele was the woman with the pink hair. Adele bustled from the car to the door, balancing a paper plate full of sandwich quarters and cookies in one hand and a styrofoam cup of coffee in the other.

"I'm so sorry I didn't give you a chance to grab a bite to eat," she said, "but I hope you'll forgive me. I brought something even better than food. This is Cheyanne Bascomb. Cheyanne, Ana. She says she'd be thrilled to handle the children."

I looked at the young woman. Not only did she have pink hair, but there was a pink and purple butterfly tattoo on her neck, and the light glinted off several studs which pierced her nose and eyebrows, as well as her ears.

"Are you sure?" I asked, incredulous.

"Absolutely." Cheyanne grinned. "I love kids. I run a daycare center in Waabishki. It will be fun to spend time with some who are already potty trained, and can follow directions. There are lots of games we can play."

"I told Jerry to come," Adele continued. "We need to designate a room for this."

Jerry had joined our small group just as Cheyanne was delivering her promise to help, and Harvey poked his head out the front door at about the same time. We all entered the school building. It no longer looked dingy nor smelled musty. The primary aroma was fresh paint. Although I knew most of the rooms were still neglected, the hallway had been painted and the floors cleaned and buffed. Light fixtures had been fitted with working bulbs.

Jerry led the way to the end of the west hallway and opened a door which led into a classroom twice the size of any of the others I'd seen.

"This is the old kindergarten room," he explained. "Everyone in town over the age of fifty learned everything they need to know, right here."

The room had large cupboards beneath the windows, and there was plenty of open space for relay games or forming circles.

He turned to Cheyanne. "Do you think you can uphold that tradition, Miss Bascomb?"

She laughed again. "I'm not sure we can accomplish that in one evening of playtime, but we'll try to keep the cherubs from pulling out each other's wings."

"Good enough," Jerry agreed with a chuckle.

"Maybe I can get some of my friends to help. Don't worry about a thing."

"And we'll get the painting volunteers in here tomorrow," Jerry promised. "One more room shouldn't be a problem."

39

Adele, Harvey and Cheyanne drove away, and I sat down on the front steps to eat the lunch my friend had brought. Jerry moved around to stand in front of me, a couple of steps lower.

"Take a step that way if you would," I requested, pointing west.

"Why?" he asked, although he did shuffle to the left.

"Sun's in my eyes," I said, stuffing a pimento and cream cheese sandwich quarter in my mouth.

"Ah. Glad to be of service, madam."

I spent the next few minutes eating, while Jerry watched me. My mouth was still full of chocolate-chip cookie when I thought about washing dishes.

"Is the plumbing working in the kitchen? Will there be hot water? It will be so much easier for Janice and her helpers if she's able to wash some dishes while the catering is going on."

"I'll find out," Jerry said. He looked down at me kindly with a bit of a wistful expression on his face. "I want to thank you for all the effort you've put into this event."

I stuck out my lower lip and blew upwards to move a stray hair that was hanging in my eyes. "It's not a problem," I said. "It's just that there's a ton of stuff to prepare, and the building is going to be great, but I can't count on any of the amenities one usually expects in a facility. That makes it a bit stressful."

Jerry shifted, and I squinted as the sun glared in my eyes again. "Oh, sorry," he said, repositioning himself so that his shadow fell across my face. "I think it will be worth all the work, on so many levels. Have you talked to Cora?"

"I have. And that's such a mystery to me. She really is jealous; she all but said it! Thinks you and I are spending a lot of time together, and she feels neglected."

He rubbed his hands together and smiled. "Perfect. I told you I knew her."

I swallowed the last of my coffee and started to stand, assuming we were done talking, but Jerry motioned for me to sit down again.

"What?" I asked.

He seemed to change his mind and instead beckoned me to come. "Let's take a walk. That way the sun won't be in your eyes, and it will look good for adding fuel to the green fire."

"Out back? Did I tell you I took a look at the river to see if someone could have floated a body from the school to Jalmari?"

"Really? It seems as if it would be too shallow here."

"That's what I discovered."

"No, let's walk through town. Much more reliable for being seen." He stuck out his elbow and I slipped my arm through it. We looked at each other and stepped out in the direction of downtown in a very good imitation of an old fashioned Sunday stroll, but without fancy clothing or a parasol. The sun had become so bright I thought the parasol would have been quite useful.

We'd only gone about half a block when Jerry's body language lost its casual feeling. He stiffened slightly and leaned toward me. "There is one thing I want to tell you about. I've been working on tracking that phone call you received."

When I stopped and glared at him he held up his free hand in protest.

"Don't get all legalistic on me. I talked to Tracy. She thought I might be able to talk to some people without creating such a stir as if she went after them. After all, you've been doing some sleuthing on your own."

I sniffed, but I was curious. "Did you learn anything?"

"I learned that Mavis Fanning is devious and ruthless when she wants something," he said seriously. She's a client of a very high-pressure lawyer in Emily City.

"What does she want that I have?" I asked, totally mystified.

"I wondered that too. I thought maybe we made the wrong woman jealous, so I did some digging."

"She's mooning over you so much she's threatening me?" I was incredulous. "You have a bigger ego than I thought."

"Well, it was only a possibility. But everyone I asked seems quite certain that she and Harold are happy together. He's always meek around her, although a good leader when he works alone."

"He does seem to get around," I said. I recalled hearing that he'd been a teacher, principal, and was of course, now the city manager.

"The note from your car seemed to focus on the school building, so I checked into more of the recent history on it. There are five people who have been connected with it in the past couple of months. First, there's Virginia Holiday."

"Yes," I said, "but she was just handling the property."

"True enough," Jerry said, "but let me finish the list. There's Jared Canfield, who was killed there and who had a Holiday Realty card in his wallet."

"With the numbers 1-8-4-5 written on it. Whatever that means."

"How do you know that?"

"Tracy told me," I said, gratified that I knew something he didn't.

"OK, so he had an appointment with her, on some day, at six-forty-five in the evening."

"You don't think it's a year?"

"Twenty-four hour time. Lots of men use it, a habit they picked up in the military."

"Huh," I said. "Who else?"

"There's Harold Fanning, who did all the paperwork for the city when the building was listed with Virginia and then when the city took it back. There's me, I really did buy it. And there's Mavis Fanning."

I looked up at Jerry's face. He didn't seem to be guessing. "How does she fit in? Adele said she wants it, but why?" I blurted out.

"Yes, she wants the building very badly, to start a gym and fitness club. She feels that I robbed her of the opportunity because she couldn't get the down payment together quickly enough. And I guess she thinks you talked me into buying it."

"How on earth did you find all this out?" I asked. "You're getting as good as Adele at digging up dirt."

Jerry smiled down at me with pleasure. "Why thank you. Now we'll have another jealous woman in town."

I felt like stamping my foot. "Seriously. How do you know this?" I asked.

"Not so difficult. I took Harold out for an evening at a nice club in Emily City. Told him as community leaders we should become better acquainted. He loves Mavis, but finds her a bit frightening at times. It's amazing what men will share when slightly drunk."

"So now we know that she really does want the school, and why, but we don't know that she's the one who called me. Harold didn't know about that, did he?"

"No, but I did find out one more thing. I called their daughter Claire myself."

I glared at Jerry.

"Just stop. I had Tracy's blessing."

I wiggled my head from side to side, giving in to his ability to do as he pleased without consequence.

"It was an interesting conversation. When she understood that I was a friend of yours and was concerned for your safety, she admitted that she thought she knew who had the phone."

"Now that is interesting," I said.

"She said she'd been thinking about it a lot since Tracy and you called her. She knows she had it a few days before parents' weekend, and that it wasn't there the next time she went looking. She wanted to loan it to another friend."

"What are you saying?" I wanted him to spell it out.

"She thinks her mother took it out of her drawer, but she can't prove it."

We walked past the police station and through the park in the center of town, circling the block, and finally returning to our cars which were still at the school. People who saw us greeted us politely, but I had the feeling they were trying to assess our relationship as well as being friendly.

As Jerry opened my car door for me, I turned to him and spoke the question that was in both our minds, "Could Mavis want the old school so badly she'd kill for it?"

40

The final week before the Harvest Ball passed in a blur of checklists and activities. Mother Nature did not favor us with helpful weather. After the glorious sunshine of Sunday, Monday dawned wet and rainy. Forecasts predicted rain, drizzle and fog for the rest of the week, with plummeting temperatures on the weekend. *Great, now we need another room cleaned to use as a coatroom*, I thought.

Tom took several friends out to his mother's place and they loaded all the Oldfield furniture into his truck and covered it carefully with a plastic tarp. Cora insisted that some of the interpretive materials be displayed as well, and she actually came into town with them, clutching a scrapbook on her lap. She'd spent the previous week collating and copying materials to fill the book, which would provide extra detail about both the Judge's family and his killer's. She was sure people would want to read more. I urged her not to be disappointed if most visitors were content to just see the skit. When Tom and company arrived at the school, it took two hours to set up the Judge's staged bedroom. Cora and I decided it worked best on the actual stage, but it had to be to one side because the band would need the other side.

Since we didn't know exactly how the college kids would make their entrances and exits, we had to do some guessing. But Cora insisted they would get it right since we'd sent them pictures of how everything had to be arranged. The stained and tattered stage curtain wasn't going to be replaced, so set changes would be made in full view of the audience.

We pulled the scrapbook apart and mounted all the pages, the nightshirt and the gun into a locked display case on the outside wall of the former school office.

Todd Ringman had tripled up his jobs and taken on custodial duties as well as fixing the boiler and plumbing. He said he needed to stick around anyway to be sure the heating system was working right. The floors had been cleaned and buffed, and I suspected he'd used some sort of anti-fungal cleaner on the woodwork because the general odor of mold had been replaced with a medicinal smell. That sent me scurrying to the drugstore for cinnamon-and-spice heated fragrance diffusers.

Todd had also located two tall ladders, and in between receiving even more deliveries of both decorative and useful items, and directing volunteers as to how to arrange the tables in the hallway, I climbed and descended and hammered and taped and adjusted décor until I was exhausted.

The front page of the paper on Wednesday carried a full spread of photos designed to entice people to the Harvest Ball: the front of the school, wheat shocks being delivered, Sherri Sorenson's handsome team of Percherons hitched to the wagon that would bring people to the school, Janice Preston and Jimmie in white aprons smiling broadly and holding trays filled with food, kids cutting and pasting paper lanterns, and more.

The article provided assurance that the Ball was a family event; people of all ages were welcome. Although nursery care would not be provided, games for kids old enough to follow directions would be organized by Cheyanne Bascomb of Happy Kids Daycare in Waabishki. People were encouraged to "come as you are;" no one should stay away for lack of fancy clothing.

On an inside page was a sizeable column proclaiming the many prizes that could be won with the purchase of raffle tickets at the door, proceeds to benefit the county animal shelter. There was also a listing of every person and every business that was known to have offered items or volunteered time. I couldn't imagine how Jerry had kept track of all those donations. It was more evidence of how good he was at reporting small town news. He was like Adele, except that his family, for four generations, had made a legitimate career out of knowing what everyone was doing. It was suddenly easy to understand why someone might hold a long-standing grudge against the Caulfields, perhaps for revealing some family secret they preferred to keep hidden. After all, at the core of the recent mysterious events was an apparent threat directed at Jerry, not at me.

I pondered all this as I decorated, and resolved to keep track of the Fannings at the Ball. The evening was bound to be filled with distractions, giving someone a perfect opportunity to carry out a "nefarious deed." That seemed so unlikely, and I laughed at myself for thinking in Shakespearean terms. And yet, there had already been one very real murder. In this very building.

On Thursday, Jerry's weekly rush to get the paper out was past, and he caught me climbing down off a ladder for the hundredth time. Or the thousandth. My calves couldn't tell any more, they were so sore.

"This place looks positively gorgeous," Jerry raved. "You've accomplished a miracle. It smells wonderful too."

I had to admit that the odors of damp leaves carried in on all the feet that had passed through the doors, bales of hay, the ripe grain, and the spicy oil had combined to create a delicious autumnal aroma.

"Wait until the pumpkin and apple tarts arrive. By then the woodwork will smell good enough to eat." I teased.

"I love how the hallway looks like a sidewalk café. The pots of chrysanthemums sure brighten it up. Let's bring in more leaves. It's impossible to keep them out anyway."

"Works for me," I said, mentally adding a rake to the list of things I'd need to bring next time.

Jerry switched topics. "I came by to ask what you're wearing Saturday night."

"Wearing? I don't know. Jeans and a sweater, I suppose."

"Oh, no you don't," he said, shaking his head. "You are the unofficial hostess of the Harvest Ball. Everyone knows how much work you've put into it, and that you will be my date."

"You're kidding, right? It's 'come as you are.' Your own paper said so," I protested, stooping over to pick up the end of an electrical cord. "Look at this."

I pushed the plug into an outlet and garlands of tiny lights clustered within orange and red lanterns glowed and winked through the construction paper bars. "It's even better with the big lights out."

"I'm serious. You need a nice gown, and I need to know what color it is."

"Gown?" Now he had my attention. I frowned. "I don't know if I still have anything one would consider a gown. What are you wearing, tails?" I joked.

"As a matter of fact, I am. The suit was my grandfather's. It fits me quite well. Dark gray." He stuck his hands in his pockets.

"Oh bother! Jerry, I don't have time to shop for a dress," I whined.

"Sure you do. This afternoon. I insist. Go to Emily City. I've arranged for Adele to go with you," he announced.

I placed my hands on my temples and squeezed, rubbing my fingertips over my tired, closed eyes. When I opened them, Jerry was holding out a folded wad of money.

"Take it," he ordered.

"No thank you," I said. I was tempted to say a lot more.

"You have to," Jerry insisted.

"Indeed, I don't have to do everything you tell me to." Suddenly, I'd had about enough of having Jerry's plans direct every moment of my life for the past several weeks. I reached down and yanked the light plug out of the socket.

"I'm not explaining this well," he countered, letting his hand drop to his side.

"You're not explaining it at all," I said.

"Look. This is part of the ploy. I'm not trying to tell you what to do. But you've got to be dressed up, stunning, the Belle of the Ball. Cora will be so angry that I've had my head turned by a pretty young woman she'll be ready to pop a corset stay."

"I don't think even Cora wears a corset," I said dryly.

"Ok, probably not. Anyway, when I make the big announcement that I've purchased the building for her museum and I would like her to be my bride again, she'll be overwhelmed with joy that I want her instead of a glittering bauble..."

"Glittering bauble! Give me a break. You should be a playwright. No, make that a scripter of soap operas."

41

Nevertheless, I gave in to Jerry's request. It turned out that Adele had very good taste in clothing when she was shopping for someone else, and she knew of several small specialty shops in Emily City. We finally chose a black floor-length dress in a soft fabric that draped nicely. It was neither a sheath nor full. The top had a bateau neckline, and it came with a black lace jacket. I owned a jade necklace and earrings that I thought would work with it. As a final splurge, with my own money I bought a mossy green clutch purse to complement the jade.

"You've got to call Jerry right away, and tell him about this," Adele admonished. "He'll want to order flowers."

I looked at her askance. "Whatever for? You'd think this was the prom. It's a family night with hay bales and a horse wagon."

"Not for you, it isn't. Jerry is serious about you being his hostess. I'm sure he's thinking way beyond this weekend." She puckered her lips and gave a mincing little shrug.

"Um... Yes, I'm sure he is," I agreed as I pulled out my cell phone. But I knew Adele had no idea exactly what he was thinking.

That evening, Chad called to report that he and three friends would be leaving after Brittney's last class on Friday and should arrive by midnight. I reminded him that I had no extra beds and they would be strictly in camping mode at my house.

"Not a problem, Ma," he said cheerfully. "The girls are bringing a blow-up mattress and Ryan and I will just sleep on the floor. The girls can have that little room I used before."

"There are two small rooms off the living room—one each for men and women. You can consider it the weekend dormitory."

"Anything is better than the dorms," he said with a laugh.

"Glad to oblige, but you'll have to fight over the one

189

bathroom," I countered.

Jerry had urged me to take a break from the decorating on Friday. It was hard for me to let go. I'd been concentrating on getting everything set for so long it didn't seem right to just stop working on it. But the truth was the school was ready to hold the biggest party of the decade in Forest County, and despite the intense effort it took to pull it off, the facility was pretty much in working order, and the decorations were looking good.

By Friday evening, the black dress was pressed and safely hanging in a plastic cover in my closet, the jade jewelry was cleaned; I'd shined my low black heels and located black underwear. I'd had to buy a pair of stockings, since I could find none in my drawer with no runs. The number of times I'd worn a dress since moving to Cherry Hill could be counted on one hand.

I'd been grocery shopping, made a huge bowl of taco salad, filled the freezer with ice cream, the refrigerator with milk and pop, and the cupboard with cereal, salty snacks and cookies. A bowl of fruit sat on the counter. I hoped I was ready for the college kids.

It was a good thing I'd taken the day off, or redirected my efforts at any rate. Getting ready for four young people and a dress-up affair was a project in itself.

I dozed on the couch until I was awakened by laughter and pounding footsteps on the terrace. Just as someone knocked, I opened the door and the kids piled into the living room. The rain hadn't really stopped all week. In fact, it was still drizzling, and water droplets glistened on their shoulders and hair. The boys were lugging large duffel bags with pillows and folded blankets tucked under their arms. A tall girl carried an overnight case, and the other one had a backpack slung over one shoulder.

Chad stamped his feet on the mat, and despite being in the presence of friends, gave me a bear hug. "Ma, this is Ryan, Brittney and Audra."

Ryan was short and skinny with dark hair and eyes. Brittney was a willowy blond, and Audra a plump brunette. They all smiled tentatively at me.

"Call me Ana. I'm glad you made it without any problems. You'll have those two little rooms for sleeping," I said, pointing to the far side of the living room. "The bathroom's upstairs, and there's food in the kitchen if you're hungry."

That seemed to break the ice, and everyone began talking at once.

"The temperature's dropping like a rock," Ryan said, letting the duffels and bedding fall to the floor and rubbing his arms in an apparent effort to warm them.

Brittney asked, "Which way to the stairs?" and made a beeline when I pointed her in the right direction.

Chad and Audra began to sort out the equipment and poked their heads into the small rooms. One was completely empty, and I'd begun to arrange the other as an office, but all it held were a desk and chair and some boxes of receipts and mail. "We'll take the office room," Chad said.

Audra nodded approval and began lugging a large duffel into the empty room. "I'll get this mattress blown up," she announced to no one in particular.

Because Chad had been here before, he knew his way around the kitchen. The kids were soon munching on pretzels and cookies and downing bottles of pop. They quizzed me on how to get to the school and if they'd be able to arrange their props and practice the skit before show time. I gave them all the necessary information and headed upstairs to my bedroom.

I could still hear their laughter and chatting when I drifted off to sleep. As much as I liked living alone, it was nice to occasionally have young people in the house.

42

My alarm went off at eight. I quietly made coffee and slipped out the kitchen door with a few snacks of my own in a tote bag. There wasn't a peep coming from the other side of the house where the young people had crashed sometime after two a.m.

Thankfully, I arrived at the school before anyone else. I knew the day would be one long parade of deliveries, challenges, and probably a good many small snafus to sort out.

I walked through the building, checking out all the rooms that would be in use. Most of the activity would be centered in the main auditorium which would serve as ballroom, theatre and general meeting place. However, the front hallway, looking lovely as a sidewalk café, would also be highly used. The setting was better than ever. Someone, Jerry I presumed, had brought in several brightly painted doors and fastened them somehow against the inside wall, increasing the appearance of a row of small shops with outdoor tables. There was also a life-size statue of a dog, with tongue lolling, seated beside one door. Whoever brought it had added a collar and a leash which trailed on the "ground"—the obedient dog waiting while its master shopped. The sprinkling of autumn leaves on the floor and the pots of chrysanthemums completed the atmosphere.

Down the hallway to the left, the first room on the outside wall was ready to receive the food. It was painted, cleaned, and filled with two rows of long tables covered with plastic. Against one wall was another row of tables, already arranged with piles of foam plates and cups, napkins, and disposable flatware. Condiments were on yet another table which also held three large beverage dispensers. I presumed they were empty at this point. Trash cans flanked the doorway, both inside the room and in the hall. The biggest problem with the food service was that the kitchen was the opposite direction, down the main hallway. Although Jerry had managed to get the refrigerator, stove and hot and cold running water working, the cafeteria itself had badly-damaged walls and wasn't useable. The caterers, Janice, Jimmie, and whoever else they recruited, would have to run back and forth between the kitchen and the "food room."

The next room to the left was designated the coat room. It probably would have been good to organize some sort of check system, but there hadn't been time. We'd managed to borrow a good many racks and hangers from churches and businesses. And we'd put extra tables in the room. People would have to fend for themselves, and hopefully wouldn't leave valuables in their wraps although I realized small town folks had a different mentality than I on this topic. They pretty much trusted everyone. I thought again about the grisly scene Jerry and I had found almost directly below where I was standing, and doubted that any town could count on that sort of innocence any more if it had ever been real at all.

At the end of the hall, the kids' game room was also cleaned and painted. It looked like Cheyanne might have stopped in on Friday as there were several cartons of equipment stacked against one wall. Through the mesh of plastic crates I saw balls, bowling pins, and other brightly colored objects. Several hula hoops leaned against the pile.

My last stops on the checklist were the restrooms just across from the game room. They were clean and all the stalls had doors that locked. Although the sinks were stained, they had been scoured, and the hot and cold water worked.

Beyond the lavatories, a wire gate had been extended across the side hall and locked to block access to the rest of the building. I knew there was a matching gate which was closed around the corner at the far end of the front hall. Seeing the gates made me wonder if people would be able to access the upstairs. I climbed to the second floor and found there was also a gate there, closing off the upper hallway. I checked, and it was locked securely. At the far end I could see yet another gate which would stop people who came up the stairs at the east end of the building.

Everything seemed to be prepared as well as could be expected, and better than I had dared to hope.

I descended and headed back toward the main entrance just in time to intercept a man and woman who were carrying large black cases.

"We're The Blue Grass," the man said. "The band. Where do we set up?"

Another man pulled open the entrance door and struggled to drag a large box on wheels through. I hurried to his aid and jammed a triangular doorstop underneath the heavy unwieldy door. Cold air rushed in and a breeze stirred the leaves on the floor. It smelled like November, not October.

"Straight through those double doors," I said. "You'll be to the right on the stage. I'll show you." Two more women with guitar cases traipsed in behind the large wheeled box.

The day's madness had begun.

Before I finished showing The Blue Grass where the electric outlets were, Janice, her husband, and Suzi pulled up in a van and began carrying in trays loaded with tarts. I directed Janice to the kitchen. She said she'd find what she needed and called over her shoulder that Jimmie Mosher and Jack Panther were both going to help serve.

Loud music was coming from the auditorium/ballroom, and I realized the band was playing a CD for their entertainment while they were setting up.

Cheyanne must have arrived in the meantime because I saw a flash of pink, head height, disappear through the far door. A young boy, about six years old, was running full tilt down the hallway, sliding on the loose leaves and yelling with delight.

"Geronimo!" he screamed. He ran up several stairs at the end of the hall, turned and jumped into the leaves. His enthusiastic leap propelled him into a table, which overturned, dumping the tablecloth and a vase of silk flowers onto the floor. I hurried toward him with the goal of finding out whose responsibility he was, and to right the table. Thankfully the vase was plastic and didn't break.

Cheyanne stuck her head out of the game room door and

admonished, "Cody, get in here this minute. You can run off that energy in this room. Not in the hall. Sorry." Her voice had changed on the final word as she turned to me and rolled her eyes.

"Yours?" I asked.

"All forty-eight pounds of him," she giggled, grabbing his arm and forcing him through the door. "He was with his dad last weekend, so you didn't meet him then."

"Ms. Raven!" the guy from the band who had introduced himself as Mick called, striding toward me. "Can we get access to that balcony? We'd like to clamp our lights on the railing."

I wasn't sure if my key set included one for the gates, but I beckoned to him and we climbed the stairs. There were several keys on the ring that I knew didn't fit the front door or the interior doors.

"That one," Mick said, jabbing a finger at a key that was entirely different from the others.

I tried it, and the gate accordioned open with some pushing, creaking and sticking. I was irritated just because a man had felt the need to point out the obvious to a female. *Better get over it*, I told myself. *There are going to be a lot of requests and directives and annoyances today.* Just to preserve my position of authority, though, I had the key to the balcony already between my fingers before we reached the doors.

"There you go. Will you need access to this for the evening?" I asked.

"It would be good," was his immediate response. "I can run the light and sound board from up here."

"I'll see if I can find another key for the gates. We don't want everyone in town to be wandering through the building," I said.

We had descended to the railing at the front edge of the raked balcony, and as I looked over, Chad, Ryan, Brittney and Audra burst into sight in the main ballroom. Mick immediately began snaking cords over the edge.

"We'll tape these to the wall in the corner," he said, "You won't have to worry about anyone tripping or getting caught in them."

"This is awesome!" Chad exclaimed, turning and taking in the décor on each side of the room. "Ma! Where are you? We're here. Where's the murder going to be?" he continued. Mick was still talking to me, but I couldn't take in two conversations at once.

Audra pointed at the stage, to the bedroom furniture, and said, "Right there, Chad. It's obvious."

"I'll be down in a second," I called to them.

Chad whirled around, hunting for my voice, and finally looked up. "Hi, Ma! We need to run through the skit a couple of times to see how it works."

There was no direct way to get from the balcony to the main floor, and on the return trip via the hallways, I ran into Todd Ringman.

"Just checkin' the mechanicals," he assured me, saluting with two fingers as he pushed open the Ladies Room door.

"Great," I said, but he had already disappeared behind the windowless panel of dark wood.

Mick must have gotten the cords plugged in because as soon as I reached the ballroom, amplified chords began to sound from a guitar. *Bluegrass means acoustic, doesn't it? I guess not anymore.* Songs were still blaring from the CD player, but the musicians began jamming over the top of that noise.

I was showing the kids the backstage areas where they could change and make entrances and exits, when the lights went out. The dim recesses of the stage became murky with no windows located there, and the loud music ceased abruptly mid-song. The quiet was so welcome, I realized my ears were ringing.

"Sorry," Mick called from the balcony. "I think our amps did that."

"I'll take care of it," hollered Todd. He motioned to one of the musicians, opened the door that led directly to the basement and said, "Th'electric panel's down here. I'll show ya'." Raising his voice again, he yelled at Mick, "Ya' might need t' get an extension cord and plug those lights in a differ'nt circuit."

"Where can I buy one?" Mick yelled back. "I've used all ours."

"Jouppi's Hardware," Todd and I said simultaneously. "South end of Main Street," I added loudly.

I heard Cody scream "Geronimo!" from the hallway.

It was just past one, and there were still hours to go until the Ball began, when the noise level was sure to be exponentially louder. I shook my head in hopes of stopping the ringing in my ears and the ringing switched to my pocket. It was my phone.

43

"Ana, I'm glad I caught you," Jerry's voice squawked from the speaker.

"It's a cell phone, Jerry. It's usually where I am." I was suddenly peeved that he wasn't here helping to direct all this chaos.

"And where would that be?" he asked as if it were an ordinary day, and not the day of the event he'd predicted to be the biggest in a decade.

"I'm at the school. Where are you? It's crazy here. We could use some help," I said pointedly.

"On my way," he soothed, as if nothing could ruffle his feathers. "Go home. Take a hot bath and relax. I want you to be cheerful this evening. I'll pick you up at six-fifteen."

"It won't take me that long to get ready," I protested. "There's a lot going on here. Two people who can make decisions would be useful."

"At your service," he announced in stereo, and I looked up to see him striding in the door.

For the next two hours both of us solved problems, helped move equipment and props, and rescued tables from Cody's continuing exuberance. We were so busy I forgot to eat the lunch I'd brought with me. Finally, the band was running through a mellow tune with no competing music while Mick gave a thumbs-up from the balcony, the kids had gone back to my house to eat taco salad, and Janice stuck her head in the door to tell us that she'd be back to plug in the coffee urns at six. I sat down on the edge of the stage and pulled Jerry down beside me.

"We may be ready," I sighed. "I think I will go home and clean up now."

Jerry patted my knee. "I want you to know that even if Cora

turns me down on the... well, you know..." he glanced around, "that this has all been worth it simply for the boost it has given Cherry Hill's morale."

"I hope you're right," I said in a tired voice.

"People have really noticed your community spirit. They won't forget," he said.

"What does that mean?"

"It takes a long time for someone with no local roots to be accepted in a small town. But you are becoming one of us. I like it."

"I like it, too," I said, offering a tired smile, but I really was pleased at his kind words. "Can you handle things from here on out?"

"I'm staying till five-thirty. Adele said she'd close early and come over to watch things till we return."

"Why don't I just meet you here?" I asked.

"Not on your life. I'm picking you up properly. Six-fifteen, on the dot." He rose and practically lifted me by the elbows. "Cheerful, remember?"

"OK, Cyrano; or maybe I'm Cyrano de Bergerac and you're Christian de Neuvillette. Anyway, tonight all will be revealed to the lovely Cora-Roxanne and we'll determine if she loves you. I'll be elegant, cheerful, oh yes, and a glittering, jealousy-inducing bauble. But I need a shower and a snack to pull it off."

44

Jerry was a terrific dancer. We glided around the ballroom floor to the strains of "The Autumn Waltz." Its haunting melody was beautifully played by the band, and the words were strangely appropriate for the underlying plot of the evening. I wondered if Jerry had requested it as the opening song. At first, we were the only dancers on the floor. Jerry had proudly announced the opening of the Harvest Ball and taken my hand to lead me to the center of the room. It was impossible to guess how many people had already arrived. Every hay bale or bench placed around the edge of the room had several people seated on it, and spaces between were filled two or three deep with those who were standing. I had no idea how many others were in the hallway, or had already lined up to pile plates with food.

Someone was taking pictures, and a flash exploded in my eyes, twice. After two passes around the room, Jerry motioned for others to join us, and couples did so, slowly. Some appeared shy or awkward with forgotten skills, but soon the floor was filled with dancers wearing every sort of outfit from tuxedos and prom dresses to bib overalls.

It was a bit of a shock to realize how few of those in attendance I knew, but I was searching hard for one particular person. She was there, standing along the west wall, and Tom was seated next to her on a bale of hay. I might have had to look twice if I hadn't seen Tom. Cora was definitely not wearing her customary faded denim. She had on a forest-green jumper with a pleated bodice that somehow reminded me of Audrey Hepburn. Beneath the jumper was a creamy silk blouse with full sleeves. Instead of braids wound around her head, her hair had been carefully pulled into a French twist, and the edge was lined with something decorative that sparkled elegantly in the light. I thought she might even be wearing a touch of makeup. She was definitely tracking our sweep around the room, but I successfully avoided eye contact.

After the first dance, I told Jerry I wanted to get something to eat and drifted toward the front hall. Adele was in the foyer, hawking raffle tickets.

"A dollar each, ten for six dollars, or an arm's length for ten dollars," she announced, over and over, as people entered the front doors.

The temperature had plummeted all day and people were bundled up in outerwear that didn't necessarily match their party clothes. Most stood on the tile cherry bomb shivering, removing gloves and unwinding scarves. Some even turned to look at the Judge Oldfield historical items in the display case. Geraldine Longcore was there with Adele, directing people to the coatroom and game room for the youngsters, and helping to collect raffle money. Children impatiently waited to have jackets unzipped and to be released for play. Adele had wisely worn a sweater, but Geraldine looked cold. I guessed it to be in the mid-twenties outside, the first really hard freeze of the season, and every time the door opened, frigid air rushed in. I'd worn my wool cape and had still been chilly.

The women were doing a fine job of directing traffic, and I told them so, then headed for the buffet line which was long. As it moved almost imperceptibly forward, I pondered Jerry's actions when he had picked me up. He'd arrived right on time wearing a long black coat over his grandfather's suit. He was carrying a top hat that might have been beaver. It was sartorial perfection on a handsome man. I invited him in, and he looked me over from head to toe, but not in a way that made me uncomfortable.

"You look fabulous," he said. "I hope these flowers will work."

He opened the corsage box he'd also brought in and removed a beautiful arrangement of four small green orchids surrounded by sprigs of white buds. The flowers were backed with loops of ribbon in a soft green.

"Oh, Jerry," I said, "that's really lovely."

"I told them about your jade and asked them to tone down

what they call 'lime-green' blossoms."

"I think it will be perfect."

He had then taken the corsage from its bed of cellophane and leaned in to fasten it on my dress. His fingers were cool against my skin as he slipped them expertly behind the fabric to protect me from the long pin he wielded with his right hand.

Already close to me, he pulled me closer and kissed me full on the lips, holding me just a moment longer than I expected.

"I sincerely want to thank you for everything you've done for me in the past six weeks," he said when we'd separated.

"I'm... You know... I still don't think your plan is going to work," I finally managed to get out, feeling a bit breathless.

"Understood. But it won't be for lack of trying." He smiled broadly and fingered his mustache.

My feelings were definitely mixed. I had come to appreciate Jerry Caulfield as a man who cared deeply about this town and who was willing to perform amazing feats to try to win back the woman he genuinely loved. And although I didn't want a romantic relationship with anyone, I wasn't immune to his attentions and gentle touch. And yet, it irked me that men thought they were so dashing and irresistible that bestowing a kiss was the best way to thank a woman. Yes, I was both touched and annoyed. I was just thinking this was probably a good thing, since neither of us could afford letting our friendship become something more, when a voice at my elbow interrupted my reverie.

"Ana," Jimmie Mosher said eagerly with eyes opening wide, "you look seriously awesome!"

He was carrying a tray loaded with cups of coleslaw. I opened my mouth to greet him but he launched into a monologue.

"Do you know where coleslaw came from? It's a Dutch nickname for *koolsalade* that they shortened to *koolsla*, and Americans just said coleslaw. Cabbage is older than snot—oh, sorry about that—older than, well, lots of vegetables, but not the kind we know with heads. That's only been around for about four hundred years."

I shook my head and blinked. "Jimmie, slow down," I said,

trying to grasp the relevance of the history of cabbage salad.

"Gotta go," he said abruptly and scooted off in the direction of the front of the line, knees slightly bent to cushion the tray.

45

My inward thoughts were pushed aside as people I knew approached and greeted me. Hunter, the oldest of the Sorenson kids—I thought I remembered he was eight or maybe nine—had his two little sisters in tow. The youngest, I recalled her name was Ruthie, was being held tightly by the hand by the older girl.

"Hello, Mrs. Raven," Hunter said seriously. "I'm watching the girls tonight while Mom drives the team."

"You're doing a fine job," I assured him. "Why don't you get in front of me? Ruthie might get impatient waiting a long time for something to eat."

The children willingly accepted that offer. Hunter must have had to grow up a lot in the past year. I recalled that his uncle Karl was planning to move to Cherry Hill to help with the implement business, but didn't have a chance to ask the boy about it because I was distracted yet again.

John Aho and his wife, Marie, passed me with loaded plates. They were laughing, and John was cleaner than I'd ever seen him, even at church. They both wore new jeans and plaid flannel shirts.

"Ana!" John said. "What a great evening, and it's hardly begun. Hurry and eat. They're going to call a square dance soon."

"I'll be right there," I assured him. Their apparel seemed better suited for that dance than my black gown.

Finally, I reached the food table, and was amazed at the feast Janice had created. There were trays the size of snow saucers loaded with sandwich buns in three varieties, white, wheat and rye. Large slow cookers filled with spicy pulled meat simmered just beyond the bread, followed by plates heaped with sandwich meats and cheese. Cups of coleslaw and applesauce were arranged next. The applesauce appeared to be homemade, not from cans. There were also trays filled with raw vegetables and fruits, and huge bowls of chips and pretzels. At the very ends of the two lines of tables were the tarts I knew Janice and her crew had been making.

Janice was presiding over the line I was in, and Jack Panther kept the other one under control. I caught his eye and nodded at him. I guessed that Jimmie and Suzi were the runners for both lines, bringing more food from the kitchen as needed. Janice grinned from ear to ear when I reached her.

"What do you think?" she asked, but the question was rhetorical. She knew the dinner was good.

"This is beyond amazing," I answered anyway. "I didn't think you were doing so many different foods."

"Stores just kept donating items and asking what they could do to make it bigger and better. There's a list over on those posters of all the places that contributed."

I looked in the direction she pointed and noted the names of businesses from most of the nearby towns, even convenience stores.

"No one wanted to be left out," she added. "If nothing else, they sent over bags of chips and things like that. Or beverages. We got lots of bottled water and juices and iced teas."

That made me recall the cash bar Jerry had been planning. It was the one aspect of preparations I hadn't been involved with. I asked Janice where it was.

"On the other side of the entrance hall. They didn't have time to clean up another room, but the table's in the hall. Just the bartenders are using the room."

"Thanks for the directions," I said with a wink. I picked up a pumpkin tart and utensils and headed for a table, balancing my loaded plates of food.

The café tables in the hallway were filled with happy people, eating and talking. Mavis and Harold Fanning were nibbling from a single plate of chips and sipping cocktails. They shared a table with a couple I didn't know. As much as I wanted to keep my eyes on them, I couldn't figure out how that was going to be possible in the crowded building.

I could hear yells and laughter coming from the end of the hall and assumed Cheyanne had things in hand there. Just once, I thought I heard a shrill "Geronimo," above the general clamor.

I'd been thinking about drinking something stronger than cider or coffee, but my hands were full and my purse was locked in Jerry's car. Nevertheless, I wandered in the direction of the bar because all the tables nearby were taken. Fewer people were buying drinks, but there was a short line and I could see two bartenders in white formal shirts and black pants and vests disappearing into the room behind them, returning and filling glasses or opening bottles.

The noise level was impressive, but everywhere I looked, people were smiling, talking with one another, and enjoying themselves. The Ball was definitely a success so far.

A group of young teenagers sat on the floor at the far end of the hall, giggling and feeding each other vegetable sticks. Sunny and Star Leonard were there. I wasn't going to horn in on the kids' fun, but I hoped I'd have a chance to talk to the girls before the evening was over. I hadn't seen them lately.

My eyes moved back to the bar just as Virginia Holiday reached the front of the line. She was even more overdressed than usual, with multiple necklaces and rings. Long multi-colored earrings dangled to her shoulders. She wore a gold lamé, high-waisted dress with asymmetric straps and a full skirt. It looked vintage rather than modern, but the style suited what I had come to recognize as her personality. The necklaces were a mixed collection of strands of colored stones, carved African wildlife charms, gaudy glass, and beads. She always seemed to think that more was better, and tonight she'd outdone herself. Her long hair hung loose as always, and a gold silk rose was pinned above her right ear. I was a bit surprised to see that she'd ordered a double Scotch, but the bartender apparently thought nothing of it, filling the order without so much as the blink of an eye.

There was an empty chair at the last small table, and I asked the occupants if I might sit there. While I was eating and getting acquainted with the couple, and the woman's mother, who had all driven in from Thorpe, I saw Alex and Shane from the canoe livery enter the hallway, laughing and shoving each other playfully. I waved, but they didn't notice me. I was glad they'd made it. They must have ridden in the horse-drawn wagon because I saw them pulling strands of golden straw from their hi-tech fleece jackets.

There must be over three hundred people here already, I thought, between rounds of small talk. Of course, I didn't know most of them, but it surprised me how many people I did know. I was just finishing the last of my tart when Jerry appeared beside my chair.

"You need to be in the ballroom. Soon," he insisted.

46

I excused myself, wishing Mr. and Mrs. Whatever-They'd-Said a nice evening. I was beginning to feel pulled in too many directions.

My throat was dry, and I wasn't willing to continue without something to drink, so I worked my way back to the food room to find a bottle of water. The Fannings were no longer seated in the hallway. I pulled a wet bottle from the tub of ice, grabbed a pile of napkins to keep it from dripping on my dress and headed for the auditorium, twisting off the cap and drinking as I went. Every few seconds someone touched my arm and said hello or waved or smiled at me. I tried to return the greetings between gulps.

A square dance was just beginning. It must have been the second or third one. I'd been gone quite a while, and one of The Blue Grass members was encouraging couples who hadn't yet tried it onto the floor. The space was tight with so many people, but six squares had formed, and it appeared that some new dancers were coming away from the walls. Chad and his friends had decided to try it and were laughing and poking each other as they took their places. Star Leonard was waiting in one of the squares with a tall lanky boy I didn't know. She lifted her slim legs alternately, as if stretching out for a run. Jerry saw me enter and headed my way. Over his shoulder, I spied Harold standing alone. Mavis wasn't with him.

From the stage I heard the caller explaining what the phrases of the dance calls meant and directing the couples to walk through the steps.

Jerry said, "The next number after this is another waltz. Do you think I should ask Cora to join me?" He sounded tentative.

I was stunned at his apparent sudden lack of confidence.

"Sure, why not?" I countered.

"What if she says 'no?' Then what could I do next?"

He had a point. "Let me go talk to her," I offered.

"Would you do that?" he asked. He sounded like a small boy hoping his sister would rescue him from some junior high social crisis.

"Heading that way," I assured him, patting his hand.

Cora was still with Tom, although now she was sitting on a bench beside him. I worked my way around the edge of the room. The harmonica and fiddle took off with a blast and the caller cried "All join hands and circle down south..."

"Hi, Cora, Tom," I said, trying to be heard over the music. "I haven't had a chance to say hello yet. I hope you aren't offended."

Tom shook his head and yelled, "I can't hear voices at all in places like this. I'm just enjoyin' the music."

Cora smiled weakly. "Oh, no. You're so busy." Then she must have realized this sounded like a continuation of her complaints during our last phone call. "Really. I understand. This is quite the party. You've done something wonderful for the community. Your corsage is quite lovely," she added.

"Well, thanks. Working on the Ball has been rewarding," I admitted, touching the orchids lightly and feeling the glow of Jerry's touch.

"Allemande left in your own backyard..." came the caller's voice.

"Have you done any dancing yet?" I asked her.

"Dancing? Me? With whom?"

"I can see you and Tom in a square dance," I suggested.

She shook her head. "Only if he learns the calls by heart. He can't hear the words."

"Chicken in a bread pan pickin' out dough..." was clearly audible to me above a jangle of banjo chords. Funny words. No wonder everyone seemed to be laughing.

"Oh, sorry. That makes sense." I paused. "Look, Cora. I have a request from someone who would like the next waltz with you, if you're willing. I hope you'll say yes. Even if it's only as a favor to me."

"Oh? Who's that?" Cora looked up at me pertly.

"Meet your honey and pat her on the head, if she don't like biscuits then feed her corn bread," twanged from the stage.

"Jerry."

Cora sat quietly, looking at me. I could tell she was trying to figure this out.

"Why?"

Why? Why, indeed?

"He's dating you. He should dance with you again," she said with finality.

"It's true; we've spent a lot of time together getting ready for this event, but you're one of the key players too. You've brought the Judge's furniture, and provided the information for the skit. It should be coming up soon."

"That's why I'm here. I'm just waiting for it," she interrupted, clipping the words.

"Let him honor you for your contribution," I pleaded.

She shifted on the bench and smoothed the jumper skirt modestly across her knees. She had really gone all out, even wearing stockings and low heels. I'd never seen her in a dress before.

"All right. When you put it that way, I suppose it would look awkward if I turned him down."

The dancers must have really caught on to the calls because everyone along the walls was now clapping and stomping their feet in rhythm with the music. With amplification, the sound was overwhelming, and I was having trouble concentrating. As I headed back toward Jerry, I glanced up at the balcony and waved to Mick who was fooling with the sliders on his control board. Mavis Fanning stood beside him. What was she doing up there?

The crowd broke into continuous clapping as I reached Jerry, and the square dance broke up. Adele stepped to the stage, and the bass player removed a microphone from a stand and handed it to her.

"There are just five more minutes to purchase raffle tickets," she announced. "The first drawing will be held immediately following the next song. Come on folks; let's support the Forest

County Animal Shelter. Avery Edwards, you haven't bought a single ticket yet." She pointed at a heavyset man with a long beard. "I know you have enough money. Cough some up! The first prize awarded is going to be a haircut, facial and manicure at the Curly-Q, to be performed by Queenie herself. The royal treatment. You know Carolyn would like that."

Avery partially rose from his seat on a hay bale, dug in a pocket and waved a bill in the air, shaking his head and revealing a set of ill-fitting false teeth as he smiled. Geraldine made a beeline for him, money box and tickets in hand. I saw other people opening purses and pulling out wallets.

"You're all set," I whispered to Jerry. "Go ask her."

He flashed me a look full of gratitude and began working his way toward Cora. I watched him bend down to talk to her, and I saw her head nod an affirmative. They stood side by side. She barely came to his armpit, but somehow they looked right together.

"All right, folks, let's mellow things out a bit with the 'Tennessee Waltz.' But I hope no one here is having their sweetheart stolen tonight. One, two, three, one, two..." and the couples were swirling onto the floor.

Cora was quite a good dancer. She and Jerry had obviously waltzed together before as they seemed to sense each other's motions. She wasn't simply following his lead with standard steps. I saw him bend down and whisper in her ear, and snug his long fingers a little tighter around her tiny waist. I certainly hoped it would soon look as if someone's sweetheart had been stolen. I ventured a tentative smile at the possibility the ruse might actually work.

47

The floor was filled with happy couples, but those who watched from the sidelines seemed just as pleased. I sensed someone near me and turned to find Harold Fanning at my side.

"May I have the pleasure of this dance?" he asked.

I didn't see that I had many options, and what could it hurt? "Of course," I answered.

Harold faced me and placed his right hand on my waist while grasping my right hand with his left. Now face-to-face with him I realized he'd been drinking enough to smell boozy.

"You are a beautiful woman, Ana Raven," he said. I noticed that his words were tending to run together.

"Thank you," I answered, trying to sound as generic as possible. We danced in silence for a few moments.

"You are a goddam beautiful woman," he repeated.

"So is your wife. Where is she, by the way?" I craned my neck, trying to look around while staying in step. I was hoping to get out of the mainstream of the secondhand whiskey fumes, too.

"Who knows? She's probably off scouting around the building."

Suddenly this became interesting. "And why is she so interested in this building, Harold?" I asked, trying to keep my voice light, as if I were playing along with a joke.

Harold stepped on my foot, but I pretended not to notice. "Her crazy obsession with yoga, of course," he said.

"What does she want to do with it?" I pressed. Harold had told Jerry she wanted to open a gym, but maybe I could find out even more.

"She's determined to open a fitness center. I've tried to talk her into other locations, but she's set her heart on this place." His words were definitely slurring, and the twirling of the waltz wasn't improving his balance.

"How badly does she want it?" I asked, wondering if Harold knew anything about anonymous calls from wayward phones, or bloody hatchets.

"Hell, how should I know? She thought it was safe in the city's hands but then the council listed it with that new realtor person. She's very strange." He added.

I thought he meant his wife was strange. Then I caught on. I was suddenly feeling glad that my formal attire made me stand out from the denim and flannel that was the evening's dress norm. "You mean Virginia Holiday?" I asked.

"Yes her, strange, but I'm talking about Mavis." He plunged on. "So she tried to buy it, but that Holiday woman had added on her fees and the price went way up."

"So Mavis couldn't afford it?"

"She couldn't afford it anyway. I'm not made of money, even though she wants everyone to think we're rich. And it would have been a conflict of interest, with me on the council. You'd think that fancy lawyer of hers would have explained that to her."

"You could resign," I suggested.

"And let her wear the pants? I don't think so." He burped, fogging me with a mixture of chips, salsa and liquor.

I averted my face, trying not to grimace. I wanted to draw more information from the tipsy man. "But then the building was turned back over to the city, right?"

"Yes, and that was another odd thing. The listing time hadn't run out, but Carolina Holiday..."

"Virginia," I corrected.

"Her. ...said we'd misled her about the condition of the place, and dumped it back in our laps."

"And then?"

"The very next day, Jerry Caulfield contacted us and said he'd buy it at the price we'd been asking for years. Odd timing, if you ask me." He sniffed.

From the corner of my eye I saw a tall woman in a slinky deep purple dress approaching us. Mavis Fanning tapped me on the shoulder and said peremptorily, "I'll take over from here."

I nodded to her and stepped away from Harold. She grasped his hand and shoulder as if she were equipped with vice-grips tipped with purple nail polish instead of fingers and steered him quickly away from me.

As the dance came to an end, I found myself near the stage side of the room and looked up into the balcony once more. This time, Deputy Harvey Brown stood beside Mick, surveying the room. I'd forgotten all about the promise from Tracy that the police would be around to help. Harvey was from the Sheriff's Department, but I was glad there was an official presence on site. Perhaps Tracy or Kyle was outside.

A rush of self-recrimination washed over me. I hadn't gotten Mick a key to the gate. He'd had to leave it unlocked. Anyone could wander upstairs if they discovered the lapse in security. Already there had been two unexpected people in the balcony. Two too many.

Adele came to the platform once again and read off the numbers for the winner of the Curly-Q beauty package, and another one for a thirty dollar gift certificate at Sorenson's, to be used in the garden shop. Each time, people fumbled to produce and read their tickets till someone cried out, "That's mine." Much applause and congratulating followed.

Jerry was waiting at the bottom of the stage steps, and he ascended and took the microphone from Adele. The musicians began moving some of their equipment slightly farther to the side of the stage.

"We want to extend a warm thank you to The Blue Grass, for providing our music this evening." He turned to his left and began clapping with his arms extended. The room erupted in clapping, yelling and whistling. "They'll be back in a little while to round out the evening. I've been told that Myra Treleaven will play and sing 'Bluegrass Saturday Night' for a finale. You don't want to miss that."

One female member of the band lifted her banjo above her head and smiled. Another round of cheers arose from the crowd.

"We're almost ready for the reenactment of an important piece of Cherry Hill History, but first, we have so many door prizes, I'll turn the mic back over to our own Adele Volger, of Volger's Grocery, who will announce more winners." As he handed her the microphone, he whispered in her ear and then left the stage. He came straight toward me.

Adele took whatever he'd said in stride and began explaining the next prize which was a dinner for two, wine included, at Chez Léon in Emily City. I nodded, recalling my dinner there with Jerry. It was where this whole plot had been hatched.

She was reading off the number of the winner when Jerry reached my side. "Should I tell her now or after the play," he hissed.

"What?" I was confused.

"Cora. Is it better to tell her about the building before or after the skit?"

"You haven't got it all planned out?" I asked.

"I did have. I was going to do it the very last thing. But I don't think she's going to stay. She said as much to Tom after the last dance. Told him to get the truck right after the kids finish." Jerry was getting uncharacteristically nervous and fidgety again.

"Then you should do it now," I said.

"That's so anticlimactic." He was almost whining.

"Well, make up your mind." I didn't like it when a leader suddenly began to waffle. "You haven't got all night," I added, probably unkindly.

"Adele will give out prizes until I come back. There are plenty of them. I have to think," he said, scratching the back of his head.

I saw Chad peek around the corner of the proscenium. I was relieved to see they were apparently in place in the wings and ready.

Jerry began to pace back and forth in front of me, even though the space was severely limited. The people who'd been in the hallway were pressing into the auditorium so they'd be sure to hear the numbers read out for door prizes, and to find good spots from which to watch the skit. Many people simply sat on the floor in the center of the room.

Someone must have delivered a message to Cheyanne that the

play was about to begin because she and a large group of children entered from the side door and she urged them toward the front of the crowd, near the stage. Her hand motions made it obvious that she was directing them to sit down and be quiet. To her credit, she must have worn the kids out with her games, because they settled right in and looked expectantly toward the front.

Jerry stopped pacing and looked at me. "OK, now it is. Thirty minutes aren't going to make any difference in her answer."

I nodded in relief and took his hand. "I wish you the best, and I hope we've done as good a job of preparing her as you predicted."

He smiled at me and leaned downward, but I shook my head and gave him a little push.

48

As Jerry headed back toward the stage, Adele finished giving away a pair of snowshoes from the Jalmari Canoe Livery-cum-sports store. Apparently Shane and Alex weren't wasting any time getting into pursuit of year-round customers. She thanked the child who had pulled the winning ticket from a paper bag and sent him back to his seat on the floor. She straightened and pulled down the hem of her sweater.

"And now, everyone, let's say a real thank you to the man who has made this first annual, we hope, Harvest Ball a smashing success. We know so many people pitched in, but without his direction and initial commitment to restoring our school, it never would have happened. The owner and editor of the *Cherry Hill Herald*, our very own, very much alive, Jerry Caulfield."

There was thunderous applause and more stamping and whistling. Jerry raised his hands and gestured for people to stop. "Thank you, thank you all," he said magnanimously, the leader-in-charge again. "I am delighted that at apparently the right time, I was able to provide the impetus for a project that you've all taken to heart. There is one person I would like to acknowledge who has played a significant role in the preparations for our Ball, a relative newcomer to our county, Anastasia Raven."

He motioned me to the stage. I was momentarily frozen in place. I wasn't supposed to be the one up there with him. I shook my head slightly.

"Ana, come on up here so people can thank you," he urged gently.

I gave in and climbed the few steps to the stage. Jerry put his arm around my shoulders.

"Ana, along with Adele, here..." he paused and put his other arm around Adele's ample waist. But he had to let one of us go to bring the mic back to his mouth, and he released me. "...took on the responsibility of making my dream for this Ball become a reality. You can't believe how many hours..."

My gaze wandered again to the balcony while Jerry embarrassingly listed a number of the decorating and organizational tasks we'd accomplished. There were a couple of teenagers huddled in a shadowy upper corner, kissing. Someone needed to go lock that gate. Mick waved at me.

...and she's feeling right at home here in our small town."

I smiled and waved when everyone began clapping, probably for Adele and me, although I wasn't positive.

Off to my right, Chad hissed loudly, "Psst, Ma! How much longer till we're on?"

I continued waving with my left hand and spread the five fingers of my right hand and wiggled them at Chad behind my hip. I was totally guessing.

Jerry stepped back and pointed to the steps. "Ladies, if you would kindly join the audience, I have another announcement I would like to make."

Adele gave Jerry a questioning look, but she didn't balk at being hustled off stage.

The room quieted. People seemed to sense that whatever was about to happen hadn't been in the publicly known order of events. I liked the feeling of being "in the know."

Jerry began. "Mavis Fanning, please come up here."

My head jerked up, and probably my jaw dropped. What was Jerry up to?

Mavis looked even more stunned than I. She had been chatting with a group of well-dressed women, and didn't hear Jerry at first. One of her friends poked her and turned her around, and she finally saw Jerry beckoning her. She minced her way to the stage, playing coy with the audience and shrugging her shoulders.

"Mavis, I have a deal for you," Jerry said.

The woman was not quite as tall as Jerry, but she could nearly look him in the eye. You could practically see sparks and questions flying out of her, but she said nothing.

Jerry took it in stride and continued. "It has come to my attention that you would very much like this building for use as a fitness center, to promote good health for our fine citizens."

I swiveled my head trying to find Harold, but couldn't locate him. It crossed my mind that I hadn't seen Virginia Holiday in a long time, either.

Mavis opened her mouth but closed it again without saying anything. She gave an almost imperceptible nod. Whispers and coughing broke out randomly throughout the room.

"I will make you an offer."

Mavis found her voice. "For this building?"

"Not in its entirety. You may have the use of this gymnasium and two classrooms for office space and what-not, free of charge, for two full years, until you find another suitable building."

"Then what 'deal' are you proposing," Mavis sneered.

"This is offered in exchange for one small item which shall not be named in public."

Mavis' face fell. Her haughty attitude disappeared momentarily, but then she recovered. "I have nothing to hide," she boasted.

From the audience came the voice of a young woman, clear and precise, "Mom, I told him you took it from my room." Had Jerry arranged Claire's presence, too?

Jerry's voice was smooth. "Mavis, it's all worked out. If you present me with this item within twenty-four hours of the end of this Ball, say by ten p.m. tomorrow, you'll have a free facility for two years. If you persist in feigning to have no knowledge of this topic, I'll have no choice except to..."

"It's a deal." Mavis said through clenched teeth. She stuck out her hand.

Jerry shook it solemnly and looked my way. I nodded in silent agreement, and earnestly hoped making anonymous calls was Mavis' only secret.

49

Clearly the audience expected the play to begin soon. They were starting to become restless, and someone called out, "Move things along."

Jerry nodded in the direction of the voice. "My next announcement has to do with the fundamental purpose of this event. Please humor me for just a few more minutes." He wasn't about to be hurried.

I looked around the room. Harold and Claire had now joined Mavis, and they were huddled together, whispering. Sherri Sorenson brushed past me, wearing a barn coat exuding odors of warm horses and cold air. She sat on the floor next to her children, leaned over and squeezed their shoulders. Ruthie scrambled into her lap. Farther to my left, Cora was still on the bench with Tom, but she looked fidgety, near the end of her social patience.

"Cora Baker, will you come up here, please?" Jerry's voice boomed through the sound system. Was this question really louder, or did it just seem that way to me?

I saw Cora jump and glance from left to right, as if she were looking for a different Cora Baker. Then she composed herself and with a dignified air, rose and walked to the stage. She raised her face to Jerry and said something, but she was so much shorter the microphone didn't pick up the words.

"She says I'm very good at wasting everyone's time," Jerry explained with a wide grin. There was scattered clapping and laughter, but people weren't sure if this was some new joke, or something more serious. The interchange with Mavis had been tense, and now it appeared there was to be another public conversation spoken in riddles with a threatening undercurrent. Children were squirming and becoming restless.

Jerry raised a hand to still the clapping and whispering which had begun. He took a second mic from a stand and handed it to his diminutive stage partner. "Cora, I have two questions for you. I'm certain of the answer to one of them but not so sure of the other."

"Get to it," Cora said tightly. For this attempt to hustle the proceedings, she received applause. She had donned her no-nonsense persona, and didn't waste a moment before saying to the crowd, "Settle down, and let the man speak his piece."

The audience quieted, charmed by the feisty little woman. I had no idea she would be so comfortable behind a microphone. There seemed to be a lot about Cora I didn't know.

Jerry couldn't hide his delight at the repartee. His eyes sparkled. "Cora, I've heard you have quite a collection of local history memorabilia. In fact, you've brought some of it with you tonight."

"You know I do. Everyone here knows I have it. If you'd come to the point, there might be an interesting skit that features some of the pieces," Cora snapped back.

"I'd like you to leave this furniture here permanently." Jerry pointed to the set stage.

"Whatever for?" Cora questioned, perplexed.

"This building is to be the new Forest County Museum, and my first question is, will you be the curator?"

Now it was my turn to grin. Cora was non-plussed. She looked up into Jerry's face, perhaps searching for motives. She looked into the audience, scanning for someone. I wondered if she was hunting for me. Everyone seemed to be holding their breath.

"Are you serious?" she managed, her voice cracking.

"I am quite serious," Jerry answered. "It's yours if you say yes."

"Yes, oh yes!" Cora said, reaching out for something solid to steady herself, and grabbing the footboard of the historic bed. When she had regained her mental and physical balance she continued, "But you said you had two questions."

"It's true. And I won't waste any time getting to this one." His voice softened. "Cora, will you marry me again? I miss you."

The audience was stunned into the complete silence of expectation. I thought Cora's reaction to this question would be even more extreme. Perhaps she would need to sit on the bed. Much to my amazement, she raised herself quickly to her full height and looked directly at Jerry. But she spoke into the microphone so everyone could hear the clear enunciation of her response.

"Why you arrogant, pushy, son of a flea-bitten dog! Gerald Richard Caulfield, you've been dating Ana Raven for a month and now you have the nerve to pose this question to me?"

Jerry looked contrite. He stuck his free hand in his pocket, and I saw the insecure little boy again. Curious faces turned toward me and my neck reddened. I realized what I needed to do and hurried to the stage.

Taking the mic from Cora, I said to her, and everyone else, "It's all been a ploy so we could prepare the building for you." It wasn't the whole truth, but it was close enough. I handed the microphone back to her, nodded solemnly to reiterate the point, and backed up into the set for the play.

Jerry's eyes were full of pleading. "Will you think about it?" He asked gently.

"I don't need to think about it at all," Cora snapped. "Of course I will. Someone needs to keep you from trying to manage the world. And anyway, I can't run a museum from sixteen miles away."

Jerry leaned over and pulled Cora to his side. The audience broke into applause once more, and I emerged from the shadows and tried to embrace Cora and Jerry at the same time.

Cora broke free and poked Jerry in the ribs. "Introduce the play, for heaven's sake. People have been waiting long enough."

From deep in the wings I heard Chad's voice. "Finally."

50

More door prizes were awarded, and then Jerry announced the reenactment of the murder of Judge Reuben Pierce Oldfield, which had occurred on November 23, 1924. He read the names of the students who had traveled from Michigan Tech just to participate in the Harvest Ball. The townsfolk seemed impressed. I only hoped the kids would do a good enough job to meet Cora's standards of history preservation.

He explained that the cast of characters, in order of appearance, were Dieter Volger, founder of Volger's Grocery and grandfather-in-law of Adele; Nora Bradley, the young wife of Zeke Bradley, who worked at Keto Brothers Oil and Service, now Aho's. John waved his hand, grateful for the recognition. The lawyer, Arnold Schoenbrunn, and finally, there were Judge Reuben Pierce Oldfield and his wife Winnifred. That was six characters and four actors. I didn't know who had multiple roles.

Clearly, the kids had coordinated with Mick, the sound and light guy. The play began, not in the bedroom, but in front of a painted flat which was handily carried from behind, so the stagehand couldn't be seen, and placed near center stage. The backdrop was a general store, simply painted, but it created the atmosphere. A beam of light from a Fresnel lens focused people's attention on the scene. Dieter Volger dusted a shelf of canned goods.

I chuckled at the portly German man with his hair slicked and parted in the middle. The butcher's apron tied around his waist served to keep the padding in place which Chad had stuffed beneath oversized shirt and pants.

From stage left, a thin young woman, whom I recognized as Brittney, carrying a basket, entered the store and greeted Dieter, who went back to his dusting. She pantomimed a careful examination of goods on an imaginary shelf near the front of the stage, occasionally slipping something under a cloth in her basket. Finally, she carried one more item to Dieter and indicated she wanted to make her purchase. "Just the one bag of sugar today, Mrs. Bradley?" Dieter asked.

"Yes, please," Nora lied, not mentioning the concealed goods. After she left, Dieter put his hands on his hips and shook his head. The stage light dimmed.

When the light came up, Dieter was bent into a large pickle barrel, with his head out of sight. Ryan, dressed in modern clothing, walked across the stage bearing a sign that read "two weeks later."

Essentially the same scene was repeated several more times, with Nora paying for one or two items, but pilfering several more in the bottom of her basket.

Finally, Dieter walked to the front of the stage and asked the audience, "Vat am I to do? She is a nice girl, *ja*? Her Zeke, he fixes my car. He fixes all the cars. I do not vant to make him angry." He raised his arms and shrugged.

For the next scene a small table was added to the set, with various cuts of meat displayed. There was a turkey, several plucked chickens (which I hoped were rubber), and a paper maché ham. Dieter once again was scrubbing the pickle barrel. Nora entered, and seeing Mr. Volger's face hidden she grabbed the ham and scurried away.

Dieter gave a yell. "Aha! I haf caught you. I see you through this knothole."

He grabbed her by the arm and Nora began to protest and cry.

"*Nein.* No more. You vill go to police vit me. I cannot lose a ham to save my Sunday drives. You vill pay for this crime." He led her off stage and the lights dimmed again.

When they came up next, a cloth had been draped over the flat, and because the store shelves had been ingeniously painted, the backdrop looked like a window and the cloth became the curtain. We were seeing the inside of a house. Nora and a thin man wearing a greasy coverall were arguing.

"You've gone and done it now!" the man said.

"Zeke, I didn't mean any harm. I just wanted us to have a nice dinner for our anniversary."

Zeke began to pace back and forth, and then said, "Well, you have to go before the Judge tomorrow. They released you into my custody until then, but I don't know what to expect next."

"They won't do anything much just for wanting a little old ham, Sugar," Nora whined.

The scene ended.

Again the lights came up, and now the cloth had been draped to completely cover the backdrop in vertical folds. In front of that was a desk on a raised platform. Judge Oldfield sat there, holding his gavel. I nearly cracked up. Chad had been transformed by means of a wig, fake beard and sideburns, and even more padding. He wore glasses and a dark suit, making it almost impossible to tell he was the same boy who had played the grocer. But I was his mother. I knew.

Zeke and Nora appeared before him, and he handed down a sentence of thirty days in the county jail. Nora was distraught, and Zeke was not pleased.

The play continued with various scenes through Nora's release, the theft of the more expensive objects, and her sentencing to a year in prison. The lawyer who recommended counseling for Nora was played by Audra, her already round frame easily believable as a well-fed professional, when dressed in a suit and sporting a false mustache.

At last the lights came up on the bedroom which had been brought in for the occasion. There was a slight rustling as the audience shifted to view this scene, which was farther stage right, to the audience's left.

The Judge was sitting on the edge of his bed and wearing a long, striped flannel nightshirt. Winnifred, Audra again but now in a nightgown and ribboned cap, bustled around the room, setting a glass of water on the nightstand, and fluffing pillows. The judge removed his slippers and swung his feet into the bed. "Now, Winnie, stop your fussing, and come to bed," the Judge said, gently shooing her away as she tried to tuck him in. This got a laugh from a fair number of people, and Winnie hammed it up. I suspected the next line was improvised.

"Oh, shut up, you old fool. Just because you're in charge in the courtroom doesn't make you king here." With this she climbed into bed and gave him a peck on the cheek.

Again the lights dimmed, and a silvery crescent moon floated above the scene, arcing from one side to the other, suggesting the passage of time.

A yellowish light began to glow softly. Winnifred rose from the bed and spoke to the Judge, who continued to snore. "You just rest yourself, dear. I'll start breakfast. It's cook's day off." She patted the large lump beneath the covers and left the scene. The yellow light grew brighter.

From the far side of the stage, Zeke Bradley approached the Oldfield "house" in a crouch, looking left and right. When he neared it, he raised the butt of the gun he carried and smashed an imaginary window. I had to admit the actors were doing a great job. The sound of smashing glass was heard at just the right moment.

The Judge roused himself from sleep, looking confused, while Zeke climbed in the window and delivered his famous line. "If Nora's going to prison, I'm going with her. She's the best dad-gummed cook I've ever lived with!"

Then he lowered the pistol and fired a shot. The Judge looked startled and placed a hand over his chest. When he lifted it away his fingers were covered in blood. There were gasps from the audience, even though almost everyone knew the local story by heart. Reuben Pierce Oldfield looked at Zeke, and opened his mouth as if to speak, then fell back against his pillows.

Winnifred rushed into the bedroom, crying, "What have you done? Ezekiel Bradley, you're a bad, bad man."

Police whistles were heard and the sound of running feet. The lights went out once more.

Everyone waited patiently for the next scene, but the lights did not come up.

51

Mick's voice boomed from the balcony, "I think we've tripped the breaker again."

Whispering began to swell throughout the room.

"I got it," someone yelled. I was pretty sure it was Todd Ringman. This was followed by the sound of heavy footfalls descending steps. I assumed this was on the backstage flight that led directly to the basement.

There was a banging and clanging, as of a heavy chain hitting metal, followed by thumping. Someone had fallen down the stairs. "Oof. Ouch!"

"Uh. Dang it! Who's there?"

At this, someone began to giggle, and then ripples of laughter and guffaws could be heard. People were hoping this was part of the show.

The chains, and the person connected to them, must have recovered, because the clanking slowly began to rise to stage level.

I sensed everyone around me becoming still. As my eyes adjusted, I saw a dark figure making its way across the stage, holding a thick threatening bar. A beam of light flashed upward from the end of the bar, onto the haggard face of a man in prison stripes, wrapped in chains. Blood flowed from a gash on his forehead.

"It's Zeke's ghost!" a child's voice wavered fearfully. There were screams from many young girls, and even the adults seemed unsure if this was supposed to be part of the play. The blood looked all too real, not overly bright and sticky as we'd seen on the Judge's hand.

The flashlight clicked off, and after a moment of silence, someone began to clap. Others assumed this signaled the end of the play and the applause grew in volume.

Just as people began to stir restlessly, wondering why the lights' still hadn't come on, there was a low rumbling sound that reverberated underneath the clapping, and the whole building shook. Not a massive shifting, but just enough that everyone noticed. There was another shock and something hard clattered to the floor. Immediately, everyone went dead silent.

"What was that?" a woman asked, her voice tentative, but clearly audible in the hush.

"It's an earthquake!" another woman screeched.

"Could be a cryoseism. A frost quake." A man's voice this time.

Another man answered, "For Pete's sake, Willard, it's not cold enough for one of those, even though it's freezing out. That was an explosion."

Then a third woman demanded, "Where are the lights? It's time to stop fooling around. You're scaring the children."

The flashlight beam appeared on stage once again, but this time it was held high and aimed out into the audience. Todd Ringman said, "The power's off now, folks. This is mor'n a tripped breaker. Stay calm 'n' we'll figger 'er out."

His intentions were good, but shining the light into people's eyes only made them flinch. As the light played across faces my eyes caught snapshots of surprise, annoyance, and even fear.

Jerry wasn't about to let the Harvest Ball end in a panic. In the spill from the flashlight, I saw him step to the stage. His voice boomed without amplification. "Now, Todd, just stop swinging that light around and lift it up and point it at me. Yes, that way. All right, Adele, come up here and bring your bag of prizes. We can surely overcome this slight inconvenience. Meanwhile, let's give these young people some genuine applause for their great performance."

A few small flashlights and some cell phones were produced by people around the room, and they all aimed them at the stage. Chad, Brittney, Audra, and Ryan, with a towel held to his head, stepped into the light and took a bow. Jerry shook their hands. "Are you all right, son?" he asked Ryan.

"I'm fine," Ryan must have answered. He was grinning and

nodding.

Adele took a child by the hand and led him to the stage. I saw that it was the energetic Cody.

"I'll just try to find out what's happened," Jerry continued soothingly. "Perhaps the band can play some songs acoustically. Maybe some that everyone can sing. Would that be possible?"

"Sure thing," one of The Blue Grass answered.

"Geronimo," Cody yelled.

Jerry left the stage and Adele took over. I was near the entrance doors, which were fastened open, at the back of the room. He made his way toward me, pausing to speak to Cora, who came with him.

Another beam of light flashed from behind me, someone placed a hand on my shoulder and I heard Tracy Jarvi's voice. She sounded all business. "Excuse me, Ana. I need to talk to Jerry."

I sidled left, and in the strong beam of her battery powered lantern I saw Jerry's facial expression sober. "What's the problem, Tracy?" he asked.

"You need to come with me," she said. "Maybe Ana and Cora too. I think we're about to get some answers, but there might not be much time."

52

Tracy hustled the three of us into the back seat of the patrol car. She let us get our coats, said we'd need them, but told us not to waste any time.

The Sorenson's Percherons were covered with blankets, tethered to a utility pole, but the street light was out. They were munching on flakes of hay, and their warm breath fogged the frigid air. Enclosed in the car, we could hear no outside noises— ordinary enough— but it seemed oddly ominous. The streets were deserted and dark, and there was no need for flashing lights or the siren to clear our way as Tracy spun the car around and drove the few blocks into the center of town.

Had there been an explosion? Was Jerry's house or the newspaper office on fire? I didn't see flames leaping into the sky. No sirens had shattered the silent darkness since the earth had quaked, but every building was dark. The power outage covered at least the north end of town, although I saw lights far ahead of us.

She sped directly down Mill Street and stopped in front of the real estate office, not even pulling to the curb. The buildings on the block were standing, but something had to be wrong. Immediately to the south, several police cars filled the street, red and blue lights flashing. As Tracy hurried us out of the vehicle, I could hear the distant wail of an ambulance from the east, on its way from Emily City.

It was a dark night with no moon, but the police flashers revealed a landscape defined by pulsing purple shadows. A broken power line sparked and jumped, turning the scene into an eerie parody of a Fourth of July celebration.

As soon as we reached the sidewalk, we could see that most of the vacant lot flanked by the newspaper office, Jerry's house and the realtor's, had caved in. There was a gaping hole with several strangely straight valleys leading off the main depression.

Men and women in uniform swarmed around the edges setting up equipment. A second or two later, a bank of Klieg lights flared brilliantly, casting hard shadows from a different direction, giving the illusion that the whole scene had just leaped several feet to the south.

"Down here," Tracy urged, leading us to a ladder that disappeared into the gloom.

"Jerry, what's down there?" Cora asked.

"I haven't a clue," he responded.

Tracy descended the ladder, and Cora followed her. I knew I wasn't thrilled to be wearing a dress for this activity, and I knew Cora liked them even less than I did. Nevertheless, down we went. Jerry climbed down last.

"Over here," Tracy directed, leading us to one of the open arms of the pit.

It was hard for my brain to process what I was seeing. There was half a person lying on the ground, covered with a blanket. A shovel handle protruded from the blanket edge. I could see a bald head, the shapes of covered arms and part of a flat torso. Where an abdomen should be, a heavy beam angled across a pile of dirt and stones. But the face was that of Virginia Holiday, her makeup smudged and smeared with dirt.

When she saw Jerry, she growled, deep in her throat, coughed and said, "I asked them to send for you. You should be the one dying here in the cold with no friends." The voice was not Virginia's graveled yet feminine tone, but that of a man. I was totally confused.

Jerry looked appalled. "Who are you?" he demanded. "You don't seem to be Virginia Holiday."

"My name is Greg Halloway. Does that mean anything to you?" the woman-man asked, glaring fiercely at Jerry.

"Halloway?" Jerry rolled the name around in his mouth. "No, I don't think so."

I shivered, and Cora pulled her coat tighter around herself. The siren had been gaining in volume, and then it ceased abruptly, just above our heads. Doors slammed and footsteps pounded.

"Down here," someone yelled, and there was a clattering of feet on the ladder. An EMT with reflective stripes on his coat appeared, carrying a large case in his left hand. "Stand aside."

He quickly stuffed another blanket beneath Virginia/Greg's head, and began unrolling a blood pressure cuff. "Where does it hurt," he asked

"Can't feel my legs. Can't feel anything really," Greg said. "Don't waste your time. I need to talk to this scumbag."

People have no intermediate feelings about Jerry, I thought. *They either love him or hate him.*

"What have I done that distresses you so?" Jerry asked. "The only Halloway I can recall was a friend of my great-grandfather. Charles Sr. and Stonewall Halloway were very close, so I've been told." Suddenly a light dawned. I could see it in his eyes. "Stonewall Halloway bought the corner lot. You must be related."

"*My* great-great-grandfather," Greg rasped. "His real name was Stuart." The EMT was working around the shivering man, but let him talk. Tracy stood nearby, and Detective Milford had arrived on the scene but stood behind the man's head, out of his sight. Milford held a small digital recorder, its red eye blinking.

"Ah, but legend has it that he drove such hard bargains and was so stubborn that he earned his nickname many times over." Jerry wasn't giving ground, even to a dying cross-dresser.

"I had to find it before the time ran out and you bought the property back," Greg continued, ignoring Jerry's comments.

"What were you looking for?" Jerry asked.

"As if you don't know."

"I really don't," Jerry said, sounding genuinely puzzled. "Stonewall was a very poor man, an immigrant, I believe."

"That's the only reason you wanted the corner back, so you'd have access to the old basement."

I realized that must be where we stood. There were remnants of walls and doorways. A main beam had cracked and fallen on Greg in his unsupported tunnels.

"But it's been filled in for years. Before I was born, I believe.

The shoe shop did have a frame section in this lot, but it burned."

Greg coughed again and blood trickled from his nose.

"He's got internal injuries. We need to get a crane in here to lift that beam, stabilize and transport him," the EMT insisted.

"You shut up," Greg ordered. "Nobody's moving me anywhere. I finally found it and I'll die with it."

"What did you find, Mr. Halloway?" Cora knelt beside the dying man, taking his cold hand between her pink ones and holding it.

"The necklace. In my pants pocket." Greg's voice was weakening.

"You dug tunnels to find a necklace?" Cora pressed. "It must be very special."

"His wife's. From Europe. Gold and diamonds. Rubies, too. Stonewall hid it in a basement wall. The story came down though the family."

"But why didn't you tell me?" Jerry objected. "If you could have proven you were a descendant, you would have had a right to search for your property."

Greg mustered some strength and tried to rise on an elbow, but he couldn't manage it. He directed the energy into his voice. "You Caulfields are all so high-and-mighty. Stonewall's son came home from a trip and found the store burned and the basement filled. Your grandfather wouldn't give him the time of day. Told him it wasn't safe to go poking around."

"I've been told they moved away after that," Jerry admitted.

"Damn straight. Your family never treated anyone... he knew..." he broke off with more coughing. The EMT wiped blood from the man's face.

Detective Milford wasn't about to let Greg Halloway die without some definitive answers. He stepped into the man's line of vision. "Do you know who I am?" he asked.

"I do," Greg said. "Sheriff's Department. I know what you want."

"What can you tell me about the death of Jared Canfield?"

"That loser with an intriguing name? He wanted investment properties. Instead, I made an investment to put you on notice,

Gerald Caulfield. That turned out even better than I had hoped when everyone assumed you were dead." He answered the detective, but still kept his gaze on Jerry.

"So you sent me the hatchet?" Cora asked.

"Delivered it in person. To warn that husband of yours."

"Crane's here," someone yelled from up above. "Get more manpower down there and put a line on that beam."

"Well, he was," Cora said softly. She looked at Jerry. "And will be again."

Jerry nodded and placed a hand on Cora's shoulder.

"He's unconscious," the EMT said. "But I've still got a pulse."

Four burly men scrambled into the hole, which was getting crowded. Tracy hustled the three of us back up the ladder. She followed us, but Detective Milford stayed with the injured man. I knew I was glad a male person wasn't climbing up a ladder beneath me. There was no way to do that modestly.

"A little more extension. That's good, now drop the cable, Mac," one of the men in the hole yelled, using arm motions to facilitate the communication.

More EMTs were already lowering a rescue basket down the side of the pit.

"I'll take you back to the Ball," Tracy suggested. "The line crew will have the power restored soon."

"She's right. People will be nervous and are probably leaving in droves," Cora said.

"Could you make a short official statement?" Jerry asked Tracy.

She nodded in the affirmative, and we drove silently back to the school, each of us lost in thought.

53

Over the course of the next week, the entire community learned a lot more about Greg Halloway, aka Virginia Holiday, who died en route to the hospital.

Most of the news spread by word of mouth, although Wednesday's paper added an extra page in order to cover the story. Jerry must have stayed up writing copy for three days straight. He hadn't been carrying a camera at the Ball, but perhaps he took photos with his phone, because there were pictures in abundance.

The costly necklace, wrapped in an ancient scrap of oilcloth lined with velvet, was found in Greg's pocket, as he had said.

A search of his apartment and office revealed a tan garment which padded the hips slightly and formed soft realistic breasts, and a wig. There was also a strongbox containing family documents showing when the property had left his family, and how he had purchased it back under his own name.

Almost every square inch of the basement of the realty office was filled with dirt which had been dug out of the adjoining lot. I must have nearly caught him digging, the day I came to the office.

No valid real estate license had been issued to a Greg Halloway or Virginia Holiday, leaving a messy financial situation for the two summer people who were under the impression they had purchased property through Holiday Realty. Mavis Fanning admitted she was thankful she hadn't acquired Chippewa Lodge. But she said she was still eyeing the place for her small private fitness club.

A background check uncovered the fact that Greg was the only living son of Keith Halloway, also deceased. Greg had a history of mental health problems, and had been institutionalized for five years. This gap explained why he hadn't known Cora and Jerry were not still a couple when he delivered the gruesome package to her mailbox.

Poor Jared Canfield, selected by the merest accident of naming to come to harm, was a man without roots, as unconnected to the human race as his killer. He had no immediate family. It was never determined exactly where his body had been slipped into the river. Somehow, Adele learned that only five people attended his funeral. She predicted that might be five more than would show up for Greg Halloway's, and once again, she was proven to be a local seer.

It was unclear who would inherit the necklace. Halloway seemed to have no heirs, although Jerry, with Cora's expert genealogical skills, began a search for any other descendants of Stuart. If none were found, the impressive piece of jewelry would go to Jerry when he bought back the corner lot from Halloway's estate. January first of the coming year was the earliest date that transaction could legally take place. With the agreement he would have first option, Jerry advanced money to cover Greg's funeral expenses. He was given a small local service and buried next to Stonewall. There was still space in the family plot. Jerry also paid off the credit card debt Greg had amassed to fund his brief professional life as a woman.

And where had the necklace come from? No one seemed able to uncover the answer to that riddle. Cora's research disclosed that Stuart "Stonewall" Halloway's wife was Prussian, a younger daughter of a high-ranking family under King Wilhelm I. It was possible the piece had been a wedding gift. An expert appraiser verified the necklace was European, made around 1860, and valued it at $12,000. Not a fortune, but certainly a worthy piece of jewelry.

In addition to the Halloway tale, the Harvest Ball was a popular topic, despite or because of its unplanned excitement. Combined with the upcoming re-opening of the Pine Tree Diner, there were more than enough topics to keep the phone companies in business, and to spur sales of pounds and pounds of tea and coffee to fuel gossip sessions.

54

"Whatever for?" Cora said, when Jerry asked her if they should wait until after the beginning of the year to re-tie the knot.

So on a blue and gold early November day, crisping at the edges with warm sunshine and brisk air, Gerald Richard Caulfield and Cora Leah Baker were married in my yard.

It was accomplished with carefully planned informality. The wonderful weather was guaranteed by simply waiting until the perfect day dawned. They had several pastors on call, hoping one would be free on a sunny day. As it turned out, Rev. Theo Dornbaugh, of Crossroads Fellowship, performed the ceremony.

Rather than offend a large number of people, the couple simply chose not to invite anyone. I was there, because I provided a nice lawn on neutral ground. I'll admit, I couldn't resist adding a few festive touches, and scurried to the florist, and the homes of several friends who still had late chrysanthemums and sedum in bloom, after I received a call in which Jerry loudly boasted, "We did it, Ana. Today's the big day!"

Of course, Tom, Cora's son, came. They couldn't really tell him to stay home. Jerry's adult children lived hours away, but they sent congratulations and more flowers.

Janice Preston dropped off some small decorated cakes, and Adele somehow managed to appear just minutes before Rev. Dornbaugh, looking smug and carrying a cozy of hot sausages wrapped in biscuit dough and a jug of punch. She thought she might as well stick around, since Suzi was minding the store anyway. She said she wouldn't hold it against us for keeping her in the dark, as long as she could be at the nuptials. I shook my head and started a pot of coffee.

At eleven o'clock, Jerry's Sebring purred into the driveway. He unfolded his tall frame from behind the wheel, and I saw he was again wearing his grandfather's tails. Diamond studs winked from a pleated shirt front. A gold watch chain was looped across his vest, the fob swinging as he walked. He hurried to the passenger door and handed Cora out. If I'd been surprised at her dress for the Harvest Ball, I was now astonished. She wore a long maroon velvet dress with matching jacket. The lapels were decorated with white lace that appeared to be hand crocheted. Her hair was again fastened into a French twist and adorned with a comb that was set with diamonds. Around her neck she wore the Halloway necklace of diamonds and rubies. The low-cut square neckline of the dress showed the piece to full advantage.

When she smiled at me I believe she blushed. She touched the largest ruby and ducked her head. "Just borrowed for the day, until we know to whom it belongs," she explained.

I thought she'd have a fit at Adele's presence, but they hugged each other carefully, so as not to muss Cora's outfit. I was coming to understand the primary cause of their feud had been Adele's anger that Cora had walked out on Jerry over the use of a building. I thought it expedient not to point out that she was now moving back in with him because of the use of a building.

Jerry and Cora each carried a box. Jerry's was recognizable as holding a corsage. He opened it and lovingly pinned a cluster of white orchids with burgundy centers on Cora's jacket. I was relieved that her corsage looked more expensive than the one he'd bought me just two weeks earlier.

Another car pulled in, and the fiddler from The Blue Grass emerged. He was dressed in a tuxedo and carried his violin case. Everyone arranged themselves on the greenest area of the lawn. The violinist bowed and played "The Autumn Waltz" in sweet tones.

Within minutes, the bride and groom exchanged rings and were pronounced husband and wife, and Jerry leaned down to kiss his blushing bride. Adele pinched my arm and winked.

"Time for some refreshments," I suggested when the two lovebirds came up for air.

"We have one more thing to do first," Cora proclaimed. "How

long a walk is it to the river?"

I had no idea what she was up to, but I said, "Less than a quarter mile to the clearing with the cabin foundation. Why?"

Cora was already slipping on a pair of sneakers, and she picked up the box she'd brought with her.

"Let's go," she said.

We began the short walk in silence, but soon our small company was chatting about everything from the fine day to the fate of the Halloway rubies.

When we reached the river's edge, Cora laid the box on a cinder block and opened it. She extracted a hatchet. I shot her a questioning look.

"The very one, Ana." She held it level in her two hands, like a presentation scepter. "Not the murder weapon, but the one sent to me. That makes it mine anyway, don't you think?"

I shook my head in wonder.

"Detective Milford said it wasn't evidence since it was not connected with any crime except possibly harassment."

Cora and Jerry stepped closer to the water. Jerry spoke up. "Cora, it's time to bury the hatchet. For good."

"Agreed, old man," Cora teased.

They held the hatchet between them and swung it back and forth. "One, two, three," they chanted in unison, releasing their hold.

The nasty weapon sailed in a high arc above blue ripples reflecting the sky. It turned over in a lazy flip, descended, and hit the water with a satisfying splash, where it sank out of sight forever.

Notes and Acknowledgements

The old school building in this book is a composite of two real schools. The exterior is based on the closed building in the town where I currently reside. The interior is very tightly modeled on the school I attended as a child. That building is still in use. There's no denying that the structures where we learned and experienced so much as children become a part of our adult make-up. Some towns are making an effort to preserve these buildings and give them a new life with a new role. This book celebrates all such efforts.

I would like to thank my volunteer beta readers: Lexi Stamper, Barry Matthews, and D. Glen Jackson. No author can catch all mistakes, and I know this book has been improved by their input. After all is said and done, I take responsibility for any errors.

In Dead Mule Swamp Druggist, Anastasia Raven takes on a more official role.

Ana's Notes

I'm loving my new life here in Dead Mule Swamp and the surrounding area. Most of the people are so good to me and kind and honest in their dealings with our neighbors. Of course, there are always a few who don't follow the rules. This case— yes, there's a reason I'm using this more official word now— seemed to wander all over the place. There were so many leads to follow without knowing where they might end. A lot of people, too many dogs, an unlabeled key, love letters... Was there one murder or four? Or none? But in the end, all those bunny trails led to... oh! Better find out for yourself.

1

Colin Mueller was dead. Isabel Adams was dead. Ham Nelson was dead. Milo Sendak was dead.

Even in a small town like Cherry Hill, in the middle of rural Forest County, people die. There were obits in the paper every week. I'd read them faithfully for over a year at my new home of choice in the Northwoods, after leaving the suburbs of Chicago and a husband who had chosen someone named Brian as his new life partner. I'd changed my surname to Raven, in hopes of remaining semi-anonymous. All water under the bridge, as they say— changes and death. But I mention these four deaths in particular.

Colin Mueller had died in his sleep in late March. He was eighty-five.

Isabel Adams was only thirty-two. She was found dead in her garden where she had been raking dry leaves from the beds in April, a victim of anaphylactic shock, stung by a bee. Her epi pen was in the house.

Hamilton Nelson was killed in August, in a car crash. He'd failed to stop at a railroad crossing, and well... he'd died instantly. Few people mourned Ham. He was fifty-six, mentally challenged, and did odd jobs on various farms. It wasn't his handicaps that put people off; it was his aversion to showers that was the real issue.

Milo Sendak took an overdose of oxycodone and went to bed. He called no one. His was not a cry for help, but apparently a well-executed suicide. The problem was he had no reason to kill himself. His first grandchild had been born on September twelfth, and his daughter and son-in-law were bringing the baby to meet her grandpa. They had found him cold and still.

The cause of Milo's death was not obvious. He'd had back trouble for years, but apart from that he was a healthy, energetic fifty-five-year-old tennis-playing businessman. An autopsy revealed the overdose of painkiller.

However, an enigma presented itself since he'd just refilled his prescription the day before, and only one pill was missing from the new bottle. How had one pill flooded his system with the drug? Had he been hoarding capsules?

When officials checked Cherry Hill Pharmacy's records for Milo's oxycodone purchases, they discovered that Colin Mueller, Isabel Adams, and Ham Nelson had also filled prescriptions for the same potent drug just days before their deaths.

The druggist, Charlie Dixon, was sweating bullets.

2

Charlie sat in a hard straight chair by the front window of the unimaginatively named Cherry Hill Pharmacy, a beam of September sun piercing the window and spotlighting his bald head. Emotionally, he probably was sweating bullets, but beads of real perspiration rolled off his pate and dripped from his ears, nose, and the fringes of hair at the back of his head. The shoulders of his blue pharmacist's jacket were actually dappled with wet spots.

I know this, because I was there when our young Police Chief, Tracy Jarvi, came to the store with Officer Kyle Appledorn to question Charlie. I happened to be purchasing toiletries, which I usually put off even longer than buying groceries. My over-the-arm red shopping basket was filled with toothpaste, deodorant, shampoo, band-aids, burn cream, and other sundries. The hard plastic handle dug into my flesh as the weight increased with each addition. But there was no way I was leaving until I saw how this turned out. I pulled some paper napkins, orange with white ghosts, from the shelf nearest me.

I worked my way slowly along the few aisles, keeping my ears open and peeking at Charlie as I reached the end of each row. I'm not a gossip hound like my friend Adele Volger, but there was no use passing up a real opportunity to get local news firsthand.

Charlie shifted his padded, past-middle-aged frame on the narrow chair and asked if he could get a towel from the restroom. Tracy raised her head. She was studying computer records behind the counter but now looked at Kyle and jerked her head in the direction of the rear of the store. The slim officer stopped watching Charlie but gave him a sideways glance as he walked away as if afraid the man might bolt. He returned a moment later with a small terrycloth rectangle.

The nervous owner of the drugstore wiped his forehead. Suddenly a panic attack took him, and he gulped deep mouthfuls of air, unable to catch his breath. He began to hiccup and then to sob.

"I don't know what you are looking for," he objected. "My records are in order. I'm very careful. I had nothing to do with those unfortunate deaths. My God! I would be out of business in a heartbeat if I weren't meticulous."

Perhaps realizing he might soon be out of business anyway when news of this catastrophe got out, Charlie broke off and shut his mouth with a snap, giving his shining head another swipe with the towel.

Tracy came and put her hand on the man's shoulder. "Charlie, calm down. No one is accusing you of killing Milo. But you need to tell us what you know about his prescription. The others too, if you can remember."

"OK. Yes. Milo has some back issues. He's got a bad disk, but he likes to play tennis, so his doctor prescribes him the pain meds because he won't quit the game. He's been taking them for, oh, maybe five years. Never abuses them, just fills the scrip every so often."

"Why did he get his medication here? He lives in Emily City. That seems odd," Tracy noted.

"How should I know? We're small. Maybe he appreciates the service. I've known him all my life. I'm not going to tell a customer to shop closer to home if he wants to give me his money," Charlie said.

"Was there anything unusual about the last time he picked up pills?"

"Nothing at all. He came in on Saturday morning. He was talking about his daughter coming for the week and bringing the new baby. Said they would get here Sunday afternoon."

"That agrees with the records. The Saturday morning part," Kyle called from behind the counter, where he'd begun studying the digital data.

"All right, Charlie," Tracy continued in a soothing tone, "what can you recall about the other prescriptions?"

Charlie put his head in his hands and waggled it from side to side. "I don't know. I don't know. I'll have to get into the computer." He looked up and cocked his head toward Kyle. "We fill hundreds of prescriptions here. You can't expect me to remember every transaction. I probably can't even guess the right months without looking."

"You should be able to do that much, Charlie. They all died the same month they filled their prescriptions."

Charlie gulped again and wrung his hands. That's when he caught sight of me. "What's she doing here?" he demanded.

Tracy turned and saw me. A look of annoyance crossed her face. "Ana. I didn't realize anyone was in the store."

"Just doing some shopping," I explained, trying not to sound sheepish.

"Well, you'll have to finish another time," Tracy said, lifting the basket from my arm and placing it on the floor. "Off you go."

She escorted me to the front door and nearly pushed me out. As I turned toward the sidewalk I saw the card in the window flip to "CLOSED."

PUBLISHED WORKS BY JOAN H. YOUNG

Non-Fiction:

North Country Cache: Adventures on a National Scenic Trail (2005 Independent Publishers, third place Regional Non-fiction)

North Country Quest: Completing my National Scenic Trail Adventure

Would You Dare?

Devotions for Hikers

Get Off the Couch with Joan

Fall Off the Couch Laughing

Fiction:

Anastasia Raven Mysteries

News from Dead Mule Swamp

The Hollow Tree at Dead Mule Swamp

Paddy Plays in Dead Mule Swamp

Bury the Hatchet in Dead Mule Swamp

Dead Mule Swamp Druggist

Dead Mule Swamp Mistletoe

Dead Mule Swamp Singer

Dubois Files Mysteries for Children

The Secret Cellar

The Hitchhiker

The ABZ Affair

The Bigg Boss

The Lonely Donkey

Other

Accidentally Yours- a chaotic collection of short works

ABOUT THE AUTHOR

Joan H. Young has enjoyed the out-of-doors her entire life. Highlights of her outdoor adventures include Girl Scouting, which provided yearly training in camp skills, the opportunity to engage in a ten-day canoe trip, and numerous short backpacking excursions. She was selected to attend the 1965 Senior Scout Roundup in Coeur d'Alene, Idaho, an international event to which 10,000 girls were invited. She rode a bicycle from the Pacific to the Atlantic Ocean in 1986, and on August 3, 2010 became the first woman to complete the North Country National Scenic Trail on foot. Her mileage totaled 4395 miles. She often writes and gives media programs about her outdoor experiences.

In 2010 she began writing more fiction, including several award-winning short stories. *Bury the Hatchet in Dead Mule Swamp* is the fourth story in the Anastasia Raven mystery series.

Visit booksleavingfootprints.com for more information.

www.ingramcontent.com/pod-product-compliance
Lightning Source LLC
Chambersburg PA
CBHW070443120726
47910CB00003B/911